DARK HEART

KAT TURNER

CITY OWL
PRESS

DARK HEART
Coven Daughters, Book 6

CITY OWL PRESS
www.cityowlpress.com

Cover Design by MiblArt. All stock photos licensed appropriately.

Edited by Tee Tate.

For information on subsidiary rights, please contact the publisher at info@cityowlpress.com.

Print Edition ISBN: 978-1-64898-442-6

Digital Edition ISBN: 978-1-64898-441-9

Printed in the United States of America

PRAISE FOR KAT TURNER

"A fledgling witch finds love with a mature rock star in the midst of occult danger in Turner's magic-heavy debut and series launch. Turner sets up a promising world that readers will be pleased to return to in subsequent installments. Paranormal fans should check this out." – _Publisher's Weekly_

"_Hex, Love, and Rock & Roll_ is clever, witty, and captivating from chapter one. Helen and Brian pull you into their world and refuse to let you go. It is utterly a bewitching love story that has it all: chemistry, mystery, _love_, but most of all– rock and roll." – _Jaqueline Snowe, author of the Shut Up and Kiss Me series_

"In _Blood Sugar_, readers can expect Turner's trademark snark mixed with magical and metaphysical mysteries, a well-paced plot full of unexpected twists, and two layered and complex characters winning their happily ever after." – _Janet Walden-West, author of Salt + Stilettos_

"I adore Cynthia and Raven! The chemistry between them is off the charts and they are both such badasses. _Fallen Angel_ is pure paranormal joy. From the scintillating opening scene to the satisfying ending, it grabbed me and didn't let me go. Kat Turner has not only provided readers with a fascinating new addition to her series, she's given them a story and characters that feel distinct and fresh. I loved every moment of it." – _Rosanna Leo, author of Darke Passion_

"_Song of Virgo_ is an intense and perfect combination of magic, mystery, and love!" – _Jaqueline Snowe, author of the Shut Up and Kiss Me series_

"Absolute magic. _Hex, Love, and Rock & Roll_ delivers thrilling suspense, steamy chemistry, and a sexy British front man. Anyone who's ever had a crush on a rock musician or wished on a star will fall in love with this debut." – _Mary Ann Marlowe, author of Some Kind of Magic_

ALSO BY KAT TURNER

COVEN DAUGHTERS

Hex, Love, and Rock and Roll

Blood Sugar

Song of Virgo

Fallen Angel

Inferno

Dark Heart

✳

COVEN DAUGHTERS ORIGINS

Embers

For my readers.

ONE

Everyone had bad hair days, but the typical frizz or limpness didn't pose an acute physical threat to others. At the very least, no venomous serpents were involved.

Rachel Harris wasn't so lucky. It was *always* the copperhead who caused trouble. It really sucked living like this, with her DNA destroyed by the manipulations of power-hungry mad scientists. Go ahead and throw witchcraft in the trash, too, because she still hadn't found anything in her spell book capable of breaking her ruinous curse.

Such was life for a rogue black magic experiment who also happened to be the descendent of a long line of witches.

Maybe someday she'd fit together all her broken pieces and make herself whole, but today was not going to be the day. Not when a routine outing was on the fast track to becoming a deadly emergency.

The fisherman was already turning gray, those telltale, stony scales crawling up the tanned length of his neck. He gasped and clutched his throat, losing his grip on the pole that he had cast into the Amazon River. She hadn't meant to harm him. In fact, she'd hoped their time together was kind of, sort of, maybe a date.

Their boat rocked, the motion sending a splash of warm water to land on Rachel's knee. The rod tumbled over the side of their motorboat with a splash. Cloudy water immediately engulfed the silver pole. Lost to the muck forever, thanks to her.

Her rescue and escape to Peru was supposed to represent a fresh start, a clean slate, a chance to bond with her fellow witches and show the bad guys they'd messed with the wrong gal. Unfortunately, her problems had slithered right along behind her, and earning the trust of the colony wasn't happening. It was difficult to convince others of your intent to save them and the world at large while walking around as the equivalent of a loaded gun.

To make matters worse, the stopgap spell she used to stave off the effects of the curse wasn't working right anymore. Problems piled upon problems to crush her spirit.

The normally fragrant river now smelled like death, its fragrance fouled by her sunken mood. Her cheeks burned. She covered her face and turned away, sick to her stomach.

"I told you not to look directly at me." She dropped her own pole onto the floor of the boat. The six fish they had caught lay in a bundle beside the fallen pole, their pale scales catching glimmers of the setting sun. At least the outing hadn't been a total bust. Not before Rachel and her stupid curse had ruined it. "You took off your sunglasses, didn't you? I thought I was clear on the danger. When you look in my eyes, it activates the snakes. If they get out, the power to kill intensifies. We've been over this."

She supposed she would have made an effective assassin or black ops military asset, turning men to stone in true Medusa fashion. If her captors had wiped her memories as they'd liked to do back then, maybe that scenario would have been preferable to what she now endured.

"Can't help it," the young man croaked, his brown eyes bugging out. His fingers scratched red streaks near his collarbone. "You're too pretty. At least when I can't see what's sprouting out of your head. Holy fuck, those things are nasty."

She was never going to fit in with the shifter colony who had graciously taken her in in her time of need. And dating? Out of the question. Unless she wanted to branch out to women, who were immune to the cruelties her tormentors had inflicted upon her in their twisted search for the ultimate biological weapon. Inconveniently, Rachel was strictly of the hetero persuasion.

Careful not to touch Copper's snappy, renegade head, she nudged the naughty snake back under her head wrap, his scales scraping against her fingertips. Her chest hurt. Her companion's comment about her nastiness stung, even though he was right. She tightened the material of her scarf for good measure, keeping the serpents quite literally under wraps. For now.

"Hold still and don't jerk around." If her hapless victim fell overboard, they'd have an even bigger problem. At this point, his muscles were so locked up he'd be unable to swim, and she doubted she was strong enough to haul him back on the boat or to shore.

"Don't. Have. A. Choice." The words broke out of his mouth in a hoarse staccato. His hands were frozen at his neck and clenched into claws. Half of his head was the color of gravel. "Slowly turning to stone over here. Help."

Luckily, Rachel had a reversal incantation from her spell book, otherwise known as a grimoire, memorized. She'd drilled it into her head after the first time an accident much like this one had happened. Word had gotten around the jungle colony fast, and now everyone looked at her like the freak she was. At least she wasn't about to earn a reputation as a murderer. She wanted nothing to do with this Medusa situation that was foisted upon her without her knowledge or consent.

Rachel swallowed hard, mentally preparing for her spiel. As the coven daughter of chaos, she wielded the most unpredictable and capricious of the elements. The overlord of her element was hardly a benevolent goddess and invoking her was risky at best. But Folly, ruler of chaos magic, was who Rachel had to turn to. So, she dug down deep in her bone marrow, pulled the swirling tempest of black and purple magic to her surface, and spoke the words she needed to say.

"Sister Chaos, I humbly request your assistance." She could deliver this incantation in her sleep at this point. She sometimes did, dark dreams of chaos magic springing up from her unconscious; tentacles the color of a deep bruise strangling her as she tried to rest. "The serpents growing from my scalp are restless. Please soothe them, and plunge them into dormancy, so my community may remain safe." The squirming feeling atop her head settled into cool, familiar heaviness. Tension in her muscles loosened. "Please return this man's flesh to its supple state and allow the blood of life to run through his veins once more."

Her fishing companion sucked in a ragged gasp and dropped his hands to his lap. Tremors wracked his fit body. A sheen of sweat made his handsome face glow as if he'd just worked out, his normal color seeping back in to replace the sickly, gray look. "I think I'm gonna puke." He looked at her without making eye contact, then sharply bent his head in the opposite direction.

Her heart cried out. Nobody really looked at her anymore, not since everyone figured out what she could do. They looked away, sidelong, over her shoulder, above her hairline, and at the ground. She understood, but it still felt horrible. Being an outcast was lonely, even if she had no grounds to blame those who pushed her away.

Awkward silence filled the boat. The current whispered along, the river undulating with life. The late afternoon sun spread a mellow red glow across the sky. Bugs chirped their consistent symphony. Rachel drew in a big breath of fishy, fertile air. "We'd better head back before it gets dark." They had plenty of time before nightfall, but they both needed an excuse to abort this mission.

Her fishing partner and now-former crush—Jeff was his name— hopped out of the boat and untied the tethering rope from its post.

She got behind the wheel and fired up the motor, taking the initiative to drive in case he was still woozy or spaced out from the unintentional Medusa-ing.

She'd burn that entire experimental laboratory to the ground if given half the chance. Call upon Megan the fire witch to torch the place responsible for ruining her inside and out.

A pungent fog of gas filled her nostrils. The motor got going, buzzing steadily as water churned near the back of the boat.

Jeff put his sunglasses back on. He must've pulled them down his nose to get a better look at her, flouting his safety precaution on impulse. After five minutes of boating in silence, her steering their vessel down a channel of water as wide as four interstate lanes, he finally spoke. "Is it true you were a scientific experiment? Did mad scientists really put magic into you?"

He had the gist. Those mad scientists had unleashed a torrent of dark magic into the world, dark magic she was supposed to help stop. Dark magic was both the entire reason she was in Peru and the bane of her existence. To say the subject of her past was a sore topic was a massive understatement. "I'd rather not talk about it."

"Fair enough," Jeff replied with a brusque sense of closure. "I was just trying to make conversation."

"Why not ask me about what type of music I listen to? There are other interesting facts about me besides the horror movie on my head."

Jeff took out his phone, totally ignoring her.

"It's Florence and the Machine," she mumbled under her breath. Silly of her to think she could have a normal outing with someone. Her problem always got in the way.

"What?" He scrolled through a social media app.

"Never mind." Rachel steered the boat back to its usual docking port at the mouth of the main trail. The nose of *Poseidon* sunk into a rut of black mud and halted with a squish. She ushered the fish she'd caught into one of the nets they'd brought and pulled the drawstring.

When she stepped out, a pit of gunk sucked up her yellow galoshes to the ankle. It was so muddy down here, especially in the winter months. Wet dirt was everywhere, slurping her into greedy, earthy mouths.

Ironic, the nonstop engulfing from a place that didn't embrace her as one of the tribe.

Jeff collected his share of the catches and leapt out of *Poseidon* with the typical agility of a jaguar shifter. He bolted onto the trail, where he gained ten feet on her in seconds. He was ditching her. She didn't care, or at least didn't expect any differently.

Soon, he'd rounded the first corner, leaving her alone to slog through a blanket of underbrush. The sun-blocking canopy of wide, bright green leaves enveloped her in all directions. Such was the jungle. A constant embrace of foliage, humidity, and all-around stickiness. Smothering, if one was feeling ungenerous.

A few more yards of walking, and the beaten trail opened to the clearing for the homestead cabins. Seemed like every time Rachel looked, there were more living structures.

Over a hundred shifters of all sorts called the log cabins home, as did Rachel's fellow coven daughters Taylor and Cynthia, along with their partners and Taylor's twins. The remaining three witches stayed in smaller cabins when they visited.

Past the living area lay the communal and industrial buildings. There was the kitchen and dining hall as big as a warehouse, the cedar library with its charming, hand-carved sign over the door, heralding readers and researchers to The Book Nook.

At the edge of a structure that housed the backup generator and other mechanical necessities, piles of logs were stacked in neat pyramids, waiting to be chopped and used for fuel. She hung a left past the community garden, several bountiful acres of produce for all to enjoy. The winter crops were doing well, soaking up copious rain.

Rachel smelled the butcher shop before she saw the blue hulk of a wooden barn with its wide doors flung open for ventilation. She didn't even mind the coppery odor of blood anymore, nor the ubiquitous, rich smells of fresh or roasting fish. She'd come to associate these aromas with people being fed.

Even though she was a square peg in the shifter colony, she couldn't deny the beauty in how the operation hummed along seamlessly and with kindness. No commerce, no power struggles, no inequality. Just shifters caring for each other and offering shelter to outsiders such as herself.

She ducked into the butcher station; a cavernous, open room lined with bloodied workstations. She dropped off her catches with Ray, the old fishmonger with gray hair to his waist and a menagerie of unrecognizable, faded tattoos on his crepe-paper arms. Rachel left and headed back down the trail, looking forward to some private moments with her thoughts to decompress.

"We both know I can help you." A deep, familiar male voice said from behind her. "Whenever you're ready to give my suggestion a try, you let me know."

Rachel's eyes narrowed on instinct. She and Timothy Tsosie had had this conversation before, and she wasn't interested. "We've been over this. I'm not going to let you turn me into a shifter." She'd had her fill of experimental procedures and wasn't keen on being any more unusual than she already was. Half witch, half shifter, all weirdo? Nah.

She glanced over her shoulder. The alpha of the wolf shifter pack was walking out of the creamery across the pathway from the butcher shop. He held two single-scoop cones, both strawberry, one in each big brown hand. His flannel shirt was rolled up to show off thick, corded forearms. Despite the inherent danger, he looked right at her, a warm smile extending to his dark eyes. "Heard the fishing trip went sideways. I thought some emergency sugar might help. Lucy only had strawberry today. Sorry. I know vanilla is your favorite."

"Word travels fast around here. If I were you, I'd keep those eyeballs on my eyebrows."

"We both know the holding spell lasts for at least a week." He gently shook the cones. "I can't eat both of these."

"It's getting weaker, which is why today turned into a disaster. This was only day four. Shortest duration of protection yet."

"Hence my original proposition."

Pink liquid was dripping down Timothy's fingers. If she let this go on much longer, her traitorous brain would fill with images of licking the ice cream off his skin, ridiculousness which would not stand. Sure, Timothy was hot with his built body, dark features, and easy grin. Beyond the physical aspects, he wielded his power with a kind of calm grace that was undeniably sexy. Too bad his idea for solving her problem was insane. Besides, she had work to do. Unpleasant work she'd better tackle before she lost all motivation. "I need to study."

"Sugar will help."

She couldn't argue. Rachel accepted the cone and allowed herself to enjoy those first few licks of sweet berry goodness. She resumed her trek back to what was apparently now her permanent home. Nearly three months and the place still didn't fit. The jungle made for an uneasy homestead. Too large at times, small and constricting at others.

"You want to talk about it?" Timothy kept pace beside her, working through his ice cream.

"What's there to talk about?" Everyone already knew the extent. Gossip ranked high on the list of preferred entertainment in the colony. It was like any small town in that regard.

"Look, I know this isn't easy for you. What happened today. What happened before. I'm fully aware you don't feel like you fit in."

"I wonder why." She pointed at her head. She kept her tone light enough to prevent sarcasm from degenerating into outright bitterness. She took another lick of ice cream, crediting the cone with lifting her mood. Timothy had the right idea there, at least. "I wouldn't worry too much about my angst. It isn't your problem."

"It is, though. Everyone here is. Not a problem exactly, but a responsibility. If you're having a bad experience, it's my job to do everything in my ability to make you as content as possible."

"You don't have to manage me. I'll be fine. I would get yourself some sunglasses though." She'd noticed more and more pairs of sunglasses shielding the faces of residents since she'd arrived, and word had gotten around. Soon, everyone would be wearing them, day or night. The men, at least.

"Don't think of it as me managing you. Think of it as me managing your chaos magic. For everyone's best interests."

The subject of chaos magic gave her an idea. They could talk shop, which beat talking about her uncomfortable feelings. "Any news on the date for the counter-ritual?"

Though the weather had cooled only slightly, Rachel had been keeping track of the days. She hadn't forgotten. The winter solstice was afoot, meaning there was a good chance some extremely bad mojo was set to erupt on such an auspicious date.

Rachel and the other five witches had a world-saving mission to get on with. After, she could turn her focus to breaking her curse. For now, though, she had a bigger problem to solve than the reptile zoo burrowing out from her scalp.

"I wanted to talk to you about the ritual, actually." Timothy worked on his ice cream. Rachel tried not to look at his mouth, or the way he carried himself with such poise. He was in his early thirties, right around her age, but radiated the aura of someone more mature. "There's been a development. We might have to change course in our approach to physical space."

The ice cream wasn't tasting as delicious anymore. The heaviness in Timothy's speech didn't sit right with her. He was worried but working to remain calm. She could hear the subtlest shake in his rumbling voice. "Elaborate." She threw the remains of her cone in a trash bin outside the supper hall.

"Grab your book and take it with you to my cabin. I need to show you something."

She didn't love the sound of his proposal. But witchcraft was why she was here, and work needed to be done, apparently. What else was she going to do, veg out in front of the television while the architects of a world-ending prophecy finalized their plan to destroy everyone?

Rachel jogged to her quarters and went inside. Her accommodations were minimalist, a living room with a couch and wall-mounted plasma screen. In her bedroom, she'd set up a standing mirror and hung both her flat and pointe ballet shoes on one of the arms. Practicing her hobby kept her sane and centered, even if the rest of her life plan was out the window, swallowed by a damn disingenuous medical study she'd enrolled in for extra cash. She wasn't likely to return to the dance studio any time soon, but she could still spin the occasional pirouette, pretending her turns in a remote jungle cabin were the same moves as the ones she'd practiced on the Marley flooring back home.

Her bookshelf, decorated with twinkling fairy lights, was stocked with the English literature classics she used to study along with some romance novels and other popular fiction favorites. College was out the window now, too, but she wasn't about to let her mind wither.

The grimoire stood out among the other books; a hulking chunk of old leather bound together by thick twine. The tome always seemed to be watching her. Peering. Studying. Sentient. The other witches swore the books were aware of their surroundings. Mute and still, but alive. Rachel had never wholly bought into their theory, it was so outlandish, but then again, who was she to cling to the notion of logical consistency anymore?

Magic followed its own set of rules and laws, physics and reason be damned. Rachel had known this from the moment the book had landed in her hands, delivered by Cynthia following a harrowing ordeal to claim it.

Rachel pulled on the thick spine, her hand and insides heavy with duty. The wheel of fate spun a web through her cells.

An unsettling, out-of-body sensation rippled through her. She felt unreal in a grotesque way, as if a malignant version of herself lived inside her and wore her skin. One of the smaller creatures on her head wiggled. She swallowed a lump of frustration.

"Everything okay in there?" Timothy's voice, muffled by the front door, cut through her musing with an edge of urgency.

She tugged her book free the rest of the way, the weight of it unusually burdensome in her arms.

It's not pleased he's here, her intuition whispered. *She's not pleased.*

"Fine." Rachel's voice swung up at the end of her reply to Timothy, her tone exposing the falseness of her statement. "Why wouldn't it be?"

"You've been gone a while, so I thought I'd check."

Another snake readjusted, scales brushing a rough path above her ear. Her spell, rock-solid only a few weeks ago, was now practically worthless. She had to figure out what this meant. And what Timothy was talking about. She hauled her book to the entrance of her cabin.

He waited there, his hands in his pockets, confusion in his eyes.

"Five minutes is a while?" Rachel pulled the door shut with a click. They never locked up down here. No need.

Timothy canted his head. "I think we'd better get to work right now." He tilted his gaze to the treetops, drawing her focus to the indigo dusk, where the Sirius star had pricked a silver dot. "It's speeding up. I can feel it. Did you?"

She hugged her book to her chest despite a bone-deep urge to throw it to the ground. "I felt an odd sensation. Like a force passing through me. How long was I gone?" Day had slipped to night, so more than five minutes. She'd heard stories of missing time from the other coven daughters. It was a sign of magical interference from their arch nemesis, which never meant anything good.

"Almost an hour. I have an idea. Take the book over to my cabin and we'll compare notes."

"On what?"

Timothy let out a heavy sigh. "In colloquial terms, they call them the backrooms."

TWO

As a pack alpha, Timothy Tsosie had one goal: protect the pack. His main goal encompassed a range of smaller goals. He strove to mediate disputes to ensure a resolution amenable to all parties. He offered leadership and guidance when appropriate. He pitched in with construction projects.

He was a busy man now, in charge of the entire shifter community and not just the wolves. Timothy was damn good at his job, if he did say so himself. Competent.

Despite his competence, he didn't have the first clue how to handle his feelings for Rachel Harris, whatever they were. All he knew was he had to get her chaos magic under control so she didn't inadvertently hurt a member of the tribe. Or worse.

Once a stopgap was in place, they could switch gears to their collaborative goal of saving their community from the impending magical apocalypse. No sweat, right? Just another Tuesday in the Peruvian jungle.

"What?" Tucked into the corner of his sofa, Rachel glanced up from her book. Her eyes matched the colors of the jungle surrounding them in all directions, a deep forest hue flecked by golden brown. Her sadness wasn't lost on him, a wisp of emotion floating off her like a lone, fallen leaf fluttering to the ground.

He looked away from her and back to the webpage on his laptop monitor. There wasn't anything in those webpages to help him alleviate her pain, so he threw himself into the task at hand. In the areas of researching and strategy, he had control. The emotional realm was a thornier domain. "I didn't say anything."

"You laughed. Did you read something funny?"

"I suppose there's an absurdity inherent in our situation."

Rachel joined him at his desk, standing close enough for him to catch a taste of her scent. His sense of smell was heightened anyway, and the attraction made it worse.

Her top notes were exotic flowers and spice. Underneath was the sweetness of her skin. Her sex.

Her head scarf shielded the feature that made her so insecure while also hinting at it, which somehow enhanced her appeal. Despite her easygoing demeanor, Rachel was dangerous. Deadly, but not by intent. It was hot, how she wielded this weapon that kept him at bay.

He was thinking about her way too much and had been ever since she showed up down here many months ago. Her allure was persistent, consuming, and a threat to his resolve. He reread a paragraph on the message board. "We're going to have to tackle this battle in the Other Place. Here, they're referred to as the backrooms, but I'm positive the terms refer to the same place but with different jargon."

She was standing so close to him. "How do we tackle the battle?"

"Your magic, from what I can surmise. We have to go to the Other Place to work, where magic is most heightened and therefore has the best odds of succeeding. We have to close the portal between the other world and ours and, based on my research, shift this timeline onto one where this prophecy doesn't gain traction."

"So kind of like quantum physics? The idea of there being an infinite number of possible realities, and our role is to steer the course of fate onto the one we favor?"

"You've got the gist, yeah."

"I don't want to diminish you, but how exactly do you factor in? I'd think I could go by myself."

Too dangerous. She needed protection, someone versed enough in the ways of magic to offer backup. He'd be a bodyguard, essentially. He would have done the same for anyone in the clan. Plus, he had to test the prevailing theory of fated mates being bandied about on the message board, if only to debunk it. If he was able to synch with Rachel's magic in the Other Place, according to the most trusted posters, their bond was more meaningful than a simple infatuation. Timothy was putting on his scientific hat. Conducting an experiment.

"It's my duty to protect my own. I'll be your bodyguard."

She raised a single eyebrow. "How come you didn't go along with Taylor and Julian when they went searching for Luna?"

"It's not responsible to leave a leadership vacuum, either. With Julian here this time, I don't have a leadership problem."

"What if I don't want a bodyguard?"

"I'd say this is bigger than you and what you want."

"Okay. Fair." She leaned against his desk and reclined into a seat. "Let's go have a look. I might have a way to protect you from the snakes, at least for a little while. I can't guarantee it'll hold, but if you insist on coming along, it'll behoove us to take steps to keep you safe."

"Yes. I insist." He refused to throw her into harm's way when it was his duty to protect her.

"Fine. Hold on. I'll do the quick fix so you can look at me safely. I want to try a glamor out, anyway. I've heard they last longer than my usual holding spells." She opened her book and recited an incantation. The spell hit fast and hard. A force of unseen pressure pushed through the atmosphere, catching him in an invisible blast radius that shook him down to the subatomic particle.

He was still reeling, his heart banging in his ears, and his whole body drowning in heat and adrenaline, when the visual change washed over him.

In place of the turban hiding the snakes, a full fall of chestnut hair crashed past her shoulders. A cloud of glitter wrapped her, each fleck breathing out sighs of life with every sparkle. Her eyes had transformed from their usual color to an icy, iridescent violet.

It was exquisite. *She* was exquisite, a force field in a force field, pinning him in thrall.

"From the look on your face, the glamor spell worked," Rachel said. "Disguise mode activated, yeah? You're not dying, right? You can look at me without the curse kicking in?"

He wasn't turning to stone from the inside out, but he wasn't unaffected. The effect of this spell meant something.

It was a simple glamor spell, his brain knew this. His heart, though, danced to a place where they could be something other than who they were. Where they could be themselves, unpolluted and authentic, free. He looked away and back to his screen before she caught him staring or was able to read the daydream on his face. "Do me a favor and cross-check some of these facts from the message board with your book. I want to make sure our bases are covered."

"What's wrong? Did you feel something weird, like the glamor was wearing off?"

He swallowed hard. Quite the opposite. The glamor had given him a glimpse. Not that he wasn't attracted to her in her current state despite the snakes. He was. Even because of them, partly, with the twisted aura of danger and the sinister, Biblical beauty they cast all around her. He was attracted to Rachel regardless. Even more so, though, when he looked into her eyes and caught a fleeting glimmer of the unburdened version of herself. The person ready to open her heart.

"Not at all, I felt completely at ease." He somehow managed to both lie and speak the truth at the same time. "I was just thinking of the task at hand."

"Okay. Yeah." She didn't sound convinced, but the next noises were the soft flutters of pages turning, so he was out of the hot seat for the moment. She murmured the occasional word while she read. "Your research from the boards checks out. We should be able to use my spells to travel between dimensions or timelines. It's high-level chaos magic, though, meaning there's an inherent risk."

His heart beat faster. There were other risks he'd rather take with Rachel, the sort where they gave in to each other, body and heart, consequences be damned. Where they escaped to uncharted worlds together and played at being fresh and wild versions of themselves. For now, his fantasy was off the table, so he poured himself into his project like he always did when giving in to urges or instant gratification wasn't an option.

"Good news. Excellent. I think given your skill level and my ability to shift, we'll be able to pull off a partner spell. This method should offset some of the risks. So not only will I be able to help in a physical sense, but my participation in the spell will also supply a buffer against malevolent interference. This is Julian's theory." He re-read the same sections of a few posts on the board in an unsuccessful attempt to distract himself from her proximity, her allure, the idea of what might be if circumstances changed.

Shit, he hadn't felt this way in years. Not since those initial inklings of love had stirred his now-weary heart many years ago. He'd resigned those feelings to the dustbin of history. Why the hell were they returning now, and prompted by someone who made no sense as a match?

"You're acting weird." Rachel tilted her head, staring at him, her pale fingers tracing shapes on the parchment pages of her book.

"I'm in my zone."

"There's nothing else?" Her voice had softened. She scooted closer, a strand of her hair tickling his upper arm in a silky tease.

The words slid right off the screen, off his brain. "What do you think?"

Their arms were touching. She wasn't rejecting him. She was moving closer to him, literally. Maybe they could try this on for size. Try *them* on. She seemed so at ease. Free at last. Swept up in a peculiar kind of magic with the power to dissolve her self-consciousness.

He was looking through a door and seeing a version of Rachel who fit with him. The version of Rachel who had made peace. The version of Rachel whom he saw beneath the spiny surface, the one with whom he was meant to be.

Shifters talked nonstop about fated mates. They were *obsessed*. Timothy had always imagined himself to be above such superstition, too educated and evolved to put stock in unproven lore. But what if the legends were true, and he was just jealous he hadn't found his match yet?

She dipped her head down. The moonlight streamed in past the gap in his curtains to illuminate her high cheekbones and sharp nose. Her beauty was timeless. Ancient. As risky as their mission and his infatuation. Her eyes were the color of the forest, the howling trees he ran through at night, the wide leaves kissed by golden sunset.

She drowned him in warm pools. His bliss was oceanic. He remembered nothing but this eternal moment. The rapture was orgasmic, but purer.

"I have a confession." She parted her lips.

"I'm here to hear it." If he could absolve her of every ounce of her pain and every single demon haunting her spirit, he would. Take away everything making her feel ugly inside and pour endless grace into her. "Tell me, Rachel." He laid his hand over her smaller one. "Tell me anything and everything, and I'll listen."

She moved toward him, a small gasp escaping her mouth. Her bottom lip was fuller than the top, and a perfect shade of pink that made him think of another part of her anatomy. His sex swelled, and his hand itched to wander to her thigh, but he fought off the desire despite how badly he burned to touch her in a more intimate fashion. To make her cry out. For him.

"I love how you look at me." Her declaration was slow and smooth, a controlled expression of reverence. Sexy as hell. She was in total control.

He was rapt. Enthralled. Enchanted, and utterly bewitched. "You put a spell on me," he murmured.

Those words were the wrong ones to say. He knew so instantly by the storm cloud that blew across her gaze before she looked away, snapping the tie that had bound them so tightly seconds ago. "That's all this was? My bad magic in effect? Wow. I thought you liked me. My bad."

Regret was a wrecking ball. "I didn't mean to imply what you're thinking. Of course I like you. I more than like you." More than like you? Ugh, could he express himself any more awkwardly? He'd trashed their priceless chemistry with his careless, impulsive remark about being under a spell.

She jumped off the desk. "This can't happen again. Mixing lust and magic is playing with dynamite. We both know this."

"I wasn't feeling lust. Not exactly. It was so much more. It wasn't the glamor spell. What passed between us was authentic and meaningful." He reached for her arm, but she was too fast in pulling away.

"Maybe, but it's still not a good idea. I thought you were all about being safe. Well, we were right on the edge of doing something profoundly unsafe and you know it. Lust. Magic. Dynamite. A bad combination. Let's not forget again." She snatched up her spell book and pressed it to her chest as if calling upon it as a shield. "Okay. Back to work. If I'm understanding correctly, we have to line up the contents of my book with your research to find the specific area of the backrooms, Other Place, whatever we're calling it. Once there, we can get ahead of what's coming."

"Will you please talk to me? Pretending this didn't happen isn't a solution. For all we know, repressing our feelings could be fueling a spell being used against us."

She glanced at him sidelong. "Have you been studying magic, or did you just make up this theory?"

Made up theory. Oof, she was perceptive. "It stands to reason. Don't a couple of the other witches have similar stories?"

Before she could answer, two knocks on the door cut short their rapport. Timothy cast Rachel a *to be continued* glace and went to greet his visitor. He opened the door to Julian, a fellow wolf shifter whom Timothy had come to consider as somewhat of a brother.

They shared brown skin and dark hair, tribal traditions (any Ute versus Navajo rivalry was evoked only in jest), and both found satisfaction in a long hike or hard day's work. There was so much more depth to their friendship even given those commonalities.

Timothy and Julian shared a deeper, more brooding bond. Both had found the community after a long series of struggles to fit in, leading to intense ambivalence about what set them apart from those in the human world. Without words, they could look in each other's eyes and find solidarity in their shared sense of difference.

Speaking of appearances, Julian looked distraught today. He'd piled his long, black hair in a hasty-looking topknot, as if he'd rushed over. His long-sleeved t-shirt and khaki pants had a thrown-on quality. Then again, the man was a father of toddler twins, so an occasionally haggard aesthetic was an occupational hazard.

"What's up, man?" Timothy greeted his close friend with a pat on the upper arm. "You good?" What a dumb question. He knew the answer. It was plain as day, etched into the groove between Julian's eyebrows.

"None of us are good right now." Julian spoke with such graveness, Timothy wished they were having this conversation sitting down. Yet he also sensed there was not a second to waste. He and the other shifters shared a sort of low-grade telepathy. This gift allowed them to read emotions and thoughts through subtle inflections and gestures. "I think you'd better come outside and see for yourself." He slid his gaze to where Rachel stood with her book in hand. "You'd best join us. I have a feeling we'll need to reference your book."

THREE

RACHEL SHOULD HAVE KNOWN. BY HER OWN ADMISSION, TO SPRINKLE lust into magical practice was to play with dynamite. Yet she'd lit the fuse herself and jumped into the explosion.

She'd allowed herself to succumb to simmering temptations, getting close enough to where the fuse was nearly sparked. From now on, she'd keep those urges at bay and hold Timothy Tsosie at arm's length, where he belonged. Unfortunately, what they'd done, or almost done, couldn't be taken back.

Here she stood, her feet sunk into the quicksand of her error, the firecracker in her hand sparkling its way to impending doom. Timothy stood beside her, calm and immobile, his stare tracking Julian's broad back and dark ponytail as the other man ducked down a forest trail.

They exchanged a glance. They should follow Julian. Following Julian was what they were supposed to do. She should follow Julian, but she didn't want to. This was her fault. Predestined, perhaps, though such an explanation felt like an excuse unable to absolve her of accountability.

A humid blanket had dropped in to cloak the evening air, the effect heavy and stressful. The energy was burdened. Big. Changing, and not in a positive direction.

Julian looked over his shoulder. "You two coming?"

You flew too close to the sun. The voice of the coven sister of chaos, ruler of the magic system and perennial source of woe, crooned in Rachel's head. Folly wasn't an ally. At best, she surrendered bits of valuable information involuntarily, piloted by the whims of a blinding ego. *Now you drip to the earth as tears of wax. Mere droplets in my palm.*

Rachel took off walking behind Julian as if she could outrun the whispers in her head. Timothy caught up to her.

In all the taunting, though, Folly gave out clues. Whether tossing breadcrumbs of occasional support amused Folly, or if she accidentally slipped up when her hubris got the best of her and she couldn't help but brag, Rachel wasn't sure. But one fact remained. She was worth listening to. The other witches had used Folly to their advantage, and now it was Rachel's turn.

Rachel dug her precious clear crystal out of the pocket of her cargo pants and squeezed her palm around the chunk of rock. She opened her hand to examine this artifact of hers, benign on the surface but apparently symbolizing so much. Four raised bumps pockmarked one side of the stone, creating the appearance of a miniature animal with stubby arms and legs.

"Will it help?" Timothy asked, every word coming out smooth in an intentional way. He was in damage control mode already, regulating his emotions so as not to infect others.

"I'll know more once I see what we're dealing with." She took a big step forward, overtaking him.

Timothy stretched his arm to the side, shielding her, and got in front.

"You don't need to protect me," Rachel said. "You aren't indebted to me because of what almost happened." She swallowed, a mess of emotions swirling just below her surface. What had they done, exactly? What did it mean, on multiple levels?

"I'd protect anyone here." He caught up to Julian's heels. "It's my duty."

She wasn't sure if the comment made her feel better or worse. Was she fishing for a certain type of answer from Timothy? Assurance? Validation? Selfish either way, to place the issue of them in the foreground when a bigger situation was afoot. Childish, to mix up priorities in such a superficial manner.

Rachel trekked down the trail, grateful for the sturdy hiking boots and flannel she'd thrown on to protect her from scraping branches spiking out into the path. This trail was darker than the rest of the jungle, trees and their massive canopy blocking out whatever light the moon or stars would toss their way. A monkey shrieked overhead, foliage rustling from its movement. Her pulse picked up. She was used to the animals here. They were a backdrop now more than anything, but the anticipation in the air heightened her senses.

A hot kick thudded into her chest when she saw the reason Julian had led them here. A line of light slashed through the air, gas-stove blue in its iridescence, alive with a vibration.

She squinted against it, turning her hand into a visor, making sense of the senseless like she'd been doing ever since she snapped back to consciousness in a demonic dungeon, touched her hair, and discovered she'd never be the same again.

The luminescent cut was around five feet long, its height looming above the heads of the men.

A noise issued from the pulsing slash, a mechanical buzz more artificial than, or at least distinct from, the typical insects.

"This isn't good," Timothy said. He walked to one end of the line and back, surveying the portal.

Was the glowing blue slit moving, changing? She couldn't look directly at it for as long anymore. It hurt her eyes. A gauze settled over her thoughts. This thing was sucking her in. She'd heard stories about a portal down here before, a malevolent thing capable of pouring forth nasty spirits from the Other Place. Those who wished them harm had gotten past a sealing spell and kidnapped one of Julian's children. Baby Luna had been rescued, and everyone had assumed the portal had been closed, except now the threat was back.

"You need to seal this immediately," Julian said. "She's plotting. Changing. The stretch of portal wasn't nearly this long when I first spotted it."

Julian meant Folly. She was the only one formidable enough to lay claim to this handiwork.

The lower end of the line stretched down, gaping, a sadistic grin of interstellar sapphire leering before them. Images danced in the newly formed maw; sparks mixed with formless, floating apparitions. They were going into Rachel. Taking up residence. Her head was alive, worked up, the glamor spell long since broken. "I can't seal it." Folly was going in through her. Sending spirits into her so as to render her an earthly puppet.

"Rachel, try to fight the haze. You have to seal this. Close it fast, before it does some real damage." Timothy's idea wasn't bad. The blue expanse pulsed, grew, glared at them with all the strength of a fierce horizontal sun. He was wrong, though. He lacked the information necessary to counter this malignant presence hadn't been sent into his head. Not like it had been delivered to hers.

This was how the apocalypse began. She knew this in her bones, the deepest pit of her gut brain. She opened her spell book.

"Hold on." The alpha put up his hand, blocking the glare with his forearm in the process. "We don't know what the best approach is. Whether the right approach is for you to act solo or with your sisters. We have to go into the Other Place with a plan intact. The last thing we need is a rash decision."

She connected with his brown eyes and saw fear in them, fear he tried to hide from everyone who depended on him. Something else was in there too. Concern for her. The preliminary pain of loss anticipated.

"I can feel it accelerating. I am so tuned into this. I've never been more sure of anything. We won't have another chance. I have to do this my way."

"What way?"

"You said so yourself. The backrooms. A battle in the Other Place." She showed him the crystal before giving it a squeeze. The points of the limb-like stubs bit into her palms. "This here is my key. My lifeline. I understand now. I was the only one ever authorized to use it. Not Helen. Not Megan. My role in this is to return this rock once and for all to its rightful place. Lock the door. Lock this evil presence out of our lives for good."

Timothy took both of her hands in his. "We'll take the others. There are six of you for a reason. Lean on your coven for support. Draw on them."

She shook her head. He had a misguided notion of how the prophecy worked. "Not at first. I have an individual trial. A test. If I pass and move on to the next level, then I bring them in. But if I try to skip steps, everything gets worse."

Julian paced the length of the blue cut. "I still say we seal it. Once it's blocked off, we sit down and have a look at solutions from a level-headed place."

"She'll gain too much strength and use the extra time to her advantage." Rachel knew Timothy could see the movement under her scarf. Everyone tried so hard not to look that it became even more obvious when they were looking. "This needs to be me, now, and I need to be alone. I'm the coven daughter of chaos. Scarab picked me because of my element. To bring me closer to Folly for use as a conduit. I'm more attuned to her than the others. Closer to her, whether I like it or not. So I'm the one to begin this thing. The natural choice." Scarab had somehow channeled Folly in their ritual. She had to stop them, too, before they harmed anyone else or rode the coattails of this apocalypse for their sick advantage.

Timothy's lips had parted. He looked at the ground, then back up at her. The light made for a cold, eerie backdrop, like being underwater in a pool. "You're suggesting we go right to her and fight head on. Your idea is bold and brave but so risky. Nobody has beaten her at her own game yet. Only subdued her and kicked the can down the road. This time, what if there isn't a stopgap available? The solstice is coming. The big ritual. Scarab is plotting behind the scenes to take part in solstice mischief because scheming is what they do. We can't afford to get lost in an unwinnable battle. I say we go back to your spell book and devote some attention to crafting our approach to the Other Place."

"No. I go now. If I can lock the door, there will be no ritual. Scarab will know this. They'll sense it. I'll take away their access to this dark energy they want so badly. Stop it before it starts." Stop them for good before they hurt anyone else like they'd hurt her.

"That's a lot of responsibility for one person," Timothy said.

"I'm not just any person." Rachel looked him square in the eye. "I'm the coven daughter of chaos. This is my mission. I'm sure of it."

"I'm going with you," Timothy said. "My reasoning from earlier still stands."

His reasoning was sound, but she wasn't about to throw him like fodder into Folly's path of destruction. A shifter wasn't equipped for such an opponent. Despite how much he wanted to help and protect, he wasn't a witch. He wasn't built the same. "No way. Too dangerous."

"Think of it this way. You'll need to have your chaos magic under maximum control before you're ready to bring the others in and face Folly as a group. I want to help you."

"We've already ruled out reshaping my magic through shifting techniques." What if she accidentally transformed into a half-woman, half-snake and couldn't shift back? Hard pass.

"I can help you structure and shape your magic. I know you're not crazy about the idea, but please give my theory a chance. If you gain the ability to shift, to change your form at will, then it stands to reason you'll be able to work with the serpents to your advantage. Turn them from a nuisance and a burden into allies in their own right. Merge them with you so they work in your service instead of as an adversary."

Timothy certainly made a convincing case. Not shocking, considering how good leaders were typically skilled at winning others over to their point of view. Still, she wasn't about to let him bulldoze her into submission. "What if your approach fails, and I get stuck in a different form and can't shift back? What if I lose control of my magic?"

"We'll take it step by step. Go at an even pace. I'm here for you, Rachel. I won't let you down. I want a resolution to this prophecy more than anyone. Closure is all I want. Peace for us down here."

The portal had grown to a cavernous orifice. The hole exerted aggressive pressure now, a magnetic field physically pulling her towards the threshold.

A black hole. A dying star, pulsing its last gasps. She could finish this thing off. Instead of fighting the force, which worsened the discomfort, she could move with it. There was something spiritual about the choice to move with an energetic flow instead of resisting it.

She and Timothy were holding hands. She hadn't realized this until she began to pull away, already missing the comfort of his warmth, his hold, before their clasp even broke.

"We go now, then," she said, letting go of muscle tension to give the portal more leverage, "and put this curse to rest once and for all."

"Wait." Timothy pulled on her hand, putting his strength into the resistance, his stare pained. "We go in at the exact same instant."

Warm winds blew a song across her face in a murky, heavy jungle kiss. She'd never quite gotten used to the atmosphere leaving its mark. How romantic it would be for those breezes to lift her hair, to carry the strands upward as she and Timothy said their goodbyes. Not so. At least, not right now.

But Rachel had a plan. Timothy would not be joining her on her journey for multiple reasons. When she returned, though, he'd look at her with fresh eyes. Eyes that saw the real her and not her curse. "You aren't," she said, her tone gentle yet firm. "Stay. Defend everyone here. I'll do my part, and you do yours. This stops here. Now. With me." She let go of his hand.

Her statement must have had a finality to it, a gravitas suggestive of grim outcomes, because Timothy blanched like he'd seen a ghost. He lunged forward, screaming her name, but Julian held him back from leaping into the portal and following her into the abyss.

The energetic pull of the rip in space sucked Rachel up into a vortex, twisting and pulling until she'd lost all sense of direction, orientation, and physical coordinates.

A kaleidoscope of lights pulsed behind her lids. Queasiness turned her stomach inside out. The moment of freefall, of being upside down, was formless, boundless, and endless.

She didn't care about the discomfort. She had a quest. A mission. A duty. She was the pivotal coven daughter, the only one with a shot. The only one equipped to face Folly and walk away victorious once and for all.

Rachel came to her senses, sick and coughing, pain pounding through her head. Her knees wobbled. Blurry auras ringed the edges of her vision. A few deep breaths settled her enough to take stock of her surroundings.

She stood in the center of a hexagon etched black against a white floor. The walls and ceiling matched the slab under her feet, six squares of blinding, colorless monochrome. The Other Place had welcomed her into its deranged embrace, and it was up to her to navigate the toxic ties binding her to this sunken realm.

Rachel got right down to it. She had a baddie to beat. "Sister Folly, I, a chaos born, arrive now to claim my birthright. Your era of disillusionment and discontent ends now. You are unfit to rule at the heart of our magic. I am the heir. The successor. The breaker of chains, cycles, and prophecies." She gulped. "I order you to retreat to your small corner of the Other Place and seal yourself off once and for all."

Her book had outlined the steps to dethrone Folly and claim the seat at the center of the magic system. Rachel's heart hammered against her ribcage. Her book was right. It had to be. She hugged her book hard.

Once Folly was banished, the hologram prophecy would end in an instant. The portal would seal automatically, and Rachel would take her rightful place. She'd cleanse the magic, purge it of so much evil, trickery, and deceit, and usher in a golden age. This was the end of Folly's dark dominion. It had to be.

Seconds ticked away in agonizing, endless beats. Rachel's mouth dried. Her scalp was still heavy with the serpentine mass. The curse wasn't lifted yet. She shifted on her feet. Her book had to be right about the steps to untangle the malicious tentacles from the core of chaos magic.

It had to be.

Had to be.

Had to be.

Nothing is happening!

A spark no larger than a teardrop twinkled against the snow-sheet flooring. Relief loosened Rachel's muscles. Finally, movement. She wasn't sure toward what, but action beat stasis. She had to believe in optimism, or she'd slide into despair.

Rachel remained hopeful until Folly's disembodied, androgynous voice crooned, "Big things always start small."

The speck popped, jerking against the ground, and ballooned into a larger version of itself. Four corners jerked into relief. The object twitched again and swelled, its movements glimmering in flickers of light. A couple more growth spurts, and there sat the clear crystal.

Rachel's heart sunk. The object she was supposed to neutralize and return sat before her, stolen from her possession and sentient with Folly's spirit, taunting her.

Folly was in no way compromised by the spell. In fact, her essence teemed stronger than ever, centered and seething. Rachel held her ground and put on a show of confidence even though she was shaking. "So what, you crawled out of the crystal mountain to terrorize us some more? Or were you never trapped there at all?"

"I like you." The crystal pulsed with a pale, icy glow in time with Folly's words. A dark heart pumping cold blood. "Do you know what I like more than you?"

"Destroying the world?" Frustration pulled Rachel into a dense knot, constricting her chest. "Psychologically tormenting everyone you encounter?" She hated that this fiend was her elemental sister. Everyone else got a real element. She was stuck with a malevolent mess.

Folly laughed a smooth, round, sinister chuckle. "Close. I do like both of those things. Very much in fact. But more than destruction and torment, and more than you, I like games. Do you like games, Rachel?"

She was already in one. She didn't like it, but the only way out was through. And the way through Folly was to keep her talking, because her pride often swallowed her, and she was prone to fall into self-sprung traps. "Sure. I like tennis. How's your backhand?"

"Outstanding. Your hair looks lively today. Not as limp as usual. New moisturizer for the scales? Anyway, I was thinking more parlor games. Games of chance or skill. Cards. Charades. Dice. What do you say? Want to play a game, my dear child of chaos?"

Rachel would rather play a game with Jigsaw himself and saw off her own foot in the process. But she was smart enough to know when Folly was giving her a head start. A chance. This was chaos magic in effect—an opportunity to establish a set of rules only to turn those rules on their head and completely rewrite them. As malevolent as Folly was, this invitation was her giving Rachel a shot to engage in a fair-ish fight and prove herself along the way.

This was her shot to halt the prophecy. Halt the prophecy, break her curse, and see if maybe, just maybe, there was hope for her for a normal life. One including Timothy Tsosie—or not.

"I'd love to," she told the crystal.

The rock pulsed with light wordlessly, as if attuned to Folly's breathing. "Winner takes all," Folly said.

"And *all* is what, exactly?"

"You know the stakes." The sister of chaos's voice was soft, disarmingly so. Maternal, almost. Almost. Rachel could not let her guard down.

"Give me the rules," Rachel pressed, her palms sweating.

Six points of light flared on the face of the hexagon, one at each juncture. Folly continued to talk through the crystal. "You will succeed where each of your coven sisters failed. You will use your chaos magic to rewrite each of their stories in your own mind. By slipping into their skins, you will stitch together their storylines and yours. Once the six of you converge as a single unit, you simply declare yourself victor. Then I will fall into nothingness forever, and you will ascend to the apex of the crystal mountain. From there, you do with this world and the Other Place as you wish. Hologram, no hologram, absolute personal power or democracy, all up to you. The other world and this one will belong to you, wholly."

Doubt crisscrossed her in heavy ley lines. Rachel knew better than to trust Folly. This was a trick. Some means by which she'd *spell* her own demise. "I don't believe you. Why would you ever agree to this? If you lose, it's over for you and your precious hologram."

"I know."

"I don't understand. Why would you assume so much risk?"

"Simple, really."

"Elaborate."

The crystal spun in a lazy circle, its tip lining up with glowing points at the junctures, stopping briefly in a teasing dawdle before resuming its spin. "You'll never win."

Rachel straightened her spine. Indignation burned through her in a hot streak. Her competitive side had been activated. "We'll see." The world was at stake. Folly might be right, but Rachel would at least give her a hard-nosed battle.

Another hollow laugh of mockery and malice. "I'm humoring you because you're of my lineage, and I'm genuinely curious about the extent of your powers. Your chaos magic is an unfocused pile of slop, and I'm intrigued to see how adept you become with it before I put you in your proper place for good."

"What's the next step?"

"Spin the crystal. Where it lands, you go. Each of those points of light is another portal. A portal within a portal to take you to a different node in space-time, a specific coordinate in the plane of your world. You've been a dimensional traveler before, though you may not remember."

She didn't. She'd been mind-wiped then, totally under the command of the mad scientists at Scarab who'd brainwashed her, turned her into an experiment, and stuck her with the cursed wig she now wore. "And once I'm there, then what?"

"Figure it out."

Rachel needed an order to figure it out, as crazy as it sounded. Her confidence surged. She'd figure it out. She would. Rachel spun the crystal. It whirled in a circle, slowing before stopping to point at a glowing joint between two planes. The dot of light morphed into the symbol for spirit, and a forceful tug yanked Rachel through the floor.

FOUR

RACHEL SNAPPED BACK TO CONSCIOUSNESS AMIDST ANOTHER WORLD OF white. Except now, her senses told her she wasn't in the Other Place. Her nose and cheeks stung, brushed by frosty breezes. The air smelled of campfire smoke, and coldness filled her with nostalgia for her Midwestern home in December. A bulky coat buffered her against the elements, and a wool scarf draped her neck, its scent musty and comforting.

A pair of purple boots with rounded toes, the brand with evergreen popularity, stared up at her like an extra set of eyes.

She drew her gaze away from her shoes and to her surroundings. She stood in the middle of a frozen lake. Her hands were empty. No book.

The panic instinct kicked in fast, a sizzling bolt to her solar plexus. She pushed aside the fear and exhaled a deep breath of misty white vapor. The ice beneath her was sturdy. Stable enough to walk on. She'd be fine. She did have to figure out what the game was.

Chaos magic, she'd learned from her book, was game based. Altering the rules of reality through the use of symbols, sigils, and conscious, intentional decision making was a central component. Kind of like a more potent version of the butterfly effect. Or manifestation on steroids.

A few tentative steps on the smooth ice sheet, and she'd found relatively sure footing. The lake was larger than a couple of football fields, and round. Ringing the perimeter were barren trees, their branches crisscrossing like brown capillaries against the blue sky. An assortment of two-story houses was visible beyond the ice. At least she'd landed in civilization.

As she minced to the edge of the frozen water, picking up the pace once she'd settled into a confident gait, she was able to make out a paved trail surrounding the lake. People walked strollers and dogs; some held hands. Some more tension in her loosened. By all appearances, this was the everyday reality she was used to. Not some upside-down alternate dimension where the laws of physics and logic didn't apply. She'd heard stories of weird, irrational places from her coven sisters and had no desire to experience them.

Coven sisters, the wind whispered, its sharp gale penetrating the gap between Rachel's coat and her skin. The eeriness of the statement made her shudder more than the cold.

"What about them?" she asked, fishing for a clue. After another ten feet of careful walking, she made it off the lake and onto the path.

A husky, redheaded man in a heavy-duty flannel shirt passed her right as she stepped on the pavement. "Cold enough for ya?" he asked in an affable tone, his accent thick with the rounded vowel sounds of an upper-Midwestern intonation.

The instant she made eye contact with the man and his kind, dark blue eyes, a fresh bolt of panic pierced Rachel. She'd forgotten all about the snakes. He'd start to turn any second, and she'd have to cast a spell right here in public. Her hand flew to her scalp on instinct to tuck someone away. But there were no snakes. Only wavy brown hair, the kind she'd had before the experiment. Rachel stroked her own hair like an idiot, stunned. "Sure," she stammered out.

"Rachel!" A different man shouted from the middle of the lake, urgency in his cry. He was too far away for her to recognize.

"Are you okay?" the man in the flannel asked, clearly sensing her distress or confusion.

"I'm fine." Not exactly true, but there wasn't a way for him to help.

Rachel's mind spun. She was information overloaded, sensory

overloaded, and unsure of where she was. Strange input was coming at her from all directions.

Things got stranger when she saw Helen pass by on the trail.

Her sister witch wore a dark, puffy coat and boots like Rachel's. Same brand, the color baby blue. She was talking on the phone. Did these details mean anything? Rachel jogged to her, catching up after a couple of feet. "What's going on?"

"Rachel, wait!" The man on the lake called, closer now. He wore a flannel similar to the male stranger, except in green. Everything was symbolic. Doubled. Mirrored. Rachel struggled to catch up with her thoughts, her interpretations, but the meaning was always a step ahead.

Helen looked bewildered. "Do I know you?"

Her heart sunk. Something was off. This was a different reality. "Do you remember anything about the coven? Peru? The prophecy?"

Helen's eyes stretched wide. She drew back, let out an awkward laugh, and looked straight ahead. "No. Sorry. Maybe you have me confused with someone else." She picked up her pace and returned to her phone call before quickstepping forward in what appeared to be an effort to get away from Rachel as quickly as possible.

The new man finally walked off the lake and joined her on the trail. He was handsome, with dark eyes and brown skin. Sturdy build, husky, like he labored outdoors.

She didn't recognize him, yet he was unflinchingly familiar. He was uncanny. Like she'd known him in a past life. Déjà vu took hold. Recognition for so many things dangled barely out of reach, yet it all felt so meaningful. The man carried a beaten, leather-bound book larger than a dictionary. Her spell book. He had her spell book. Her mouth dried. Shock waves knocked her out of body. "Who are you? How did you get my book?"

"It's me, Timothy. Don't you remember?"

"I don't know a Timothy." If she didn't know him, why did the sight of him strike her with mysterious recognition? Had she dreamt of him? Did he remind her of a relative, a famous actor?

"Shit." Timothy's jaw hardened. "This is part of her game. She cleared a part of your memory to make it more difficult for us to work together."

"I'm not sure I understand." Her stare bounced between the strange man and her book. "Give me my book." She motioned for him to hand it over, which he did. The weight comforted her. At least one thing here was consistent. "You never told me how you got this."

"You dropped it. I picked it up and followed you here. Through the portal. I'm positive you're going to need this. We both will. I think I have a pretty good grasp on the test you're being put through. But we have to be on the same page here. Literally. Because every move you make, every word your utter, and every person you interact with, is your chaos magic in action. You'll need to be wielding it with total precision if this is to have a good outcome."

For the first time since before she'd been experimented on against her will and turned into a biological weapon to be used in top-secret projects contracted by militaries and private defense firms, Rachel seriously considered the possibility she was going crazy.

Here she was, in a strange place with no money or identification, talking about magic spells with a man who seemed to have drifted up from the depths of her subconscious and walked across water to deliver her a grimoire. At least he was attractive. "We have to try Helen again. She's our only connection to this dimension and the one we came from."

"She's not as much of a connection as you might assume." Timothy puffed up his cheeks and blew out a white gust. "She won't remember you. We're in a version of reality where she never activated her craft. This timeline is the result of a constellation of completely different choices by many people. It's like here, none of the mess with the prophecy or the witches or Scarab's rituals or anything of the sort ever happened."

Rachel played with the thick, healthy hair she'd grown to miss. "Can we stay here instead?"

He chuckled. They shared a lingering stretch of eye contact. A pleasurable rush of tingles made the shared stare taste sweet. She didn't know him, or at least didn't remember him, but she'd like to. "I wish. But it won't matter. This timeline will eventually fold into the one we know, just by a series of different events. Then we're back to square one anyway. Our job is to align them on purpose."

Rachel opened her volume to the chaos section, her section, and read a couple of paragraphs. The encounter with Folly had been mysterious and occulted, as encounters with Folly usually were, but not useless. One thing Folly had said, the comment about stitching the threads, resonated with Rachel. "I have to bring the timelines into alignment somehow. Got it. Tie up the loose ends. If I want the result I desire, circumventing the prophecy, then I have to custom-make all these realities to fit my goal."

Timothy nodded. "They're like loose ends. Versions of events where some decision somewhere along the way leads to the launch of the hologram prophecy."

"And I've been inserted into these realities to undo those choices with different ones." She snapped her attention away from the book and to Timothy's brown eyes. "It's a test. To see if I'm good enough yet with my chaos magic to control the environment with my will. To retrofit these anomalous realities so they sync with my wishes." She got chills. "If I can accomplish what I've outlined, I take her place. It's a test to see if I have what it takes to unseat her and claim rule as Sister Chaos."

"I think you've got it," Timothy said in a soft, almost reverent voice.

"Where do you come in?"

"You'll need to incorporate shifting into your chaos magic. I'm not completely sure how yet, or when. But my role is to guide you through. And to protect you." His Adam's apple bobbed. "As your bodyguard."

"Shifting what?"

"Your shape. Your physical form. Possibly to prevent the snakes from coming back, possibly to head off some other outcome. I'll do partner work with you to collaborate on your magic." He looked deeply into her eyes, confident yet somehow also vulnerable. "If our bond proves to be viable enough to sustain such a connection."

"So you know how to teach people to shift their shapes? Are you a witch too? Or wizard or sorcerer or whatever?"

"I'm a shifter with a sensitivity to magic. Julian, a fellow shifter, has helped me attune myself to be fit for partner work with the coven daughters. I'd turn into a wolf right here to show you, but I'm afraid I would scare these people."

She stared at him.

"You still all about staying in this timeline? Because it's going to get weird." He teased her with a fast wink. They both laughed, the levity clearing cobwebs from her brain and heaviness from her midsection.

"You know what?" she patted the cover of her book. "Sure. Can we walk and talk? I'm turning into an icicle."

They merged onto the middle of the trail and assumed a medium pace. He said, "I don't know about you, but I didn't make it here with my wallet or phone. Which I'm sure was intentional. You?"

"Nope. This is all I have from my old life." She tapped her finger on the book. "So thank you." Connecting with her magic, even if only remembering the book, opened some valve to release the flow of her memories. One in particular involved Timothy and made her blush.

"We might be able to use chaos magic to turn a random piece of paper into a credit card so we can check into a hotel. Such a thing is possible."

He was right. Cynthia, the air witch, had used magic to transform matter in everyday objects. Timothy's idea, though good in theory, didn't feel right. It felt like stalling. Side-stepping the heart of the matter. "I think we need to get to Helen first. Somehow convince this version of her to make the choices required to steer this reality on the track we need."

The wind picked up, billowing blasts across the lake and onto the trail. Flecks of snow glittered in the space between ice and sky. It was as if Cynthia was speaking to them, arriving on cue in elemental form. Taylor, too, was with them as water crystallized into its frozen state. What would her sister witches do if they were here in the flesh? Plow ahead, or stop and plan?

He asked, "How confident do you feel about the Psyche Splitting spell?"

His proposition came out of the left field along with those frigid blasts. Everything was topsy-turvy. A sign, but one without a clear referent. Rachel shivered under her jacket. Folly was in the air. Every time things weren't quite right, a little eerie or just off enough to throw balance into disarray, she was there. "What's Psyche Splitting got to do with Helen?"

"Nothing, as far as I know. I need to go back to the community. I can't abandon them."

She felt heavy, like a burden or distraction. "So go back." She wasn't being manipulative or sarcastic. Timothy had obligations. They'd flirted and almost kissed, but flirtation didn't automatically rocket her up his priority list. Such thinking was immature.

His dark eyes pinned her in place, the effect making her shudder deep down in her belly. His presence radiated confidence, calm and assured. No wonder he was a leader. It came naturally, as if lodged in his bones since birth. "I can't leave you here all alone."

"Of course you can. This is what I have to do. You have your own obligations."

"We did partner work to get here." Timothy gestured to her book. "I'm calling the glamor spell step one. Therefore, I'm a part of the spell. To cut and run would ruin the magic. I can't risk it."

"Ruining the magic is a stretch." Whether he was being paternalistic, acting as a responsible leader, or, as her lonely heart teased, fishing for an excuse to stay by her side, Rachel couldn't say. The bottom line was he was correct. Breaking the link after initiating partner work, if he was right about how they'd set the spell into motion, was tantamount to pulling a loose thread on a sweater. One small tug and the entire thing unraveled. Slowly at first, then all at once. "Besides, I'd rather not cast a magic spell in the middle of a public place."

People were already staring. She exuded weird without even trying. Perhaps it was the arcane book. Maybe they'd seen him walk across the water calling her name, a spectacle evoking both a surreal, religious flair and the trappings of romantic fixation. Unless passersby had pegged her as out of place using some ineffable, intuitive sense. They could smell inter-dimensional trespass on her, a cast-out odor, the funky disquiet of chaos magic brewing.

"Over there." Timothy turned his head in the direction of a one-story, yellow building flanked by a concrete patio and picnic tables. A restaurant, clearly closed for the season, named Sea Salt & Brine. "There's gotta be a space to hide."

She barely knew this man, but his approach made instant sense as a feature of his core personality. Constantly tracking, scouting, and assessing his environment. A shifter had such gifts, it seemed. No doubt they'd been particularly useful for surviving in the jungle and ensuring the survival of others.

She listened to him. Trusted him. His presence moored her. He was a natural buffer against chaos gone amok. She was glad he was with her, even though she was remiss to admit as much and look desperate.

A quick walk through a small playground, steps crunching over snow-crusted sand, and they made it to the patio of Sea Salt & Brine. Timothy zeroed in on a banged-up door, once green and now eaten by plaques of rust. A padlock hung open and limp. Hinges creaked in protest when he pulled, but the door gave.

The smell beyond was dusty but now necessarily bad. "You saw this from far away?"

Inside the restaurant's side door was a dark storage room with cardboard boxes piled in sloppy heaps. Unwanted paperwork littered the ground. The door squeaked shut, landing ajar so only a sliver of light seeped through the crack.

In the unlit space, her senses heightened. Her heartbeat drummed. A sweet, spicy smell issued from somewhere and nowhere. Magic was in the air. He stepped closer. "It's more like I felt it. It's hard to describe. My senses have been more active lately. My peripheral vision, sharper. Intuition in overdrive." His voice was so sexy. She could smell him, woodsy and cold. A surge ran through her center.

What was happening? "I don't have enough light to read by." Her words came out as a husky whisper. Her equilibrium was off, like dizziness was incoming. She grabbed his arm for stability. He was sturdy and muscular. "Oh, God, I can feel it."

"The magic's here? Already? We haven't even said the opening words to an incantation."

Chaos had her paradoxically both blinded and empowered to see everything, all over the place, and all at once. Purple and black, glittering in void-deep indigo tones, her chaos magic slithered from her deepest parts to fill the space in the storage room.

The dark heart pulsed and pumped, above and below, in her chest and her sex, positively throbbing. The dark heart had birthed her and called her home.

She couldn't pass this up. They had an opportunity now to do next-level partner work by bringing their bodies as complementary forces into the equation. Megan, the fire witch, had talked about stuff like this. More potent than reading from the book by unlimited degrees. "Now.

You're up for a good split, right? Equally here and there in perfectly divided measures?"

"What are you saying?"

He knew. She could smell it on him and hear the intonation of arousal in his voice.

Rachel filled her fist with the material of Timothy's flannel shirt and pulled him closer, communicating with her body. Inches away from her, she read his desire, and vice versa. Her eyes had adjusted to the light enough to make out the spark of lust in his lidded brown eyes. The way he gazed down at her, both knowing and awestruck, as if he couldn't believe it but understood there was no other way. Couldn't fathom any other way.

Lust, magic, and dynamite. Caution flew away in the cold winds. If the rules didn't apply anyway, she'd sure cast them aside with a bang.

The dark heart was hammering now, ripe and hungry, an organ both sexual and life-giving. It existed both outside of her and inside of her, this ravenous flesh spurting out thick ropes of indigo, violet, and magenta to fill every corner of every universe and dimension. She wanted the juicy, viscous substance to fill her up too. She was greedy for it. She gasped. Her clit was aching. She was wet. "Inside me."

His lips parted. He placed a hand on her hip, steadying her. She used the stabilizing force to rock forward, her head thrown back, grinding against him. He got hard. She couldn't take much more. Neither could the dark heart, slamming in tandem with her own pulsations, eager to expel more, and more, and more. This magic was hers, and this was how to embrace it.

"You're sure?" his tone was gruff with gravel. He wanted her just as badly. Right here and now. "This is the spell? And this is you talking?"

"Yes. It's me. *And* this is the spell. I won't get possessed. She's not capable of it. Please hurry. We have to work fast." She was in her right mind all the way. But the chaos magic was frantic now, spewing streams of vibrant color in all directions, in danger of burning out before they added their own libidos to the mix.

"Rachel," Timothy whispered, fumbling with his button and zipper. The sound of metal on metal, his pants giving way, made her moan. "I can't resist you. At least let me kiss you first. Touch you."

"No," she breathed, the magic so intense now it blinded her, fireworks spurting behind her eyes.

Rachel tore her way out of her boots, then her pants and underwear. The cold air tickled her skin, illicit and decadent. She hiked her leg around Timothy's waist, gripping him for support. One of his hands stayed on her hip. The other held her shoulder, his touch as erotic and assuring as the situation would allow.

She reached into his open fly, past the fabric of his underwear, and grabbed his hard cock. Perfect length and girth for her, angled up at the target. She maneuvered him, twisting her hips until she had the perfect angle. "Pull out in time," she panted, now completely unable to see.

He surged forward and pushed into her in a single thrust. She cried out.

She bounced on him, craving a release both from sexual tension and the magical intrusion. Were they even the same force, libido distilled and unbound?

He filled her up just right, the friction stroking her inside and out, pleasure building into bliss before tipping over into insane craving. She came fast, hard, her voice breaking into a yell as a dark flower blossomed so violently, she was sure she'd get sucked into an event horizon and torn to pieces.

She was shuddering, coming down in aftershock quakes when he moaned and pulled back at the crucial moment. Hot seed splashed her lower belly. He cupped his cock at the head, rubbing a spot below the tip, and muttered a soft curse as one more spurt shot out.

Breath vacated Rachel's lungs. She screamed silently, vise-gripped by some new sensation of both climax and pain. The dark flower collapsed in on itself before exploding into a black sun caged in a network of shimmering lace. Every square in the network had six identical sides, a perfect hexagon.

"The prophecy," Folly crooned from some forgotten corner of a lost universe. "Comes to you."

FIVE

Timothy ran down a scraggly jungle path, ducking and weaving to dodge roots, fallen branches, and leafy ground debris concealing the threat of hidden snakes. Wildlife chittered and skittered as unseen things fled his approach.

He didn't have one nanosecond to worry about the creatures inclined to stand their ground, red in tooth and claw, but he didn't know why he ran.

His headspace was as bright and luminescent as the midday sun that pierced the overhead canopy and shot its rays onto his head. His muscles burned with force and determination. He smelled his sweat, but not fear. Only focus.

He was unsure if he was running toward a goal or away from a menace. "Rachel," he called out, mentally scrabbling backward. They had transported. Not to the Other Place, though, to a different version of their usual world. One where outcomes differed based on an alternative set of choices made. With her help, he'd split his psyche in the interests of protecting her there and protecting everyone here.

Timothy stopped and caught his breath, blood whooshing in his ears. He was in two places at once. Or, at least, he'd tried to be, tried to perform to the level he expected of himself.

The terrain around him floated into familiarity. Carvings on a tree trunk, a particular cluster of pink and orange flowers sprouting from the shallow part of the creek like illusions of wading flamingos. Once oriented by trusty signposts, the run back to the town was simple, quick. They called it a town now, not a camp or base. A town full of shifters and others who looked to him for stability. He wouldn't have it otherwise. This was his calling, but he was honest with himself enough to admit his seams were frayed.

Timothy caught up to Julian near one of the storage sheds, where Timothy's fellow wolf-shifter chopped wood, the blade of his ax glinting in the sun before slamming down to split a log. Winter was coming, and though temperatures in the southern hemisphere typically stayed mild, they'd all learned to never take preparation for granted.

Before Timothy could get a word out, Julian spoke. He looked drawn and severe, like he'd seen or heard things he'd rather not have. Timothy hoped he was projecting.

"There you are." Julian wedged his ax in a crevice in the stump. "I wasn't sure how much longer I'd be able to distract myself here."

"Did Rachel come back?"

Julian wore a grim expression. "The two of you tried Psyche Splitting, right?"

Timothy's heart sunk. "Tried" did not imply success. "We were trying to work in two places at once. I was at least. There and here. My plan was to contain the threat on both fronts."

"I need you to see something."

"She's not..." he went into freefall. If Rachel was hurt, or worse, because of the damn spell, he'd never forgive himself. "Julian, you'd better warn me about what I'm about to see. Because I can't be having a breakdown in front of everyone here."

"It's not what you think. Come on." Julian led Timothy to a clearing behind the dining hall, about ten feet from the edge of the creek, the area hidden and unremarkable enough to where nobody cared to go back there.

A defunct well poked up out of the ground, dingy bricks circling a dead hole, the bar long stripped of its bucket.

Except today, the sight was far from unremarkable. The five

remaining witches stood around the protrusion, holding hands, swaying in silent harmony.

The sight of the women locked in a ritual trance was jarring enough, and even then he wasn't prepared for what hovered over their heads.

A dark cloud, denser and more void than anything made to carry storm waters, seethed in the open space, ripe with hostile sentience. Inky tentacles bled outward from the center mass, fat and sooty tendrils grasping at nothing in particular with primal, curling motions. His stomach sucked in on itself. He didn't have to analyze the situation much to discern who had encroached into their vicinity. He knew it was bad.

"It's begun," Timothy said, the continued presence of the cloud sickening him.

Invisible poison leached from its core, a hateful center glimmering in a spectrum of deep purple and magenta tones. If he looked close enough, he could make out a delicate network of pores, or scales. Hexagons, hundreds of them, linked together to make the shape of a honeycomb. Worse, they were multiplying before his eyes, dividing to reproduce in their blackened womb. Doubling, quadrupling.

"They have it self-contained for now," Julian said. "But it's pregnant. Ready to burst. And if it does, it's game over. The five agreed that Rachel had another part to play and didn't need to stay here and hold the circle. I hope they're right and Rachel is working on her part as we speak."

Horrors unfolded in Timothy's imagination. Other Ones, monstrous creatures from Folly's depraved dimension, spilling from their gestational chamber to run amok in the jungle. From there, the honeycomb trap would spring, and the life force of the community would be feasted upon by Folly's minions as they grew stronger and leaned in to their era of rule. All shifters would be trapped in energetic pods and used for food supply for the Other Ones, who feasted upon the rich essence of magical beings. Once strong enough, the monsters would come for humanity, and then all was lost.

"I disagree. They need Rachel. She needs to be here." Something was wrong. Why didn't she split like he did? Or did she end up in a mistaken destination? Either way, he had to find her and correct the course so they could complete their mission in both dimensions.

Timothy had an idea. There was plenty of research on the fabled

Coven Daughters Prophecy, most of it teeming in dusty, obscure corners of the Internet, but obscurity didn't make the source material any less valid. During his years spent researching this subject, he'd sharpened his tools of discernment, taking note of the useful information and leaving behind the true crackpot garbage.

With the witches indisposed, he had to figure out what happened when Psyche Splitting spells went wrong and if there was any chance of outside interference. Scarab had been dormant for awhile, but the company with a penchant for using dark magic for their unorthodox rituals likely hadn't given up. They'd gone underground, where they plotted their next move and waited for the perfect moment to strike. Aided by Folly, they'd surely find an opportunity.

"Can you keep running interference here?" Timothy asked. Someone would eventually get curious and wonder where all the witches had gone. Or stumble across the spell accidentally, having wandered behind the dining hall for whatever reason. Pandemonium would ensue, a cat which Timothy wouldn't be able to easily re-bag.

"I'll do my best," Julian said. "But I have to get my kids soon. I can't tell you how long Taylor will be tied up back here. You'd better hurry."

Julian didn't have to tell him twice. If he could determine what had happened with Rachel's split, where her other form had gone, he could go back to her in the alternate Minnesota and help her re-cast. Once she was established with the others in the jungle, they could resume. Then there was the issue of getting himself back to Sea Salt & Brine without the aid of a witch or spell book. Luckily, Timothy had a storehouse of knowledge to turn to. He jogged to his cabin and got to his computer as fast as possible, impatiently swirling his finger on the trackpad to wake up the machine.

The message boards were a strange, heady world made up of a mishmash of conspiracy theories, baseless speculation, and the occasional nugget of gold. One of the most credible posters had been an escaped victim of Scarab experimentation much like Rachel.

Back in his days as one of the top contributors to the boards, he'd gone by the name Mad Dog Margarita and amassed a cult following. Now he lived in the shifter colony. There were others out there like Mad

Dog, one step ahead of Scarab, who knew nearly as much about the prophecy and magic world as the shifters and witches in Peru.

He clicked, read, clicked, his heart in his throat, his stomach knotted into his ribs as he mined for clues. He tumbled down rabbit holes but dipped out just as fast, remiss to use too much precious time. He was an accomplished dabbler, a quick study in this mission.

The book wasn't necessary. He'd garnered as much, pieced together a kernel of needed hope.

After post after post had tumbled over him, all feeling significant and meaningful without offering up much evidence in the affirmative, one made him sit up and take notice.

He didn't recognize the username, and the directions were vague enough to be useless to the untrained eye, yet the totality of it all stuck a fishhook in him. A tiny beak, implanting meaning while pulling the meaning out of him.

His breath caught. His pulse clamored deep in his ears. The meaning was inside, not outside. The words said as much. He didn't fully grasp them, yet he got it way down low.

HeartoftheMountain8647:

What scholars of the Coven Daughters Prophecy still don't get is the books are a trick. A trap. A ruse. See, Folly wants everyone to be reading these books, studying them, obsessing over them. I wish the witches wouldn't do this anymore. All they're doing is helping her re-write our reality in her language and erode the veil. It's like giving her new ammunition. The real magic is never on the outside, in a book of spells or series of chants. It's on the inside. Work from the inside out.

SOURCES? HA. TIMOTHY WAS VERSED ENOUGH IN THIS TYPE OF research by now to know he was flying reckless and blind, given over to the realm of speculation and guesswork, of flimsy links and manic collages where facts were strung together to make a composite that held form only in the mind of its creator. The people here weren't vetted. Conspiracy theorists, attention-seekers, and all manner of nutcases thrived on this message board.

But just because they were crazy didn't mean they were wrong.

The dark heart beat inside Timothy. It always had, ever since the first time he had shifted his shape into the wolf totem, involuntarily and with much horror. His heart beat for Rachel. The force of chaos generated when their eyes met, an amalgam of passion, purpose, and terror capable of knocking them both flat in unison. He had to get to her. Unite in the mission. And he knew how.

Timothy beat feet to where he'd left Julian and the witches, finding the women still looped around the well, their faces whorls of blankness, features made slack and blotto from the trance. They moved as one, murmuring too softly for him to decipher. He called for Julian, who arrived at once.

"You're in charge." Timothy met his wolf-brother's dark eyes.

Julian looked at the unholy cloud, its gloom writhing yet fixed in suspension, tentacles grasping at air. He looked at Timothy. Then back at the cloud. "What do I tell everyone? In the interests of not causing a panic, what do I say?"

Julian didn't ask Timothy what he was doing, or why, and he certainly didn't try to talk him out of what he'd already decided. Timothy respected Julian for this gesture. Whether it was best classified as deference, or a leap of faith, or radical acceptance, didn't matter. The flow could only be facilitated or protested in vain. Impediments weren't an option.

Timothy put his hand on Julian's shoulder, offering a small comfort while commanding attention. "You tell them when I come back, we're all going to be safe for good."

Skepticism passed across Julian's eyes in a fast flash, and Timothy saw what went unspoken. *Will I be lying?* He didn't have an answer, and they both knew it. But at least he had a solution. The idea for one.

"You got it," Julian said.

Timothy gazed into the fecund center of the void until the goddamn abyss gazed back, each of those honeycomb hexagons peeping and surveying, appraising him, like endless pairs of eyes. Spider eyes, bug eyes, a nest of them breeding in their womb tomb.

What he had to do was take these eyes, collect them, and make them his. So they would watch on his behalf, fling his perspective far and wide into every dimension ever to exist. Then, they'd be brought to heel and stripped of their power.

I'm going crazy. Everyone who fucks with this magic loses their mind eventually. This outcome is by design.

He shut the voice down, drew upon his wolf, and drew into himself. The burning pain came first, taut, hot pressure of muscles stretching, tendons tweaking, organs breaking free and resituating. Then the collapse, the crunch, as his face caved in, his eyes folded forward toward his nose, and new flesh formed a snout. He looked monstrous in this stage. He didn't care. The entire process was monstrous, a necessary evil.

In wolf form, he was dialed in enough to connect, mystical and mysterious. He'd become a radio tuned to the proper wavelength. His vision was gray and muted, his center of gravity lower. He gazed right into the center of the terrible, pregnant pre-storm and howled loud enough to shatter the sky.

The cloud trembled, shook, every molecule in its wake quaking with inhuman rage. His blood vibrated. Eyeballs strained in sockets. His eyes could see. His eyes took from the hexagon eyes, claiming for the colony what evil so badly wanted to steal.

He was sucked through a straw, the next thing he knew. His canine body, fluid and boneless, slipped through miles of pipeline. Screams wailed at him from all angles in a layered cacophony of discordant voices. White-hot light brighter than a thousand suns drowned his vision, and dull pain thrummed in his marrow, but he was moving. Going forward. Taking steps, not standing still.

Maybe he was dying, or headed somewhere worse than death, but it beat the lifeless impotence of inertia where he lived without Rachel.

Timothy snapped into sentience in the middle of a street. Daylight. Snow. Cars swerved, honked. Metal giants bore down on him, headlights glaring with a mix of shock and hostility.

He smelled gas and oil and a faint garbage stink, odors emanating from the blacktop. For a split second, he froze against the onslaught of stimuli, adjusting to his low center of gravity. He was the wolf. He was fast.

He ran out of harm's way, dashing down a sidewalk. People screeched and jumped to avoid him, their prey instincts kicking in to inspire the flight response. Timothy had no interest in attacking anyone. He only cared about finding Rachel. This had to be where they'd ended up before. He recognized the smell of the air, the precise temperature, and the feel of the snow under his paws.

"Nine-one-one?" a woman shrieked behind him, her voice on the verge of breaking down. "I'd like to report a free-range wolf running down Hennepin Avenue. Correct, there's an adult wolf loose in downtown Minneapolis. Gray and white. Huge."

Minneapolis! He'd thank the lady for confirming he'd transported to the correct location, but she wouldn't handle an interaction well. More to the point, he needed to hide himself and shift before he ended up tranquilized by animal control or worse. But first, he needed to locate Rachel's scent and track her down.

He ducked down an alley, away from more witnesses, and took a moment to gather his sense of direction. He could smell the frozen lake, its freezer-like humidity tinged with a mineral bite. The sun's placement helped him determine direction. He slunk behind buildings and cars, edging closer to where they'd parted company, until at last he caught her scent.

The top note of Rachel's aroma was fresh and floral, the soap and bath products she used mixed with her natural uniqueness to form a sweetly earthy fragrance. But the true distinction lay on a lower level. The ground floor was where the darker layer persisted, the subtle, musty richness. The taste of the oak barrel in which the wine was stored. The dirt in which the vines took root. The deep stuff. The chaos magic.

Once he got a hold of the magic trail, his nostrils flaring as he chased its path, tracking her down wasn't hard. He found her standing on the porch of a painted bungalow, her arms folded over her book, peering in the front window as if she was trying to see around the drawn curtain. A wooden sign was planted in the snowy lawn, signaling this was a business of some sort.

His footfalls silent and weightless, he glided up the steps to meet her. "It's me. Don't scream."

She turned around, and her eyes widened, but she caught herself before a reaction hit. "Thank God." Rachel crouched and threw her arms around his neck, tucking her book in the crook under her arm. "The spell failed. I'm so sorry."

"No need to apologize. I don't think it failed, per se, it just worked differently than intended. I'll explain as soon as we're inside. Which I need to be soon. People are making emergency phone calls."

Rachel rose to her feet and paced the porch. "The good news is, I found out where Helen works. Bad news is nobody's here. Her home address isn't listed anywhere."

In the distance, a siren wailed. Probably not animal control, but it did remind him of his predicament. "Do you see a blanket or anything lying around? I need to change, and my clothes didn't come with me." Occasionally, garments hung on in the shift, other times they fell off or were completely destroyed. Unfortunately, Timothy was dealing with the latter scenario.

She took off her coat and laid it over his back. Underneath, she wore a wool sweater. It occurred to Timothy that this was the most they'd undressed in front of each other, despite having given in to passion. Or sex magic. Or whatever intersection between the two they'd carved out of a combination of desire and urgency. They needed to talk about the thing between them, but not now.

With the coat as a shield, Timothy concentrated on nothing more, nothing less than returning to human form. The pain and distress in this direction wasn't as bruising, for whatever reason, but it took over enough that the sensations were all he could focus on while he gritted his teeth, tensed his muscles, and got through it.

He'd lost touch with his surroundings entirely until a new, unseen, female voice demanded, "Who are you, why are you stalking me, and why is there a naked man on my porch?"

SIX

IT WAS SO VISCERALLY STRANGE AND UNCANNY, LOOKING INTO Helen's familiar eyes from the perspective of the outsider. Eyes she'd come to know well for their empathy and no-nonsense kindness now stared at her with shock and more than a trace of fear.

The person she'd come to know as a sister had morphed into a stranger, never having existed here, replaced by a clone.

Rachel didn't blame Helen. After all, she'd shown up on the front porch of the woman's business, a naked man in tow, rambling about failed spells and her successful efforts to track Helen down. She was lucky that this person who was a member of her coven in another dimension, wasn't aiming a can of mace at her.

She had to say something to break this standoff. Think fast. Helen owned a yoga studio and was into crystals and chakras, energy healing, Tarot, and all the rest. They'd talked about the lot of it. Manifesting on the full moon, somebody having a planetary stellium in Scorpio, angel numbers. Those elements were present in this reality, at least in theory. She had to have some affinity for off-the-wall subject matter introduced without conversational warmup.

"Do you believe in magic?" Rachel asked.

Helen blinked. Her lips thinned. She wore her brown hair in a ponytail and had on athletic leggings and a tank top with her studio name, "Light & Enlightened," written whimsically on the front in violet cursive. "I'm not sure I understand what you're driving at. How can I help you?"

It was weird to meet Helen in her element, to encounter her as a slightly frosty stranger. Rachel kept talking to stave off an impending feeling of dissociative horror threatening to suck her deep into the bowels of her own mind. She was stunned this was happening and vaguely terrified. "Divination? Prophecy? The butterfly effect of choices rippling through one dimension to cause a domino cascade of effects in another?" Yes, her speech toed the edge of what a rambling lunatic might deliver. But the vicinity was legitimate. She had to hit Helen where she lived, literally and figuratively, to have a shot. "I guess you could say I'm searching for common ground here as quickly as possible."

Helen appraised Timothy, a wince transforming into a half-cocked wink. Rachel told herself the erstwhile spirit witch was amused, not threatened, by this baffling display of near nudity. "I'll bite. Sure. I believe in the fundamental reality of occurrences that don't necessarily obey, or that exceed, scientific principles. I believe everything in existence is comprised on energetic vibrations." She was holding back, which was fine. This was a start.

"We're from another dimension," Timothy said, Rachel's pink winter coat pulled around his front, the hem too short to cover much beyond mid-thigh. He was so poised, wearing the ridiculous coat like it fit him perfectly. He'd really dialed it up to eleven by dropping the dimension line. Rachel respected him for the choice. There was no point in soft-pedaling the reason behind their visit. "Or another plane of existence, however you want to think about it. The point is, she's telling the truth, and you need to listen. The fate of the world depends on it."

Helen laughed in a bewildered way, but she hadn't slammed the door in their faces yet. "This is the most interesting thing that's happened to me all year that isn't bad. Sure. Come in." She stepped aside and made a motion with her hand, still eyeing her guests with incredulity, her mouth curved in bemusement. "Better the two of you stopping by unannounced than a debt collector or my estranged mother, now that there's a perception that some money has turned up." She walked to a nook transformed into a cozy kitchen thanks to a plug-in kettle, a hot plate, and a mini fridge covered in new age-y stickers. Above the sink, a stained-glass window took in light to infuse the atmosphere with an ethereal kaleidoscope of primary color aided by the glow of the winter sun. "You guys like tea?"

"Please." Timothy rubbed his hands and blew on them. Neither he nor Rachel inquired about Helen's offhand mention of her personal issues. Rachel figured the background matter worked to their advantage. Helen wasn't in complete control of her life from the jump. Weak points had her rattled, the debt collectors and mother. Perfect staging ground for opening to a drastic change in routine.

Helen pushed a button on her kettle, and a blue light came on. "Why are you naked? Does your ass practically hanging out of a woman's Old Navy coat have anything to do with the urgent matters coming from another dimension?"

"I can shift my shape. I had to change to come here, and my clothes weren't with me after I transported."

Okay. Timothy was choosing to stick with radical honesty. Interesting play.

Helen ripped open paper bags and set two tea bags into mismatched cups. One was Halloween themed with the words "boss witch" painted on the front, the cutely scribbled play on words accompanied by a tiny purple witch hat. Rachel took this as a sign from the universe. Witchy topics of discussion were on the table. She felt required to make such interpretations of the mundane aspects of her environment, because otherwise the situation was too absurd to bear.

Rachel said, "There are planes of reality where the laws of physics don't work the same." Including here, apparently, because Timothy had used his shifting ability, and they'd cast a spell back at Sea Salt & Brine. Maybe they'd christened this dimension with the principles of magic by virtue of their very existence. Rachel experienced this possibility as at once a privilege, a blessing, and an impossibly heavy burden. "Can I have the tea in the witch cup?" The mug would work as a conversation starter.

"Since we're full speed ahead, can I tell you about this recurring dream I've been having?" Helen handed over the mugs, heeding

Rachel's request, the cup warm in her cold hands. Her gaze had changed to expectant. She picked at the black nail polish on her forefinger.

"Yeah." Rachel's mind was open to any new information. She had to find a natural inroad or acquire tidbits to help her grasp her specific task. Her book made for a heavy weight. "We're all ears. Anything you want to share, we're grateful to receive."

Moving with the fluid ease befitting a business owner, Helen led them down a narrow hallway, past what looked like a small bedroom converted into a space to house racks of clothing, a shelf of yoga mats and other accessories, and a round table covered with neatly arranged crystals and candles.

Light & Enlightened was so cool, a vintage bungalow, all hardwood and homey smells. Perfect for conversion into a yoga studio. A little crunchy, not too neo-corporate, bereft of the post-gentrification, hipster vibe tending to infect trendy neighborhoods. Rachel was a bit bummed that small talk was not in the cards. She'd like to get to know Helen better outside of the crucible of the damn prophecy.

"We have men's wear." Helen gestured to the racks of clothes, a sidelong glance sneaking out when she turned her head to address Timothy. "Unless you want to hold out in case you need to shift your shape again." It wasn't clear how seriously Helen was taking this yet. But she was affording them her space and time, which was the most important thing for now.

"Clothes would be great," Timothy said. "I'll pay you back somehow, but I'm sorry to say that I don't have a card or cash. The society where we live has moved past money."

"Yeah, it's fine. We can barter or something." In the next room were two lush, blue velvet couches, an abundance of plants of indeterminate authenticity, and a front desk. Three different signs advertised a sliding scale and a donation-based class on Thursday nights. "Must be nice to escape the soul-crushing rat race of late-stage capitalism." Helen peered at a computer monitor on a desk before walking away from it and sitting down on one of the sofas.

Rachel caught frustration in Helen's voice and noticed how the front desk was covered in papers resembling bills. Helen must've been at her studio during off hours catching up on financial stuff, and she didn't seem enthusiastic about it.

While Timothy dressed, Rachel sat on a couch opposite Helen and nursed her tea. A sip of ginger lemon comforted her, and she launched into the bottom line as best she could. She had no game plan. "There's a way out of the endless race. Of the grind. We found it, and now we have to save it. You can go there with us. In fact, you're already there. Another version of you, I should say. Coexisting with this one."

Helen lifted her eyebrows. "I'm pretty new age-y, but I confess I'm struggling here. You guys aren't high, right?"

Timothy emerged from the clothes closet in gray sweatpants and a navy t-shirt with "yogi" printed on the front in block, collegiate-type lettering. He looked so sexy, casual cool, weekend masculine chic. Rachel entertained a brief, fleeting fantasy of what it would be like to wake up with him on a Saturday morning, kissing while the sun rose. She quickly got her head back in the game. They'd used sex magic, but she had to be mature about it. No feelings.

"We're sober," Timothy said, taking a place at Rachel's side on the couch. The new clothing smell on him further stimulated her imagination. They could be different versions of themselves in this world, trying on new clothes and new personalities while on vacation from paranormal drama.

Except not really, because paranormal drama was the precise purpose of their visit. Such things hemmed her in and followed her wherever she ran, a psychic crown of snakes to accompany the tangible counterpart.

Timothy went on. "She's telling the truth. There are parallel worlds, probably more than any of us will ever experience. Some are sunken, hellish, while others are fantastical. Still others are little more than slightly different versions of each other. The last category, those are the ones we have to move through to do our job."

Helen had gone poker-faced. "What am I like in the dimension where you travelled from?"

Rachel went for broke. "In the other dimension, you're a witch. You can teleport easily and manipulate matter with your thoughts. Get inside people's minds, use telekinesis. Think of it like the self you are now, but turbo charged. Controlling your environment with crystals and color energy. You're incredibly formidable at your craft. You're one of the most powerful women I've ever met."

A scoff, but more self-deprecating than sarcastic. "I sound overpowered. How's my love life? I want to live vicariously through this other me. Speaking of hellish dimensions, please tell me she's not on Tinder."

"You're married to a famous rock star who inadvertently programmed dark magic into his band's songs."

At the very least, her account, which was true, ought to pique Helen's interest. Get her mind away from past due notices and Tinder tragedies and steer it to scenarios where she didn't have to worry about garnishments, left swipes, and ghosting by mediocre men.

Rachel could liberate Helen from those dull and pointless shades of hell.

"You're sure you're not on drugs? Like, this is outlandish, you guys. I've smoked pot and done shrooms. I won't judge."

"You still haven't told us about your recurring dream," Rachel said.

"What a coincidence you bring my dream up at this exact moment. Are you a mind reader, too?"

"There aren't any coincidences. All three of us know that. The timing of the dream subject happened for a reason." The notion of dreams as auspicious synchronicities seemed like something Helen would believe.

"Okay." Helen uncrossed her legs. She fidgeted with the string on her tea bag. "I didn't think you'd actually be interested. It can be so boring to listen to other people's dreams. Everyone thinks their dreams are weird, cool-weird, but most are actually pretty basic."

Timothy leaned forward. "We won't be bored. We're here to find you because we need your help. Anything you have to offer is valuable."

Helen spoke. In the dream, she and her business partner went out for brunch, then to the farmer's market. A typical Saturday. Then, on a lark and through seemingly random chance, they saw a concert. The timeline skipped forward to Helen walking with one of the band members from the performance, someone she knew and admired, and was attracted to. They held hands as they cut through a dusty outdoor parking lot. Fairgrounds, Helen thought. She was proud to be with him, and strikingly content. Vividly living in the moment, warmed from the inside out. She remembered this key part with unforgettable clarity. Later, Helen and the man picked up a boy from a daycare center. The child wore a leather jacket and had long, curly hair. He played with colorful blocks. Things began to dissolve into a blur of color, like images covered in film. Subsequent events unfolded at a greater distance and lacked immediacy. She mourned the losses.

Another jump, and Helen found herself in the mailroom of her apartment building. Her memories began to fade, slowly, then all at once. Then she woke up.

"I've been having this one for years, on and off. The content is always exactly the same. The images, the order of events, what I'm wearing, the color and placement of the cars in the parking lot. This might sound crazy, but I've started to track and chart the dates of the dream's arrival. Kind of like keeping track of your period." She laughed. "The dream shows up on astrologically significant benchmarks. Solstices. Equinoxes. When the moon is in my sun sign."

"What's your sign?" Rachel asked, both to deepen her understanding of Helen's dream cycle and out of curiosity. She'd long enjoyed astrology, even if only as a fun escape.

"Pisces." Helen rubbed her hand over her face and groaned. "This is so embarrassing."

"Being a Pisces? It's okay, I'm a Taurus." She'd read somewhere Taurus was easily embarrassed, so it seemed like a good icebreaking joke.

"No, the question." Helen's eyes were foggy. She waved her palm in front of her nose, like she was trying to push thoughts out of her head. "There's a song with the same title. It's a whole thing. With the dream."

"Brian Shepherd's band, right?" Timothy asked.

"Yeah." Her cheeks and nose had gone pink. "He's the subject of the dream. The man I'm walking with. It's like I have this infatuation with him I can't shake. I had a crush on him when I was younger. My first crush. This all sounds so juvenile."

"I don't think crushes ever really go away," Rachel said. Now was probably as good as any time to drop a bombshell. "He's the one you're married to in our dimension. Brian Shepherd. Your dream isn't a coincidence or a fluke. It's trying to steer you. Tell you something. If not the dream itself, the magic behind it. The guiding force."

"You promise me this isn't some kind of prank?" Helen sucked in a breath. "Because I feel really vulnerable right now, and honestly a bit foolish."

"We're not messing with you," Timothy assured. "And we need to merge these timelines. Does part of you want to see what the other version of your life is like?"

"What happens to my studio? Everything I've worked for?"

"You still have it. You come back here now and then to teach and catch up on work. But you and Brian have been spending a lot of time in Peru lately, where our colony lives. It's been a good fit for you, being in nature and away from the grind. You still teach yoga."

Helen's stare had turned incredulous. "Why do I feel like this is how people get recruited into really scary cults where they end up drinking the guru's bathwater or eating dead flies to prove their devotion?"

"I know it seems farfetched and full of red flags." Timothy held the studio owner's gaze. "If I were in your shoes, my skepticism alarm bells would be ringing too. But ask yourself this. Haven't you wanted to know what's behind the dream? Why it's happening, and what you're supposed to be doing with the content? How it might be a sign there's indeed more to this world than what's been proven?"

"Of course. I tried all sorts of lucid dream techniques to get control of the narrative while I slept. Tried and failed. It's as if the dream story is stubborn. I feel so heavy on those nights, sucked in deep. When I try to go lucid, I feel this force pulling back on me. Keeping me exactly where I'm supposed to be, if what I'm saying makes sense."

"Perfect sense." Rachel would have to gloss over the darker details of who was controlling Helen's dream, the realities of those more nefarious aspects of magic and otherworldly portals. Timothy had alluded to some stuff, but she had to tread carefully now since the subject matter was so personal. Scaring Helen away could ruin their plan. "My thought is you'll need more substantial tools than lucid dreaming techniques to really make this dream work for you."

"What tools would those be?" Helen's eyes narrowed. She'd slipped into a moderate retreat. Rachel had to pull her back. No evasiveness or sugar-coating. Entice and tempt.

"Have you ever experimented with witchcraft?"

"Maybe? I don't know. According to the nuns from my Catholic high school, probably. Do moon manifestation rituals count?"

"You can change your life this way," Rachel said. She fished in her pocket until her fingers closed around a smooth, hard chunk. Fortunately, despite the game with Folly in the Other Place, her talisman had made it with her to the alternate Minnesota. She showed the rock to Helen. "Does this mean anything to you? On an intuitive level or from your dream?"

Helen recoiled with a grimace. "If my business partner were here, she'd say this sounded like a snake oil sales tactic."

"I have a story about snakes." Rachel tugged on a lock of her hair; the strand still mercifully normal. "Using magic solved my snake problem. This craft can work for us."

"I know you're apprehensive," Timothy said. "It's valid. But we need you. And you might not know it yet, but you need us. Everyone does. Along the way, you could get closure on this dream issue. How good would it feel to finally be able to make sense of this baffling event that won't unhook from your life?"

"You know what?" Helen slapped both of her thighs. Rachel braced herself for a rejection. Then what? "I'm in. This might be the dumbest thing I've ever done, and I've made plenty of dumb mistakes in my life, but at least I'm trying something new. I want to go to my house, though. Not here."

"Fine." Internally, Rachel released a massive exhale. They were moving forward. To where remained to be seen, but the events of the last hour had felt like some form of stumbling, messy progress. "Venue shouldn't matter. I have some spells committed to memory and an idea of how to stir you into the mix." She'd break out the book if Helen seemed receptive to a deep dive.

With any luck, this version of Helen bore traces of magic, the dragon bloodline, the special sauce allowing her to tap into their shared craft. There was one way to find out.

Helen walked to her desk and slung a patchwork purse over her shoulder. Keys jangled in her hand. "Venue absolutely matters. I don't want my business partner to show up here unexpectedly and catch me chanting in the middle of a pentagram or whatever. We're already on thin ice, and she'll think I've lost my marbles once and for all."

"We don't work with pentagrams." The last thing Rachel needed was for Helen to think they were about to dip into the brackish pool of dark magic or Satanism. Diabolical practice was the purview of their enemies.

"Whatever. I'll call you a rideshare and text you my address. My car's a mess. If you guys try to sacrifice me or something, you won't get away with it." En route to the front door, Helen tossed a dry look over her shoulder. Sarcasm, but only a touch. Which was fine. Her trust wasn't cheaply earned.

"We mean you no harm," Timothy said. "But if it would make you feel any better to let some people know you're having new friends over, go for it."

"Nah. I don't want anyone to know I've officially gone off the deep end due to obsessive dreams about my adolescent celebrity crush. Let's go. I'm so intrigued to know what's going to come of this. I can't take it anymore."

Once Helen's back was turned, Rachel looked at Timothy and bent her shoulder up in a half-shrug. He returned her gesture of mild celebration with a tick of his lips. As they exited behind Helen, he held the door for Rachel, the chivalry unexpected but not surprising and certainly not unwelcome. She brushed her knuckles against his, meeting his eyes on the way out.

Who knew what they were, and what they might become? All Rachel knew was they'd scored a win this afternoon, and they'd done it by working together. If magic was their love language, or at least where they connected best, then she was happy to see where the dimension-blending project led. Bonus points if they averted catastrophe.

She was happy to have an ally in Timothy, a partner in crime. What was about to happen with Helen, her nocturnal conundrum, and any latent magic swirling under her surfaces remained to be seen. Rachel was prepared to solve those mysteries.

But once their driver finished navigating a snowy network of interstate and city streets to arrive outside of Helen's high-rise apartment, Rachel's optimism dampened. An unwanted guest had arrived, forever lording over Rachel's magic but never on her side.

SEVEN

TIMOTHY HAD BEEN WRONG. BACKWARDS, EVEN. HE DIDN'T NEED TO redirect Rachel's chaos magic to help her shift her shape and channel the source from within him to break her curse. He needed to link himself to her chaos magic and build a chain. Once he did, he'd be able to close the portal, send the dark cloud back across the veil, and seal the gap permanently.

Julian and Raven, Cynthia's partner and a fellow shifter, had talked about partner work linkages. Timothy hadn't understood until now how integral his role was to be, though. How everyone in the chain would have to pull from chaos magic. Before a chain reaction could happen, Rachel had to assume her seat at the helm. Her magic had to be the mightiest of all, the generative source to flow unimpeded to everyone else.

His vision had told him so. A flash, a mere suggestion, but that was all it took. One image piercing through the blankness of an otherwise failed meditation, a snapshot hurtling through the blackout behind his eyelids so fast someone might as well have thrown it at his head.

Seated on the floor of Helen's apartment, holding hands in a three-person circle with the two witches, Timothy arrived at this conclusion along with the dead end of many failed attempts.

Helen broke the silence first. Her grip had gone limp a couple of minutes before she talked, her body language admitting defeat before she officially spoke it. "Didn't you say we were supposed to experience fast results? Or at least get clues something was happening? I don't mean to be impatient, and I'm trying to give the benefit of the doubt, but it's been two hours."

At Timothy's opposite side, Rachel dropped her hand. She pinched the bridge of her nose. "I don't know why I can't even see into your mind, let alone the external hive mind. All I need is a little peek to be able to get a glimpse of the choices you need to make to jump timelines. But the inside of your head is a black box. Or blocked. I can't crack it."

Helen stood up. She had an uneasy look on her face, furrowed brows and a pursed mouth. "I think this was a bad idea. It was really great to meet the two of you and think big on a spiritual scale, but maybe this isn't for me."

"We need to use Rachel's book," Timothy said, more sure than ever. There was no mistaking what had flashed before his closed eyes. The text to end all texts, beaten, tough leather with the sigil of the coven daughters etched on the bloodlines. Nobody knew where those books came from or what series of events moved them into the hands of their owners. All he knew was the book needed to be in the middle of their circle. Immediately. The book was screaming to be seen. "And we need it now."

"The big leather book?" Helen eyed the grimoire on the floor. She crossed her arms over her chest. "I didn't ask at first because I didn't want to know."

Rachel said, "Yes. It's a book of spells and witchcraft. It's called a grimoire. It's sacred. Authentic." She turned to Timothy. "Why do you think we need to bring it in?"

"It appeared to me," he said. "And spoke with its mind, demanding to be read. I think it wants to be involved in this process and won't allow us to progress unless we bring it in."

"Nope." Helen stuck her hand out palm-forward. She didn't sound like she was joking about her rejection. "I'm afraid I'm going to have to ask the two of you to leave. This was interesting at first, but the way you're talking is giving me the heebie-jeebies."

What happened next shocked Timothy. Rachel rose to her feet with confident grace, went to where Helen hovered by the door, and placed her hands on their host's upper arms.

Helen struggled for a second and failed to wiggle free. She went limp. Her lips parted. A thread of gray smoke curled out of her mouth and faded into Rachel's hair. After, Helen stood like a decommissioned robot, her eyes fixed on some nowhere point in the void, her expression dazed.

Timothy rushed to her side. Helen's chest rose and fell, but she was no longer herself. "What did you do?" Timothy didn't mean for his question to come out like an accusation, but it did.

When Rachel turned to him, a shot of fight or flight jolted his pulse. Her eyes were solid black pools. The brown waves of her hair, though not serpentine, moved on their own accord, animated with strange life.

A tingle sparked between his legs. She'd never looked so beautiful. Dark. Taboo. Wrong. Sexy, drenched in her elemental chaos. He wanted her more than ever. He had to remain calm and in control of his raging desires. "Answer me," he said.

"I don't answer to you." Half of her mouth ticked up into a sneer. "Or anyone except my whims."

His cock stiffened. Still, he took a step back. This wasn't right at all. A fatally seductive unwholesomeness had intruded into the apartment. He liked it and hated it at the same time. He understood the meaning of the word temptation like never before.

Without warning, the inky veil dropped from Rachel's lids. She sucked in a fast breath and muttered a swear word. "She's okay." At least the statement rang true. "I did a simple mind pause spell from memory. Basically, I removed her thoughts from her head and placed them in mine. That's what the snakes do, even if you can't see them. They're like storage containers. When men turn to stone, it's really their essence leaking out and making its way into snakes' mouths. I've been trying for ages to get control of it, but those spells are hard. Looks like I finally made progress."

"What happened when you went away?" His mouth tasted bad. He'd never be able to purge that memory of Rachel, some twisted, perverse version of her with blacked-out eyes and a sadistic sneer. "You were gone, and someone took your place. Another presence." He knew who'd come in to act as the replacement. They both did. There was no need to name Rachel's interloper, and invoking her by saying her name enhanced her power.

"I know. I was half-in and half-out. It's the final stage of my trial. I have to take control of the chaos magic without leaving myself open to possession. I could feel myself in there with her, but I was weak. Feeble. Overtaken. I need to get stronger. You're right—we need to use the book."

But when Rachel went to the spot where they'd left the grimoire, it wasn't there. "Shit." She ran around the apartment, peeked under the couch, and upended a chair cushion before throwing up her hands. "It's gone. The spell I did spirited it away somehow. I bet I was tricked into giving it up."

Rachel wouldn't be able to marshal chaos magic without her text. It was too mighty, the central tent pole of the entire system. Folly knew this and stole her book to disempower her. Their enemy would not give up her toehold without a fight, but battling for dominion was the only way. As an unbroken circle, the witches, shifters, and other nodes in the network had to pull from chaos magic and send it back to Rachel, cleansed and fortified.

"I'll go find the book. You stay with her." In part, he proposed this plan as a practice run. It was time to up his game. He had to figure out how to consistently transport with objects, guide his travel, and order the chaos he'd soon have to master.

"I can't let you. The chaos magic could take you over. You're not equipped enough yet to face it head on." Her cautionary skepticism challenged him to rise to the task.

"I made it here." He pointed at the ground. "No small feat."

"Sure, but you had the portal to guide you." Rachel laid her hand on his forearm as if the gesture would slow down his train of thought. "It's harder without it. We both go."

"We can't leave her here." Helen loomed large in Timothy's peripheral vision. "She might have a bad reaction. Or wake up and do something rash."

"We take her with us." Timothy closed some space between himself and Rachel. "I'll wake her up once we arrive in Peru. Show her the new world. Once she knows we're serious, we return her to here and get back to work merging. She'll be more committed. It'll help."

A vehement shake of her head shut down his argument yet again. "We're kidnapping someone. Crazy."

He had to admit that sparring with Rachel heated him up. "So crazy it just might work."

Once the buzz of banter faded, Timothy shared a long look with Rachel. Past the surface of her, the color of her eyes, the angle of her nose, her smooth, tawny skin, he saw her nucleus. He didn't mean that as a metaphor, a way to express how he noticed the dimensions of the attraction penetrating beyond skin-deep physical appeal. Those things were obvious. Her tenacity, her smarts, her dedication to beating staggering odds were all admirable. The leader in him saw the leader in her. When Rachel spoke, or even looked like she was thinking, he sat up and took notice. None of those impressive traits defined her nucleus.

He saw deeper. He saw to the otherworldly force that made her unlike any other person. Beneath the qualities making her an individual person, he glimpsed her affinity to those more unpredictable elements of her magical gift, curse—whatever it was.

Timothy danced where the dark heart beat, and he saw the space. He craved to touch the darkest part, taste it, hold it close. She'd pulled him in with her own spell, a marvelous, wicked collision of supernatural stuff and those unique pieces of herself.

He took Rachel's hand. "We're in this together. I need you to trust me in these next steps."

"Sounds like a warning."

"It's a precaution." He laid their clasped hands over his heart. "I think I know what we need to do. First, we have to get the book back in our hands."

Rachel linked arms with the zoned-out yoga witch. "She's going to hate me after this unless I find a way to mind wipe her without letting her know she's been cleaned."

Tinkering with people's minds and memories was an ethical minefield, but Rachel was correct. They'd have to find a solution. "You lead the charge. I'll focus on tying my concentration to yours. A yoke should allow me to build up my own magic."

Nervous energy sputtered out in a few fast wiggles before Rachel centered to stillness. "This is all so risky."

"The alternative is worse."

"True." Rachel squeezed Timothy's hand. The gesture felt good, both a call for comfort and an assurance they were a team.

He held on, his thumb poised on her wrist, the pad of his flesh tracking her pulse. The thrum of life pulsing inside of her soothed him in an undefined way, entwining the threads of their shared being.

She called upon chaos, her tone confident and direct, and dove into an incantation designed to get the three of them to Peru.

Timothy lost his bearings fast, the edges of his perception dissolving into a velvet void. This place of unspeakable secrets hailed him, lulled him, engulfed him. Subsumed in a magnetized sea, he fell.

Next, he ran. Muscles pumping. On fire. His vision sharp, center of gravity low. Night. The air was crisp, fresh and cold, but no snow. Scents of earth and tinges of rot-sweet decay infused the mélange. He ran with the wolves, barreling down a trail. Forest flanked him, them, on either side. So much running, chasing, pursuing.

Things often worked this way when it came to traveling by magic. There were twists and turns, long routes, detours. He'd learned to be patient and go with it as opposed to struggling. A degree of acceptance got him back on track faster.

"Rachel," he'd called the word in his mind, as no sound came from his mouth. In his ears, only the whoosh of wind blew through as he charged toward an endpoint understood only by wherever his mind had been before he'd arrived here.

Beside him, a pair of yellow eyes lit the night. A wolf the color of the void. "We can talk with our minds," her unique intonation returned to him telepathically. "Helen is with us. I sensed her energy."

Relief flooded him. At least they were together, and in one piece. Before he could gather his next thought, the familiar jungle landscape opened to a clearing made of short grass pockmarked by tree stumps. It resembled one of the formerly lush forest areas, clear-cut and turned into pasture for livestock.

Timothy hated the destruction of the forest, but the way the environment adapted fascinated him. This newly formed prairie was like a Midwestern field surrounded by jungle foliage. It was alien, out of place, and utterly original. A testimony, a monument to change.

He and Rachel stood in the eerie place alone, facing off.

"This is what you wanted, right?" Folly's voice disseminated from the ether. "For her constitution to resemble yours?"

"What does this have to do with my chaos magic?" Rachel didn't open her jaw to speak, but he knew Folly heard. They shared a mind.

"*Your* chaos magic." The ruler of the magic system laughed, mocking them with poisoned sarcasm. "Do you know what a synecdoche is?"

"Part to whole," Rachel said.

"And whole to part," Timothy finished.

At almost the same moment, they moved closer to each other, the body language more profound than their earlier mind meld.

"You have two black holes inside of you," Folly said. "Everyone does. If you can use them to your advantage and control them, the book is yours." She left. Her disappearance registered like a swift, abrupt change in emotion.

"This isn't good." Rachel's irises were twin hoops of gold against endless sky, glitter sparkling against onyx. A tree line, now clear cut, had once blanketed the ground against the unfiltered stare of the naked sky. "She read our intentions easily and used my spell to turn the magic against us. Which is why we're here, being manipulated, and put to a test."

If they could solve the riddle, they'd get the book. Based on the stories Timothy had heard, Folly was going easier on Rachel than she had the other witches. This made sense. The elemental sister of chaos was partial to the one who wielded their shared element. He thought out loud. "There's a Native American proverb about having two wolves inside of us. It's not from my tribe, but it still resonates. The idea is each of us has two wolves inside of us, metaphorically speaking. One is fueled by hate, anger, envy, and other negative emotions. The other is based on compassion, kindness, and love. The one that grows stronger is the one we feed."

"Interesting." Rachel's chin tipped up and down in a nod. "A symbolic interpretation. I could see Folly putting us through a trial. Testing our emotions. Allegiances. Something about this theory doesn't quite connect, though. Like I don't see any outcome where she'd reward us for choosing love."

"Not her style, I agree." Could the black holes represent the normal range of human expression plus the dark heart of magic? But this idea didn't make sense, because Folly had said everyone, and not everyone had the access Timothy and Rachel did.

Helen ambled over. Her pelt was a steely shade of gray dusted with white. Her paws were white, too, like she'd stepped in snow. "Hey there." Her tone carried an edge of accusation and more than a little fear. "Which of you two would like to clue me in on what the hell I'm doing here and why the fuck I'm in the body of a wolf? I trusted you guys not to do anything out of pocket. This better not be permanent. I did not sign up for this." She had the same golden eyes, twin flames illuminating the night path. Hers appeared more grounded in a body. His and Rachel's stood out like fireflies floating in darkness.

This was it! A bell rang through the innermost layer of Timothy's intuition. He wasn't yet able to articulate or even fully form his thoughts, but he'd figured out the riddle. The answer was right in front of them.

Rachel did her best to reassure Helen while Timothy gathered his theory into a coherent point.

Rachel said to her sister witch, "It's temporary. We have to go through a series of trials before I can take over the magic system. The first involves solving this riddle so I can reclaim my book. Once I have it, we're in good shape."

"Take over the magic system?" Helen cried. "You didn't tell me any of this. And who's putting you through a trial? I don't like this at all. By the way it sounds, you have an enemy. One more powerful than you. Right?"

"For now," Rachel said.

Helen gaped.

An intervention was called for, and what better way to redirect than to solve a problem? Or at least lay out the first step. "It's our pupils."

"Excuse me?" Still indignant, Helen scoffed a huffy noise. "I can't believe I let you two weirdos do your crackpot experiment on me."

Timothy forged ahead. Everyone had to hear this. "The two black holes inside of us are our pupils. They take in light. Swallow it. Absorb it.

I remember reading somewhere, in a poem I think, that when we forget, the memory falls into the black holes of our pupils."

"Fascinating," Rachel said with glee, and Timothy beamed internally. He'd provided a solution, brought goods to the table, and pleased her. He loved doing those things and felt most like himself when he was able to. With Rachel involved, the sense of satisfaction magnified. "It ties into our sense of sight. If we forget something we see, and we forget almost everything we experience, then the visual memory is lost to the black hole. Stored there. Like essences in my snakes."

Helen did not look won over by any of this. "I'd ask about the snakes, but I'd rather keep my blissful ignorance."

"It'll make sense soon," Timothy said. "Just try to stick with us. With patience. Faith."

"Not like I have a choice."

Wrapping up her point, Rachel offered a final thought. "Those black holes can work for us if we can control them."

Far off in space, stars and constellations twinkled, each a pinprick puncturing the ebony to let in light. Though not always the most metaphorical, poetic man, tonight a literary sensibility was working for him. He could be intellectually flexible. He had to be to lead well. Versatile creativity was a friend who kept him mentally limber. "I think I have an idea how. We enter the black holes in ourselves. Climb inside those worlds and recover the lost memories."

"Except not our memories per se," Rachel said.

"Correct." He was humming along now. On the wave. Buzzing with the pleasure of figuring things out. "The forgotten memories of everyone in our lineage. Our generational inheritance that's been lost."

Right now, the inheritance was in the wrong hands, and the prophecy was moving forward. Minutes were crucial. They had to recover the collective mind from Folly's control, and soon.

EIGHT

THE AIR WAS WET AND HEAVY, FERTILE. SEDUCTIVE GLIDES OF WIND caressed the fur covering Rachel's body. A storm was coming. She'd been here long enough to recognize the patterns.

Not only an atmospheric storm, but an energetic one too. She'd certainly been around long enough to notice *those* patterns. Her flesh prickled, her senses on high alert. She looked into the bottomless pools of Timothy's eyes. "There is a very good chance this is a trap."

He held onto her attention with his gaze alone, conviction and calm strength radiating through him even in this changed form. Especially in this changed form, which he wore so well as a literal second skin. It was odd and vulnerable, meeting him like this. Her, upended, her grip on reality unfurled, amazed and terrified with the pounding head rush of possibility.

If you could swap your body, change shape to become unrecognizable, anything was possible. Possibilities felt endless, at least.

Timothy, on the other hand, had never looked more natural. Himself, wholly, in his element. Inside and out, his second skin was more than an alternative form, a different body. It was an aura, an essence, and it was sexy.

"If it is a trap, I'll lead us out with your help. We have to try. This is a backroom. It has to be. All signs point to us falling in deep into the Other Place."

"What about my book?" It suddenly felt like a crutch and an excuse.

"Once we're done, you won't need it, Rachel. You'll be more powerful than any book. Your actions will write the last chapter in your book and close it."

A shiver ran up her spine. He wasn't talking out of turn. Timothy was correct, and he'd researched. The books of the coven were sentient, self-authoring, telling the grand story through a combination of the witches' will and the text's individual contribution. In collaborative, symbiotic fashion, a witch and her book crafted reality as they went. A witch and her book were the ultimate example of mixed authorship.

Which didn't mean she was ready. "What if I fail?"

"You won't. I've got you." In those simple words alone, she'd never felt more nurtured, held, and nourished. Perhaps Timothy was like this with everyone, or perhaps she was special. Perhaps it didn't matter.

"What about me?" Helen's tone wasn't angry, but it was insistent, a voice with a tactile quality that grabbed and shook. "Can I please go home? I'm over this."

The gales were picking up, whistling through the trees as they mingled with bugs and monkey shrieks in a cacophony wrapping all three wolves in a crucible.

If Helen returned home and remembered the jungle excursion and her transformation into wolf form, she'd have a hard time explaining away how she'd experienced an event of great paranormal magnitude. Rachel was by no means finished with her coven sister. She'd send her back. But with an unforgettable calling card.

Moving a person from one clearly defined point to another was intermediate chaos magic, advanced, even, but she could do it. "This isn't over. You're going to remember what happened tonight. I'll be back for you."

"I can't tell if that's an assurance or a threat," Helen said.

"It's just reality." Rachel concentrated on the magic within her, pulling the purple-black current into a whirlpool. She steadily urged her tool closer and closer to the surface. "A statement of fact."

"We need your help, Helen. Can I ask a favor of you?" Timothy was much more diplomatic, switching gears to empower Helen by offering her the chance to say no.

"Fine," the wolf-witch said.

"When you get home, you'll remember being here, as Rachel said. I need you to write everything down. Start writing the second you return to consciousness and don't stop until you've purged every last memory of your encounter with us. I won't go into too much detail, but keeping a record is crucial. You journaling your experience will be a tremendous asset."

"You're playing a huge role here." Rachel's magic was churning now, racing in circles of perpetual motion, a frantic snake eating its own tail to feed their shared tale. "These notes you take will conclude the book of chaos. Once it's done, I'll have the advantage I need to end this mess once and for all."

"You guys are crazy." Helen's already small eyes narrowed. "Drop me back off at home. It's been interesting, but I'm done hanging out. Not my style. Sorry."

She'd have to get used to their style, because her stint with the witches was far from over. But now wasn't the time to argue. For now, the chief requirement was that Helen understood the importance of the timeline merger. If she completed her writing exercise with this in mind, her mindful focus would enhance the chaos magic.

At the end of the day, all chaos magic was the use of signs, symbols, and insignia, backed by intention and earnest belief, to alter the flow of reality in one's favor.

When companies splashed their brand logos everywhere, implanting their image in the minds of potential consumers, they used a banal form of chaos magic. Rachel abided the same principle, but with loftier designs than selling coffee or shoes.

She turned to face Helen and stared her down, keying in on those twin black holes, their endless depth, those places which sucked up memories and tossed them into the oubliette of the past. Past, forgotten, recovered, fabricated—memory was such a strange phenomenon.

How truth could dance with falsehood and interpretation so fluidly, how two individual accounts of the same event could contrast in every important detail.

For now, Rachel lost herself in the black holes, taking Helen with her into the dungeon, the two of them falling as one. Rachel sucked in air; her lungs tight. She had to maintain control, or she'd fail.

She ran through the breathing exercises to help her stay centered, pushing Helen into the black holes, folding her in on herself, without going there as well. She pulled the chaos magic up from the cells of her marrow, a glimmering ribbon rich with the secrets of the ages, and poured into Helen's eyes.

Woozy, half-lucid, she pictured the Minneapolis apartment with its unique specifics. A patchwork quilt chair. Tile backsplash over the sink. Plants hanging in macramé, the chunky material dripping from the ceiling in braided ropes.

Along with the magic, she coaxed those images out of herself and directed them into Helen, imprinting, eye-to-eye. Planting memories of the apartment. How interesting to consider how the impressions sent to Helen might reflect Rachel's perspective on the apartment, supplanting the old ones and taking precedence.

Her reverie on mind magic was cut short when Helen shrunk to half her size before contracting again into a form smaller than a breadbasket. She folded over as if made of taffy, the golden iris glinting in a spark before she was gone.

Rachel closed her eyes and concentrated hard, picturing the apartment, the plants, the tiles. Helen lay on the couch in her clothes, asleep but beginning to stir. Relief took a pound of weight off her soul. "She's ok. She made it. It worked." On the heels of her relief, an onslaught of messier, tangled emotions thundered in. A tremor shook her foundation. She fought to cover it, maintaining her strong stance. Her eyes itched. "Give me one second to recalibrate before we tune in with each other. I think the blast of magic took it out of me."

In the darkness, Timothy's presence was an anchor and a shield against what felt like an endless brewing stew of mayhem and rural night. His attention brought her some place safe, even if only symbolically. She guarded her tender places, not because she didn't trust him, but because she owed it to him to also be strong.

The winds had picked up, the air smelling of minerals and autumn, dampness infused by the turning leaf of decay. A cold splat wetted her nose, two more following.

"Rachel." He spoke her name slowly, a lull between the syllables, saying so much wrapped in one word. "I've got you. You're so strong, and powerful, but please know it's okay if you ever can't be. I'm here, so you don't always have to be strong."

She wasn't ready to surrender. Being so different for so long had taught her tough truths. Safety came in hiding. Others worried themselves sick over her, they always had, and she refused to subject anyone new to her personal drama.

There had been her parents, rushing her to doctors and therapists after the latest spell, as they'd called her fits, the irony unintended. Seizures had mixed with a waking version of a night terror to create a truly horrifying blackout which left her screaming through chattering teeth or a locked jaw, immobilized in her own bodily prison of living rigor mortis, begging for someone, anyone, to help.

They'd tried and failed, and tried again, blaming themselves. Same with the doctors and therapists. Everyone was wrong, though. The problem wasn't some medical affliction or disease. Ballet had helped her control her body some, but mundane interventions would never suffice as solutions.

Rachel's fatal flaw, the sinister stuff buried inside of her, rested in the coffin of her dark heart.

Trapped inside, her magic attacked her other systems like a paranormal autoimmune disease. The experiment had brought it all to the surface, which was what Scarab wanted. Perhaps Rachel wanted surfacing too. An opportunity to unleash her demon, where at least she could face it on the surface. Maybe she'd walked right into Scarab's clutches, subconsciously flipping her middle finger at the red flags.

She had nothing to say to Timothy in reply, not now, so instead she closed the loop with a curt nod. "Let's see if this works." To acknowledge him for the value he'd brought, his good ideas, she said, "I think you were right about using my chaos magic to shift. It's given me more control."

"Thank me once we've merged these timelines and saved the world." He winked with one wolf-eye, a gesture so uncanny and self-aware she couldn't help but laugh. They were so weird, here together, much more than human yet painfully so in the most authentic ways.

Herself again, Rachel narrowed her attention to the centermost pinpoint of each of Timothy's pupils. She made herself small yet mighty, a laser, distilled into a beam with the ability to slide into the mind of another. Warm, pleasurable energy spread through her, a sensation that bordered on the sexual and euphoric.

The rain was coming down harder now, stinging wetness in diagonal sheets, but the ocean bath of golden energy inside blocked out the elements.

"Do you feel it?" His voice was a low murmur, appealing, but so reverent she could tell he was talking about their meld in earnest, with no innuendo. "Me into you, and vice versa?"

It was like sex. Mind sex, spirit sex, a muscular wave pulling her essence into his and back again while he fed her in steady pushes. She gave herself over to the flow, sliding with the pushes and falling with the pulls, until her ego was gone, and what remained of her self, if such a concept even applied, was subsumed by this pumping intensity. "I feel it," she heard herself say. "In me, with me, all around me. The magic, what we're doing, and you. God, you. You're in there. We're joined. It's like nothing else."

His heartbeat filled her ears. She saw the muscle in her mind's eye, four chambers and their ventricles, the stuff of life spurting, circulating in its infinity loop of petrification—putrefaction—*purification*—and nourishment.

"I've never experienced anything like this." His speech was a low moan in an awestruck baritone, hotter even than telling her he was about to come. Similar, though. Same vibe.

She shuddered all over, her breath thready, her whole self steeped in gratitude because she got to luxuriate in this delicious madness.

"We have to break past the barriers of our individual minds," she heard herself say, pulling a theory from what she'd gleaned by studying her book. "The first step is a pair bond like this. From here, we move outward. Into all minds, everywhere, all at once. The dark heart. We become it and overtake it."

A stabbing pain exploded behind Rachel's ribs, followed by a ricocheting agony that made her suck in her breath. All she could do was brace herself to withstand the agony and hold the line of the meld, keeping Timothy's essence unified with hers despite her misery.

The pain stopped as quickly as it arrived, and seconds later, she fought to remember why she was hurting in the first place. She stood on a bridge. Her form was human. Her feet were bare.

The structure was made of wood, sturdy as far as she could tell, and stretched over a swollen creek rushing by in a busy current. Beyond the bounds of the water lay stretches of patchy grass tapering into barren dirt. It wasn't a pretty landscape, more like how she might imagine a track of neglected, industrial acreage on the outskirts of town.

Her dress was indigo velvet swirled with whorls of ebony, the colors of the magic. The hemline of the sumptuous material grazed her ankles. Quite the striking aesthetic contrast to these rundown, decrepit surroundings.

"I'm going to go out on a limb and say we didn't transport here on purpose," Timothy said beside her. He wore a three-piece suit in the same color as her dress. She hadn't but a second to consider how dashing he looked before his next words served an ominous portend. "Because I'm pretty sure neither of us could have dreamed this craziness up." He pointed across the bridge, where a delicate mist dropped a coy veil on a structure in the distance.

About fifty feet away, in the middle of what looked like an abandoned lot, sat a building. Sat was the wrong word. The hulk of a building floated in midair. The architecture was modern, mid-century, with a blocky, bomb-shelter look made up of tan brick and a second story jutting out like a cardboard box stacked on top of a smaller counterpart. It wasn't ugly, exactly, but it was imposing and striking.

What lay beneath, though, rocked her world.

A disembodied eyeball the size of a football field propped up the bunker, its gray iris catching glimmers of light. The live eye looked left to right, up and down and this way and that, glancing at everything and nothing. The lashes were long, slipping down in a black fan when the eye blinked in its monstrous, massive appropriation of normal eyeball behavior.

She was too stunned to move. She looked at Timothy. He gawked right back at her.

There was no telling where they were anymore. The Other Place? Some impossible, forgotten dimension? Only one thing was certain: they had to march to the eye. The bridge led directly there, no other turnoffs or pathways.

In unspoken agreement, Timothy took Rachel's hand. She squeezed his fingers. At least they had each other. Their anthem rang out unspoken, tried and true.

They began the trek, steps moving as one, their handclasp tight. Rachel tried not to look at the eye, but not looking somehow made the uncanny eeriness worse, so she kept watch on the target. For all she knew, the eye was a helpful presence. A guiding force. Nothing sinister need be assumed.

Her goodwill toward the eyeball flew out the window when the massive orb ceased its random movements, and, seeming to sense their approach, pinned her in a sharp stare.

Every nerve in her body froze at the exact moment a single command walloped her in the gut: *run.*

NINE

TIMOTHY HAD LONG AGO MADE PEACE WITH HIS INSTINCTS. THEY were usually right, their injunctions a whisper buried in the innermost corners of him, lodged below the navel.

The gut feeling. He'd read somewhere that the gut was like a second brain, and he believed it. As a shifter, he had to get even more comfortable with ways of knowing that exceeded the bounds of typical understanding. Subtle changes in the air. Premonitions drifting in from beyond the bounds of the five senses. A look, a scent, body language nobody else would catch.

His instincts had served him well over the years, yet here he stood on a squat bridge, wood softening to rot under his boots, facing a horror at the edge of a wasteland.

Yet choices were scant, and the value of pressing forward despite obstacles and doubt was one of the main lessons he'd taken away from the message boards.

Maybe Rachel's book was in the bunker beneath the orb, or maybe the fortress hid an even more valuable secret. The eye had to be guarding something, keeping watch, unseen tendons keeping it twitching in jerky movements.

"What does chaos mean to you?" He turned to Rachel to avoid staring into the eyeball. It rose up to meet the foundation of the building, stone and brick merging with the bottom eyelid in a curve of stone to flesh, flesh to stone. "To me, I think of erosion of boundaries. Entropy. A loss of order and rules so total we almost can't imagine how they were ever there in the first place."

She laughed without much good humor, though not maliciously. "I really don't think now is the time to philosophize."

"I know we need to go in there. I get it. I do wonder if we are able to understand our territory to the best of our ability, if it gives us an advantage." He started walking, the planks of the bridge spongy, but not enough to stop the creak.

"Spoken like a true shifter and an alpha. Mapping the terrain in order to understand the enemy and gain dominance over the ground." A sparkle flared in her eye, and she leaned slightly toward him, the lush fabric of her dress trailing behind.

Given the circumstances, the flirtation came with a bit of irony, as any emotion besides grim determination or abject horror felt out of place. Her break with expectation was refreshingly irreverent. His muscles loosened even as he remained hyper-vigilant. He lightened up just enough for his head to clear but not so much he let his guard down.

"Sure. Of course. Don't you think it's a good quality, being aware of one's surroundings and maintaining a keen sense of where one stands in relation to their situation?"

They crossed the bridge and ended up in the field, where a few acres of scrubby, sunbaked grass sprouted up in tufts. The ratio of dirt to green created a lifeless effect, as if the ground had been salted.

The eyeball bunker loomed before them, spanning the distance of a few city blocks. Up close, the layout of the building was nonsensical. There were doors on the second story that would open into dead air. Given the arch over the eyeball, the lower level would have to be a slanted, sloping funhouse.

"I know where we are in relation to our situation." Her pretty features twisted into a grimace. Rachel kept her eye on their unwanted destination.

"Fucked?" They weren't. He'd see to it. But some sarcasm and observational humor helped to put others at ease. Himself included. He hated the sight of the eye, lifeless but busy, mute, and overfed with input. He had to cope with the monstrosity somehow.

She laughed. "Yeah, but I've felt that way ever since I woke up in an occult dungeon with a head full of snakes. I've been in fucked freefall for a good long while."

They'd have ten minutes to trek before they reached the bunker and had to figure out what to do. It was in his best interests to get to know Rachel a bit better and learn the history of her predicament.

He'd left her alone before they'd gotten involved, even though his attraction to her kept him up at night, twisted up in sweaty sheets, rubbing himself raw. She had a vulnerability hiding beneath prickly jokes and a cool exterior. Since they were committed to working together in a major way, mutual trust was paramount.

Dead and dying grass crunched as they closed the distance. The day was mild, similar perhaps to early autumn in the middle of the United States. A strange smell blew through the air, and he didn't like it. Acrid, chemical. Polluted. He had no faith that anything good was happening in the fallout shelter. "Did you ever have any contact with the people who hurt you? Do you remember anything about their faces, defining characteristics, anything?"

She shook her head. "Either I blocked it out or the drugs they used induced some type of amnesia. The only connection I have to that day is this." She pulled the crystal from a pocket in her skirt. "It's so weird. I can't tell if it's a false memory, fabricated somehow, or if this was used to backfill or implant memories in me."

"What would be the false or backfilled memory?"

"My whole history with this thing." She turned the rock over in her palm, its plated sides catching flickers of light from the watery, cloud-blocked sun. "While I was under, knocked out on anesthesia, I swear I had a dream about it. A vision. Floating right there in my mind's eye. And you saw how Helen reacted when I showed it to her. Like it was a dead fly."

"I wish I would have asked her about it." She stuck the crystal back in her pocket. "Or more accurately, I wished she would have been willing to say more. I felt like she was holding back. Or was so horrified by the sight of it she slipped into denial."

"It's in your hands for a reason." Up closer, the eyeball was even more grotesque. Blood vessels snaked across white flesh in red ropes. Wrinkles on the eyelid cut deep enough to engulf him and Rachel. The vulnerability of this thing was an obvious front. It would be too easy to jam his fist or a random object into the soft jelly. So simple as to be stupid. Nothing in this world ran on a direct line of logic. "At least, I have to believe there's reason and order left somewhere. Or else I'll go crazy."

They'd gotten close enough to where they stood in the shadow of the building, a few feet from the eye. Timothy had the sudden, nonsensical thought of diving right into it, penetrating its black hole, and mind-melding with this nightmare like he and Rachel had combined their powers to travel. Desperate times, drastic measures, and unhinged impulsivity anyone?

"What?" she said, her face tilted up at the structure, her eyes scanning as the Cyclops giant appraised with its same twitchy pattern.

"I didn't say anything."

"You scoffed. It was funny."

He was surprised she'd caught any vocalization he'd made. "Oh. I had a random thought about plunging myself into that black hole pupil and seeing where I ended up."

His quip startled a chuckle out of her, along with a flash of her real smile, a full stretch with plenty of teeth. "Don't you dare tap out and leave me here alone with this freak." She looked into the center of their disembodied watcher. "No offense. If you can even hear me."

The eye blinked, or that might have been Timothy's imagination. "I'm not going anywhere without you. We're in this together, right?"

Her smile shrunk to a smaller version, more wistful but no less authentic. "Right. You're the definition of ride or die."

"I'm here to protect you, so I will."

She looked at him for so long he felt a flutter in his stomach before she snapped her focus back to the bunker, breaking the thread of tenderness between them. He hated to lose their moment, but he understood. "How do you suppose we get in?"

In all directions was more of the same dry, brown-and-barely-green land. No trees. No wildlife. No rocks or debris. He'd never missed the jungle more than he did now, marooned in this dump in a remote desert. "Not through any physical means." The building part was too high above their heads.

In theory, they might be able to make it up if they scaled the eyeball, but grabbing onto the eye would likely hurt it, anger it, or both.

"Look." Rachel pointed upward.

"I don't see what you're seeing."

"There's a light on in a window. It's not a reflection of the sun."

He spotted what she was talking about. A nondescript, industrial window looked fused shut but shone with a muted, fluorescent glow within. The unease of knowing they weren't alone danced awkwardly with the *relief* they weren't alone, at least existentially.

The eyeball, not having shown itself to be sentient really, didn't count. "What are you thinking? You want to try to get their attention?" He didn't like the idea, but they couldn't stand around forever.

"Not exactly. I was wrong when I said this was the wrong time to philosophize. Thank you for bringing up the topic of chaos."

Thrown, he routed his mind back to the subject they'd barely touched. If Rachel had a notion, he'd humor it. She was one of the smartest people he knew, and her magical prowess enhanced her ability to puzzle through unthinkable situations. "How it's defined by the fundamental absence of rules, boundaries, or structure to order a series of events."

"Exactly. And I can't quite put my finger on it yet, but I think that's what we have to do here. Order the chaos. I have a theory as to why, but I don't want to get into it yet."

She was onto something. She had to be. If he wrote his part in her book, he'd be ordering the chaos magic, in a sense, by contributing to a clear system of rules and principles. "If we can get the book to stop writing, rewriting, and erasing itself, then it's a finished text. Complete. Closed. No more chaos from there."

"Correct. And if we can order the chaos in the book itself, we can bring the entire magic system into a manageable state. My mission is to take the reins." After uttering her final sentence, she clasped his hand, a gesture which sent a shiver across his skin.

He was the reins, the assist, the guide. His contribution would aid in her direction, set the needle on the compass. It had better. Shifting was a kind of chaos magic, based on their working definition. The line between human and nonhuman opened in flexible boundaries.

She'd pulled the crystal out of her pocket before he caught his next breath. In one firm, resolute motion, she aimed the point of the rock at the light in the window.

Did she know what she was doing, or was she merely winging it? It didn't matter anyway, because he didn't have a chance to stop her even if he wanted to. He felt the reaction from the structure first. A click, or a snap, at the heart of his bones. A spinning sensation followed, energy shooting through him in hoops, light he could feel.

If only he could identify this sensation, name it, and place it in the context of chaos magic. If they never saw her book again, which they might not, he had to find a backup. Had to crack this code and pinpoint the role he was supposed to play.

A cone of violet light spiraled out of the window, coils widening into a series of larger circles as they spooled toward the ground, the broad loops at the end large enough to swallow both Timothy and Rachel. Within the tube, miniscule molecules danced. The shape was a squiggly handprint. The sigil chaos magic, representing the witch's ability to manipulate her environment by way of her own hand. The symbol issued an invitation to pursue.

"The inside mirrors the outside," he said, his mind clear, though a haze had slowed down his processing. He laid his palm on his solar plexus. "Is that why you pulled it down?"

"The crystal can hold magic and transform it. If I can pull the force to me, I can see through it." She held the rock in front of her own eye. "I can use it to see. To locate my book or anything else. Like remote viewing."

"Do you trust me?"

"Why do you ask?"

"After I do what I'm about to do, follow my lead. I'm almost sure this is how we recover your book. Then we get back to Helen and merge the timelines."

He had an idea for how they'd get into the upstairs room where the symbol for her magic had originated. He reached for the glowing coil and wrapped his fingers around the phosphorescence of it.

The magical cord wasn't tangible, there was nothing tactile to latch onto, so it slipped through his fingers. But the non-corporeal nature didn't matter because what flowed down to them mingled with his bloodstream anyway, where it pumped through his body with ferocious might.

"This is crazy," she said, but she stuck her free hand into the spiral.

The next thing he felt was his feet lifting off the ground. Weightless, he levitated, carried by the magic alone. Rachel floated beside him. She clutched her crystal, the loose fabric of her dress tumbling down like a fan. "In this together," he said.

"Until the bitter end."

Stretching pressure intensified, then came nausea followed by a tight, dull sensation in his solar plexus like he'd gotten the wind knocked out. The periphery of his vision shadowed before the world went dark.

The pinch of a headache between his eyes brought him back to consciousness. White blurs swam in his vision, and his stomach rolled over, but after a few seconds, he was lucid enough to function. Rachel sat beside him, her hair mussed, the look in her eyes dazed.

One of her hands was balled into a fist. She unfurled her fingers slowly, showed him the crystal, and nodded once.

He was happy to see the rock, even though he had no idea how it was helping. The room they'd arrived in was white all over, caging them in a cube of blank computer paper. She'd mentioned a white room as part of her past ordeal.

Timothy rose to stand and helped her to her feet. "Does any of this look familiar to you?"

She shook her head. "There was much more going on in that room. This place is quiet. Too quiet."

She was right. The space teemed with heavy, silent energy. Anticipation had him tense. His short hairs lifted. He felt watched, observed, but nobody was around except the two of them. Maybe they were inside the damn eye, and it was monitoring them from the inside out.

With Rachel beside him, he got up and walked around. A series of about ten evenly placed podiums, each the color of the wall, were the only other objects in the room. He went to one and looked. Nothing remarkable about it. He tapped the hard material with his knuckles. It might have been marble or granite.

"Come look at this." Rachel's voice echoed slightly, adding to the disturbed energy of the place. It was both empty and stuffed. Haunted by an excess of possibility.

She crouched in the middle of the room, one of her palms up, cradling the crystal like a baby bird.

He got next to her, low enough to the ground to investigate. "What am I looking at?"

She pointed at a spot on the floor. "It's script. Look closely."

Sure enough, words were etched along the floor in delicate cursive. Some words were in English, others what looked to be Latin, still others unrecognizable. The stranger thing was how the script was dynamic, alive. Text would disappear, new words reappearing in its place. It was a never-ending cycle of regeneration and renewal. "It's like your book. Self-authoring. Collaborative."

"What does it want us to know by taking us here? What does she want us to know by bringing us here?" She rubbed her forehead. "I just can't figure out what we are supposed to *do*."

"The white rooms have to be significant somehow. Here we are in one. You went to one while you were kidnapped. Do you remember anything you did in the room? Any other identifying details?" Before his eyes, the text kept cycling so fast he only caught a few words, snippets of sentences, before entirely new sections cropped up to take its place.

The word "chaos" repeated frequently. So was Other Ones, Scarab, and hologram. He'd give anything for a writing utensil. Or a photographic memory.

She answered, "I have so little memory of it. There were people. I think they were people. Figures. An earthquake or explosion."

The next voice, smooth and sexless, came from an unseen source. "Regeneration and renewal." The tone was so eerie, Timothy's skin crawled. Condescending, toying, not a friend. "Self-authoring. Collaborative."

Whatever spoke was mirroring his thoughts back to him in a mocking way. They were inside his head. "Who's there? Why don't you come out and show yourself instead of playing these games?" Was the smartest move to challenge a possible adversary when in their territory and unaware of what they wielded? No, but he was sick of being on the defensive.

"We can manifest it here." She spoke with ethereal, cloudlike softness. "This is like the center of the engine. The middle node. It's guarded, but not inaccessible. Hold on. I want to try a strategy." While simultaneously mouthing words, Rachel traced a path in the floor with the tip of her crystal.

Timothy heard footsteps, everywhere and nowhere, the source invisible. "Manifest," the same speaker, or one who sounded identical, crooned. "We can manifest too, you know."

His muscles tensed. He could shift if he needed. Shifting would help in a fight, depending on who or what showed up to greet them.

"It's working," Rachel said. "I'm authoring."

He hoped she was right. "How can you tell?"

"Look over there," she exclaimed triumphantly, bolting to her feet as she pointed at one of the podiums. "Hurry."

He looked to where her index finger led him. Sure enough, a brown, rectangular object slightly smaller than a breadbox sat atop the pedestal. Instantly, he recognized the object, even from five feet away. Rachel's grimoire.

How she knew to hurry, he couldn't say, unless she heard the same voice as him. Speculating was pointless; however, instincts were not, so they rushed to the book together. She scooped her lost object into her arms and cradled it, reuniting with her beloved.

"Nice work," he said. "We'll fall into the black holes again and go back to Helen. I felt my magic strengthen being here. I'm confident it'll go smoother now." He hugged her tight, proud of her, and relieved they were about to cut out of this weird place before whatever was speaking popped into existence.

She let the hug linger for a little while, which he savored, inhaling her aroma. But this was no time to get sentimental. They had work to do.

Rachel pulled back and locked him in eye contact. "Ready to start?"

"Never been more ready."

The invisible voice spoke again, smug with a vaguely threatening aftertaste. "Not so fast, lovers. Turn around. I see you."

He looked, horror striking when he saw what he had suspected had been watching them all along, floating above where the living text had appeared, veiny red ropes straining against pallid gelatin.

TEN

TRAPPED IN THE FORCE FIELD OF HER MENACE, HER MASTER, HER maker, Rachel was struck by a few facts in particular.

First, the abyss in the middle of the eye was truly never-ending, the portal to end all portals, the stuff that not only were portals made of, but that generated portals. Ringed by an event horizon storm cloud flecked by shards of gunmetal, the wormhole called her home.

"This is a trap," Timothy said. He pulled on her elbow.

She shrugged him off, so entranced she could barely breathe. A flood of pleasure chemicals soaked every one of her cells. "You don't know what you're talking about." This wasn't his destiny. Shifters were auxiliary. Secondary. Assets, sure, but unable to vibe with the likes of the eye. Folly in her truest form, all-seeing, omniscient, calm—had arrived.

The way she floated there, right above the coven daughters sigil, was positively regal. She fit, she belonged. She began and ended. She *saw*.

Finally, the queen of the prophecy spoke, her voice smooth, collected, and devoid of emotion. "I've received some complaints throughout this adventure. Chief among those is how I've failed to provide guidance to the witches under my eye."

"You've done more than fail to provide guidance," Timothy put in with sternness. "You've tricked them. Misled them. Tried to kill them and those they loved. We aren't exactly sure why you love tormenting us, but we sure as hell know we aren't going to comply with your hologram plan without a fight."

He was right, but he'd better take a step back. Rachel could work with Folly. She was the only one who was able. She held her book tight to her chest. "He's frustrated. We all are. You're opaque. Your motives are mixed. At times it seems like you want to kill us all, or possess us and body snatch us, but sometimes it feels like you're giving us clues. Or just enough rope to hang ourselves with. Which is it?"

The eyeball queen laughed coldly. "I don't give you the rope, my darling daughter of chaos. Oh, you are my favorite. Which you already know. You witches create your own rope. You painstakingly fashion the petards upon which you hoist yourselves. I stand back and watch it happen, because I never interfere with my enemy when she's in the process of destroying herself."

"So you admit we're your enemies." Timothy sidled up close.

Rachel felt clearer of head, more like herself, less enchanted by Folly's pull. Having Timothy there was helpful. He kept her grounded. Had he not been present, she might have been totally lost to thrall by now, and then who knew what would be happening?

She sliced him a fast look to communicate her appreciation.

With his gaze alone, he reciprocated. Their connection was worth so much more than whatever toxic bond she shared with this eyeball.

"This shifter sure is a pest, isn't he?" Folly probably would have narrowed her eye into a scowl had she had her eyelid. The chilliness was palpable.

Rachel ran through fast, logical calculations. Folly had led them here, playing hide the (eye)ball and making Rachel chase her book through an inter-dimensional maze.

It was evident Timothy irritated her, but she hadn't tried to kill him yet. Same with Rachel. It was obvious she respected Rachel more than the other coven daughters, and she indeed seemed to be putting her through a series of tests. Testing her mettle to see how far she would bend before she broke. Being the daughter of chaos partly explained the favoritism, but not entirely. Folly should be battling with her whole chest to stop the witches from halting the prophecy. Yet she seemed more focused on what increasingly felt like a magical screening process.

A few more loose ends knitted together in a composite of spoken words and recovered memories. The comment about old systems withering stood out. Dimensions of forever darkness were meaningful. The old gods, dead but dreaming. Natural cycles. Regeneration. "You're dying, aren't you?" Rachel put forth. "And you need me to take over as the dark heart of the system. The ruler."

"Perceptive girl. I knew there was a reason I preferred you to your sisters. You're smart where they are daffy. More level-headed, less impulsive. Less preoccupied with petty struggles like romance and—"

"I'm not here to talk shit about my coven sisters." Rachel's ears burned. Folly's flattery wasn't wholly warranted. Rachel had decent self-esteem, sure, but she suffered no illusions she lacked flaws. And she'd been plenty preoccupied by romance lately. Or at least infatuation. "Why not just step aside to make way?"

"That would be so simple, wouldn't it?" A vein in the pale tissue bulged. "Problem is, the hologram prophecy is my life's work. My masterpiece. My mission. I've been at this for thousands of years, curating energies with the goal of the hologram in mind. The Other Ones are counting on me. This Scarab group is hard at work, unwittingly doing my bidding. I can't simply give up on what I've built. It'd be like Michelangelo walking away from 'The Creation of Adam' when it was only half-done."

God, her ego, comparing the magnum opus of an artistic genius to a sadistic plot to plunge the world into despair.

"You can and you will walk away," Timothy said. "Fuck Scarab. They're psychopaths who ritualistically murdered my kind. And I couldn't care less about the Other Ones. Disgusting."

Rachel's fondness for Timothy grew. She admired his hard-nosed courage and fearless willingness to face off with their enemy. Her own approach was more measured, but they could get a good old-fashioned game of good cop bad cop going. "He's upset. Justifiably so," Rachel said to Folly, hoping Timothy caught on that she was rolling with the bit. "But what you're saying is intriguing. You're ready to pass the torch. I'm the prime candidate. On those fronts, our goals are in alignment.

However, where we have a problem is the matter of the hologram prophecy. You're still committed, and my friends and I want to stop it. Did I get it right?"

Another haughty, ice-sharp laugh from the eye. "Quite the little diplomat you are. You'd make a fine politician, with your smooth tongue and rough attempt at turning the tables. Brava." The sarcasm hit like a cudgel.

Rachel tensed. Blatant condescension wasn't a good sign. She was losing Folly. If she'd ever even had her. It was notoriously hard to gain the upper hand when you didn't know which way was up, and confounding through misdirection and terrain-shifting was Folly's forte. "Are you saying I'm wrong?"

"I'm saying you aren't there yet."

A knot in Rachel's belly tightened and turned over. Great, just great. She'd failed some unknown test. "I recovered my book, didn't I? Surely, that counts as passing one of your tests."

"You're outnumbered," Timothy said to the eye. "Outmatched, outsmarted, and as good as defeated. Might as well surrender now and go quietly. If you do, you'll prevent a humiliating, messy fight."

"A humiliating, messy fight sounds great, actually." Folly bobbed up and down in the air. She almost looked jaunty, with her buoyant, spherical bounce. Like a Halloween-themed beach ball. "Let's give this old girl the sendoff she deserves. After all, I'm the elemental sister of chaos. Might as well make my last act a good one."

The smell of sweat, her own sweat, mingled with a steadily worsening sense of dread. Folly wasn't through with them by a long shot. "What do you want?"

"You know the answer. Chaos. Pandemonium. Mayhem. Which isn't to say I want to see you fail. I do, however, want to see you suffer and struggle. A complete mental breakdown would be a hoot."

"We've suffered enough," Timothy said. "Suffered and struggled enough for a thousand lifetimes."

"Nonsense." Folly floated a few feet back and forth, engaged in some solo, limbless dance. "You know what the apex of suffering would be? At least where you are concerned, my lovely chaos daughter?"

Rachel gritted her teeth. She was a fool for thinking she could wrest control from this interaction. But she hadn't lost hope. She and Timothy were still alive, and at least Folly was keen for some give-and-take. "I'm all ears." Unable to resist some pointed banter with this bitch, she added, "Which beats being all eyes in my opinion."

"Good one. As a reward for your fun potshot, I'll set your next travail on an easier mode. To answer your question, my greatest pleasure at this point would be for you to push forward on the prophecy and take on the mission as your own. To fall prey to the powers of my persuasion and carry out my legacy while thinking all along it was your idea. I'll go out laughing, utterly content with satiety."

"Keep dreaming," Timothy said.

"Oh, I will. I'll be spinning dreams even after my death, dreaming myself into a lucid oblivion. Metaphorically, I dream of my destiny, in bed with the old gods at last. But we're not there yet. For now, I'm still able to throw up hoops for you to watch you jump. Since you're obsessed with rope, let's play with one. For your next travail, you're to make a rope out of ashes and save your friend Helen's life. If you fail, she dies, and your snakes come back. Permanently."

Rachel's mouth went to dust. Her scalp itched. By implication, Helen's life was on the line. That was the worst part, and the threat hanging over her own head, literally, was plenty horrific. "And if I succeed?"

"I will give you one tool, no more no less, to aid in your misguided halting of my precious prophecy. You really ought to reconsider your pigheaded fixation on beating back progress. Change can be liberating."

"No, thanks. I'll take the deal." Rachel was dizzy. This challenge sounded way too daunting. Impossible, likely. How would she make a rope out of ashes? What did such a riddle even mean? What was the context? Metaphorically speaking, she was blindfolded in a dark room, throwing darts. Lost as usual. But what choice did she have but to flail at her target?

Seeming to sense her faltering, Timothy steadied her with a firm hand above her elbow. He was always there to catch her when she fell, literally and symbolically. She'd begun to wonder if they'd developed some lesser form of telepathy over the course of their journey together, picking up on subtle changes in energy and flickers of expressions. "I'm right here with you. You can do this."

"Too bad I don't know what 'this' is. It's a gaping blank that I haven't the first clue how to fill."

Folly laughed her bloodless, psycho laugh. She seemed to bulge, swollen with ego, an overcooked scallop who got the last laugh.

"We'll fill it together." Timothy cradled Rachel's face in both hands. Even as her world crumbled into entropy, she felt gratitude. She had him. She could look into the steadying foundation of his dark eyes without harming him. For now. "You and me. We're the last ones. The last chance to beat this thing. And we will; we just have to keep our wits about us and plan strategically. Keep ourselves steady and in check."

"Always the alpha." She laid her hands over his, and for a spark of a second, she forgot about the ogling, amputated presence of their enemy combatant.

"I can't do this without you. Your heart. Your magic. Your dedication. Don't falter on me, Rachel. Don't you dare."

"Okay," she whispered, temporarily freed from despair. "Okay."

"A rope from the ashes, and a witch in peril. I'll dream up a good yarn for you. Enjoy, lovers. There may be some twists and turns in your path as my whim dictates. How many days do you have until the winter solstice again? I can't remember. You'd better keep track, though, because if you haven't beaten me by then, you're in trouble. We're talking about a big ritual. The biggest. It's not in your best interests to allow it to go on as planned." With that, Folly was gone as if she had never been there at all.

Although relieved of the overbearing stare of her unwanted companion, Rachel's tension didn't abate. The next daunting task was afoot. She did some quick mental math. Her heart sunk. She tallied the days again in case she was wrong. She wasn't. She was going to be sick. "We only have three days."

"And we'll use every hour of those three days to break this curse and save our loved ones from what's coming. Right? You with me?"

"Right," she said, not fully believing her word. She'd always been a skeptical person, cynical even, someone inclined to break faulty suppositions and flimsy narratives with the sharp tool of precisely applied doubt. Now, though, her discerning mind didn't feel like an asset, and she longed for the faith she'd never quite had in anything. "I'm with you."

"All in. I need to see it in your eyes. I need to feel it. My bones need to know it."

She leaned forward and crashed her mouth into his, sucking his lips, devouring him, lost to the haze of passion and allure. He kissed her back, hungrily, showing her with his body how the intensity between them, the intensity they faced together, was two-way.

It was a strange sort of alchemy, facing destruction together while bound at the wrists and ankles by the same ashy rope. At least they were tied to the pyre as one. Their kiss said so. Their kiss sealed their conjoined fate. She broke off first, her lips achy, his red and parted. "Did you feel it?"

He moved his hands to her hips and yanked her body flush to his, pressing his stiffness against her hip. His elevated breathing somehow matched both of their heartbeats and the unspoken vibration of their pact. No more words were spoken.

Into the voids they fell, as one, surrendering to the mind sex as the muse of chaos magic spirited them away. Darkness came fast and early, smooth, a push-pull free fall into oblivion. Neither had to practice. Progress, but scary progress. They were both so close to this damn magic now. The complete submerge felt so good. Exotic. Sexual. Like being lapped at by a tongue that changed its texture. Velvet. Leather. Chrome. Rubber.

Rachel woke up gasping, euphoric waves from the dark tongue laving her all over. She lay on her back, arms and legs flailing as she writhed. An excess of friction burned her calves, and she fought to stay under the spell of the tongue. She didn't want to wake up and face reality yet. "Silk," she said, grasping for the magic cloak to drape her for just a little longer. "Feathers."

"You're coming back now." Timothy's voice was a slow drawl. She was in his arms. "Back to the physical world."

Fuck the physical world. But as she shook off the dregs of her stupor, acceptance replaced bliss. The task. Rope from ashes. Stop the prophecy. Three days. She clutched the sides of Timothy's shirt, willing a wave of queasiness to pass. "This is even worse than waking up from a really good dream, huh?"

He chuckled with good humor. "Pretty much the definition of a rude awakening." Using his fingers like a lazy comb, he stroked her hair. If they didn't correct this mess soon, he would never be able to touch her hair again. The thought was both sobering and a motivator.

The good news was, they'd made their way back to Helen's apartment. It was true what the other witches said about pair work. Spells cast with the aid of a bonded accomplice had much greater odds of success. She'd even managed to bring her book along for the ride, the trusty doorstop of all things witchy parked by her foot. "It seems rude to wake her up." The apartment was pitch black, as was the sky beyond the wall-length window of the high-rise apartment.

Beyond and below, the river pushed on, a muscular serpent made of black glitter. Two bridges stretched over the flow, a smattering of red car taillights passing over them. The drivers were oblivious to the crazy shit going down in some random, high-rise apartment at the edge of downtown. This both comforted Rachel and made her sad. Life went on, but not for long.

"We don't have to wake her." Timothy pointed into the living room.

A foldout couch had been pulled into bed form and dressed with sheets, blankets, and pillows. The sight was tender in an overwhelming way. "She's been waiting for us. Anticipating our return."

Helen had faith. Rachel could stand to follow the lead of the spirit witch there. Perhaps Helen's connection to the more delicate side of mystical things, synchronicity and auspice and the big changes ushered in by the flapping of tiny butterfly wings, lent itself to a comparatively positive outlook. And/or, she was a psychic Pisces, as she'd joked while not joking. Either way, the domestic comfort and preemptive gesture of care was a soothing treat for Rachel's jaded eyes.

"Let's get some rest." Timothy all but read her mind.

There were even changes of clothes laid out in neat piles, more loungewear from the yoga studio. Timothy swapped out his "yogi" shirt for an identical one, which made Rachel smile. She changed into pink yoga pants and a loose tank top, making a mental note she owed Helen so much more than she could ever repay.

The sheets ensconced her in a cocoon of cool freshness. Timothy got in at the same time. They lay on their sides, facing each other in comfortable silence.

"You know none of this is your fault, right?" He slid a lock of her hair between his fingers.

She had been feeling heart-heavy and sick ever since the magnitude of the task had come into relief. "What are you, a mind reader?"

It had become a bit of a catchphrase, both ironic and apt, coloring their predicament with a tone that wasn't quite humor, but lifted the gloom with a dry stroke of levity.

"I don't need to be, because I see the pain behind your eyes."

He was so close, his warmth, the solidity of him in body and spirit. On a spiritual level, even as her breathing pattern remained normal, she exhaled a load of stress. She wasn't alone. Such a simple truth meant so much more than the literal reference to companionship.

"Are you always this romantic?" It wouldn't surprise her. Timothy possessed the rare gift of charm, the authentic kind, never crossing the line into sleazy or manipulative.

"Not since I met you." She didn't even catch him moving, but he was closer now, inches away, his body heat radiating, the atoms of him pulsing pleasurably in her space bubble.

So she hung up her mind for the night, releasing the urge to problem solve any more, and faded into him. The strength of his arms, his scent of woods and pheromones. His kiss was both gentle and dominating.

Their mouths indulged their shared hunger together, in total tandem, a play of tongues in their full, dancing glory of exploration. When he touched her belly, breasts, pulled her shirt over her head, she forgot where she was. It was the most gorgeous thing. She was nowhere and everywhere, any place, and it didn't matter. Because she was with Timothy.

His lips brushed her collarbone. He used his tongue to flick her nipples one by one, teasing with every lick and suck. Next, he dipped down to position his mouth between her legs. Velvet. Silk. Feathers. She arched her back. Sensation became her being, and she exploded into a shattering crescendo, finding the paradox where bliss meets agony. After, she urged him on top by pulling him up by his hard biceps. He pushed in and out at a steady pace, the city glimmers backlighting his chiseled features to highlight every handsome detail from brow line to jaw.

His eye contact was unwavering. There was no one else, nowhere else. She caressed his cheek as another round of pleasure built inside. He kissed every one of her fingers when she broke again before pulling out and finishing silently, a shudder rippling through his muscles.

The demon goddess was alive, and magic was afoot, but Rachel would face those problems in the morning.

ELEVEN

AN UNSETTLING SENSATION CRAWLED OVER TIMOTHY, ROUSING HIM to a groggy, half-rested state of consciousness.

His surroundings were unfamiliar, but he took stock immediately, as he'd trained himself to do. He couldn't afford to slouch on his cultivated practice of sharpened vigilance. Ever. Especially not now, when he sensed he was being watched.

Rachel lay in his arms, a welcome respite. Pullout couch. City apartment. Pink and yellow daybreak spreading beyond big windows. A tabletop Christmas tree on the kitchen island, its multicolored lights having been left on all night.

A figure loomed over him. He recognized the brunette ponytail, casual clothes, and wry expression. Helen, two coffee cups in her hands. "Morning, lovebirds. Make yourself at home." She smirked as if to say 'I see you already have.'

After gently unwinding himself from Rachel, he sat up. She was sound asleep. Exhausted. He liked to think he'd been the reason, though it was just as likely their most recent trip through the cosmos had been the culprit. "Thanks for preparing the bed for us." There was an optimism in her gesture that didn't go unnoticed. She'd trusted they'd return safely. Or hoped, at least.

Helen sat on the edge of the pullout and regarded him for a moment. "Thanks for preparing us all for the end of the world, I guess." She sipped her coffee. "I'm still deciding how seriously to take this."

"Even after you traveled with us and shifted your shape into wolf form?"

Her exhalation was heavy, like she'd given that topic endless analysis from every conceivable angle. "You two could have drugged me. Made me hallucinate." She handed him one of the mugs. "The tea isn't drugged. Bad transition. Sorry."

"What would our motive be?" He drank from the cup, a potent jolt from the bitter brew washing off the sleep dust. She hadn't asked how he took it, but black was fine. Seemed fitting. Serious.

She shook her head. "I haven't been able to sleep since I zapped back here. I've spent the last four hours getting sucked into the funhouse world the two of you apparently inhabit. It's enough to turn the most level-headed person into a paranoid conspiracy theorist."

He rubbed his eyes. "Elaborate?"

She stood and beckoned for him to follow, turning her head when he slipped out from between the sheets. Timothy dressed in the clothes Helen had provided. He'd grown partial to the "yogi" shirt. Now would be a good time to cultivate a meditation practice. Help regulate his stress chemicals. Empty his mind. Maybe once the dust settled and all were safe in Peru, he'd practice some self-care to calm his nervous system. He had to be teetering on the brink of adrenal burnout.

"Meet me in my office. There are extra toiletries in the bathroom if you want to freshen up."

He took her up on the offer, ducking into a bathroom decorated with candles, incense, and art prints of Buddha overlaid by inspirational sayings. Helen had laid out extra toothbrushes and two kinds of mouthwash. She really was a gracious hostess, and her hospitality clued him in that she was at least partially onboard, or at least curious, about her odd new visitors. He availed himself of the products, relishing in the clean feeling.

Down the hall was her office. Part yoga studio and part library, the space resembled her studio with its bohemian arrangement of plants, retro curiosities, and mismatched rugs. Despite the eclectic mix of decorations, the space was tidy. Helen was already parked at a desk, hunched over a laptop.

Timothy crouched between her and a fake tree in the corner, angling to get a better glimpse of the screen. "What am I looking at here?"

He already knew. He'd looked at the page layout many times, scrounging for new clues, updates, and posts from the most reliable users. The message board had a way of sucking in anyone with even a modicum of curiosity. Timothy kept his cards close, both to avoid spooking Helen with his encyclopedic knowledge of fringe material and out of an interest in hearing her interpretation first. Assimilating unique perspectives on a shared topic helped him sharpen his own reasoning.

"See for yourself." She stood up. "Want a scone? They're semi-stale but still edible."

"Sure." He took her seat and settled in.

Much of what was in front of him was old news: speculation on the prophecy, those behind it, and their objectives. There was a lot of garbage on the coven daughters message board. The space, like any social media site, was rife with idiots and trolls looking to antagonize, misdirect, and annoy with all manner of misinformation. He'd learned to sift judiciously and only pay attention to the contributions of posters whose content he could vet or verify in some form or fashion. One of the most reliable posters, Mad Dog, now lived in the shifter colony in Peru.

Helen set a scone on a chipped plate next to the keyboard. "I need to step away before I turn myself into a nutcase, but I can't stop."

"Yep, it'll do that." He sorted through a bunch of debris before clicking on the username of one of his go-to contributors, a user called GodofWar19837. He glanced at GOW's history, and his heart jumped. GOW had several new posts. New as in last forty-eight hours. The title of the latest was "Famous Last Words."

"What?" Helen said. She sounded worried, like she sensed his change in demeanor upon seeing the new GOW posts.

He had to play it cool. Remain calm while both keeping her even keel and staying honest with her. "A lot of what you see on here is useless. Fake, speculation, malicious distraction. There's valuable information on here, but it's a cesspool too. Where all the wackos wash up."

She leaned against the wall, a bemused look on her face clashing with the dark circles under her eyes. "Okay. Good to know. Troll city over here. So, the part about the evil corporation performing blood sacrifices in an underground theme park with the goal of unleashing a horde of demons upon the earth to turn the planet into a soul-harvesting prison— what category does that fall under? Wacko trolling, fake speculation, or malicious distraction?"

Timothy winced. It was looking like he'd have to surrender the fantasy of keeping Helen cool, calm, and collected. "Real, unfortunately."

"Get the fuck out of here." She said it like, 'I suspect you're going to affirm this insanity is, in fact, real, which I cannot accept' not as in she was kicking him out. Which was somehow worse. The last thing he wanted to do was get an innocent person up to speed on the evil plot to destroy the world. He'd rather be rejected, honestly. "You can't be serious."

"Yes, unfortunately, those stories are all true. As far as I can tell at least. I've lived through some of it personally. So have people I cared about. One of my closest friends had his baby abducted through a portal by these people and their dark magic. They were going to ritually sacrifice her, but he and his wife thwarted them."

Helen stared at him.

"I am so sorry to have to be the bearer of this news." Timothy scrubbed his hand over his face. He felt like a harbinger of doom a lot lately.

"I liked your pitch for an alternate reality better when I was marrying the hot rock star." Helen fidgeted with a knickknack in the shape of a frog standing on its head.

"Think of it like taking the good with the bad." He moved each of his hands up and down like he was a scale, but the balance felt tipped in the negative direction.

"Fuck this." She shook her head so hard her ponytail smacked her cheek.

"I'm not thrilled about where we've found ourselves either, believe me. But the fact remains—we have to merge these timelines. And we need your help." Timothy wasn't going to give up until he'd recruited this tough customer.

Helen folded her arms over her chest. "I'm going to go wake up your time travel girlfriend. Let her figure it out. I'm going to back to bed."

Fair enough. There was no denying Helen needed sleep. Everyone's mood improved when they were rested, and he and Rachel could visit with the reluctant spirit witch again once she'd gotten some much-needed shuteye. "It's a lot to digest. You're right to sleep on it. We'll be around to talk things through when you wake up."

"Awesome," she said sarcastically. "Hey. Rachel. Wake up. Your boyfriend needs you to journey to hell and back and slay the dragon or whatever." A few seconds later, her bedroom door shut.

He didn't say anything to Helen about how they lived with a friendly dragon in Peru or mention how Folly manifested in dragon form now and again. Things were too tense. He'd address those subjects when necessary. The relationship with her was delicate, but she hadn't kicked them out yet. He'd give her plenty of space while she tiptoed down the path to acceptance.

Alone with the message board, Timothy honed in.

For all its foibles and unhinged detritus, this place was what he and Julian had used to save baby Luna and bring Mad Dog to Peru, where they'd broken his curse. There had to be material on here to help him do the same for Rachel. A spell to block Folly from bringing the snakes back. Such a solution would give them a stopgap, some breathing room, while they sorted through the whole "rope from ashes" riddle.

The first order of business was to parse GOW's latest posts. Timothy always got a head rush when new stuff cropped up on the message board. He admittedly succumbed to a pleasure in sleuthing, the thrill of availing himself of secret information. It made him feel like he belonged to an elite club as opposed to a shaggy band of misfits who were perpetually operating from their back feet.

"Famous Last Words" was calling to him. He ripped off the bandage and clicked on the title, hoping to have a chance to pre-screen the writing before Rachel came over. His eyes bugged when he took in the wall of text. Several paragraphs smashed into one. GOW didn't usually write like this. He took pride in organization and neatness. He must've been in a hurry. Or under duress, or both.

Halting the Song of Virgo may have felt like a victory, but at most it was a

Pyrrhic one. Scarab has merely regrouped. Recalibrated. They've been lying dormant waiting for the right time to strike. For anyone who thinks they can't perform the Ballad of Capricorn with the Song of Virgo having been thwarted, think again. These guys are masters of improvisation. The archons are coming. Titans. The veil has never been thinner. Buckle up.

GOW was as confirmed a credible source as anyone on the boards, having seeded enough classified information over the years that his status as a Scarab whistleblower, like Mad Dog had been, left little room for doubt. Now the question was, where had Scarab regrouped? Where were they lying dormant?

He had to figure out these facts so he could stop the ritual and keep the evil monsters out of Peru and away from his loved ones. Rope from the ashes, merging the timelines, and now Scarab was back in the picture. Unsurprising how they'd found a method to circumvent their past defeat and move forward with the ritual. If past patterns were any indication, they were drawing power from Folly. There were so many moving parts. He rubbed a spot between his eyes.

"This looks serious." Rachel's voice punctured his reverie.

"It is. Helen was up all night on the message boards. She pointed me in the direction of a whole bunch of new Scarab-related content and went to bed."

"Let me guess, they haven't faded quietly into oblivion."

"Not by a long shot, if God of War is to be trusted. Which he usually is. They're plotting, and the ritual is underway for the solstice."

"I have an idea."

He was all ears. "Whatcha got?"

"I want to try a spell with you and Helen. I think it'll help us merge the timelines and buy more time in the process."

As much as he wanted to bring up the previous night, to discuss what had happened, again, between them, it seemed absolutely ridiculous and ill-timed to do so now. They had to save the world, and fast. Relationship status issues belonged in the backseat.

But all those practical concerns did nothing to quell the ache in his heart, the part of him that wanted to hold Rachel all night long, to watch the snowfall with her in his arms and forget all about the dark designs unfurling before him. He wanted to drink coffee with her and talk about their hopes and dreams. He wanted to kiss every inch of her skin. But his wants didn't factor into the equation.

"We should let her rest. At least for a couple of hours. I realize we have to act fast, but we also don't want to bombard her until she burns out."

"You're right. She left us a spare key and a note about extra coats and boots. Want to take a walk?"

An escape, however fleeting, was a heavenly prospect. A chance to clear their heads would only benefit them. The spare clothes were in the front closet. Timothy slid on a brand-new pair of men's snow boots. These weren't spare items. Helen had stocked up and bought supplies in anticipation of their return and stay. Her preparations had a calming effect. Their presence might not be wanted, per se, but it was important and inevitable.

They rode the elevator down in silence, passing through a chic, sleek lobby on the way to the street entrance. It felt good to enjoy comfortable silence with someone, even if the basis was something of a lie, a ruse, a slip into denial.

Outside, winter was in full bloom, the streets and sidewalks piled high with white powder. A squirrel ran across a power line, its movements sending mounds of snow falling where it sparkled in the air. A snowplow headed up by an imposing orange scoop chugged past. Streetlight poles were decorated with twinkling white Christmas lights and topped with glowing snowflake decorations. Someone had built a snowman on the street corner. It had one arm, a stumpy branch, capped in a red glove. The nose was a wilted baby carrot.

"Do you miss your family?" Timothy asked, suddenly swept up in the nostalgia holidays tended to engender.

"What kind of question is that?" Rachel chuckled, looking at him strangely.

"Just making conversation. This season makes me pensive. Gets me in my feelings."

"I miss them. I do." They walked by an ice skating rink where people of all ages zipped around in an icy circle, living carefree. A certain, ubiquitous Mariah Carey song played over speakers. "I miss having a normal life. I've built up this whole fake persona so they don't worry too much or think I'm dead. Makes it hard to call home, but at least my absence isn't torturing them. I'm glad I never got married or had kids. It's just my parents. Still. It's hard to be alone in this way."

"I know what you mean." His situation differed from hers, but he related to the existential loneliness of having reinvented himself in the colony. "It feels a bit like I've run off to live in a commune."

"Exactly." The spring in her tone refreshed him. He was grateful to have someone to talk to about the unique loneliness they both faced. Different, so very different, from most people. With those like them, but united only in their difference, the things making them strange burst into even sharper relief. "And this had done a number on my belief system. I used to be the biggest realist. Not spiritual at all, in any deeper sense. Even given my experience when I was younger. I wrote off the spells as wonky happenings with my brain, like some anomaly. The farther I ran, the more it's like this part of me had to push itself to the forefront."

"Or be pushed." With the final showdown approaching, Timothy couldn't help but get reflective. It was as if his entire life, every choice he'd made and not made, had steered him into the version of events where he was right now. "I have to say, my entire understanding of free will has been radically altered."

"I have an idea." Rachel looked slightly mischievous as they strolled by a seasonal store displaying nutcrackers and an array of red and green gifts in the window.

"I like ideas." Hers, even more so.

She grabbed his hand and doubled back in a jog. They ended up at the skating rink. "Let's clear our minds. Have some fun. We'll go back to Helen's fresh and ready to rock."

Rachel Harris had a whimsical side, and he was here for it.

She leaned in and said in a conspiratorial whisper, "Watch this." She pulled an old receipt out of the coat pocket, murmured a fast incantation, and bam. The scrap of paper had become a credit card. "It'll work, too, because the number is tied to the account of some billionaire who wouldn't notice if a million dollars went missing, let alone the cost of renting ice skates. I picked the worst billionaire in the world for this hit too."

"The one who ruined Twitter?"

She winked, twirling the credit card between her fingers. Her performance of naughtiness delighted him.

"Money magic is dangerous," he half-warned, more to tease her. They'd passed the point of worrying about consequences of using magic. The chain of events was fully in motion. Besides, courting danger looked sexy on Rachel.

"Want to know something cool?" She guided them to the skate rental booth, where a heavyset man with beads woven into his Santa beard checked out skates. She laid down the card, and they stated their sizes.

"We won't hear any more bad news today?" He tugged off his boots and replaced them with the skates before commencing a clumsy, bladed walk onto the rink.

Rachel walked beside him in the same ungainly gait, holding his arm for support. "Ha. Not good. I was practicing while we were wolves and found out I can do partner work with my sisters without having them present. I've leveled up. I'd like to introduce this method when we're back with Helen."

He led Rachel onto the ice and took her hand, relishing their return to grace. "Can we make a deal?"

"Depends on what it is."

"While we're out here, this is our own kind of alternate reality. We're on break. No talk of magic, prophecies, the end of the world, etcetera."

He expected pushback, but her face lit up instead. Under a blue stocking cap, her brown waves flowed. The cold kissed the tip of her nose and her cheeks with pink blush. Her smile was free, her real smile. "Why not? If we lose, we won't be able to do anything like this ever again, so we might as well enjoy it. It's the end of the world as we know it, and I feel like ice skating."

"We won't lose. It won't be the end of the world." He spoke it like he meant it, willing the words to take root in his heart.

"If you say so." Her hold slackened under his grip, tension releasing as she let him twirl her in a circle. She was free, they were free. Even if it was an illusion, it was a joyous one. "Tell me about yourself. Starting with one thing about you I don't know and one thing that will shock me."

"Okay. I'll bite." Around and around they went, dodging small children and big people with childlike glee in their hearts. The scene was happy and positive, a perfect escape. A rotation of holiday classics had taken the place of Mariah Carey's Christmas staple. "One thing you don't know is I traveled to every one of the fifty U.S. states before I found Peru. My search for my kind took me to some interesting places."

"And the shocker?"

"I've never eaten macaroni and cheese." It was true. There was always something else on the menu he chose instead, and his family had never cooked the comfort dish.

"What?" Her mouth hung open. "Unacceptable. I make a fine mac and cheese."

From there, they talked, sharing stories, unfolding their personalities for each other. Timothy learned why Rachel loved the smell of barns (reminded her of home), hated knock-knock jokes (hokey and always cliché) and once won the three-legged race at the state fair four years in a row (born with superior balance, hence the attraction to ballet).

He shared his favorite stories from his cross-country adventure, including meeting other natives and learning about their tribal customs. He'd come to consider himself savvy at saving money and didn't mind riding Greyhound buses. There was always good company on there, someone with a wild story to tell.

Time slowed for them as if opening up to their need for personal respite. Soon, they'd be back on task, on target, but for one sweet, long moment they faded into snowfall and cheesy tunes and the soft pleasure of getting to know someone.

He should have known the joy wouldn't last even long enough for them to get back to the apartment.

TWELVE

RACHEL REACHED UP YET AGAIN TO SCRATCH THE ITCH ABOVE HER ear, an insatiable, irresistible nag that started up near the end of the walk back to Helen's.

Dread and denial accompanied the sensation, and she fixated on it. A pressure took root in her hair follicles. She felt them wiggling; her follicles, stirring on the molecular level with an awful, evil, mutant otherness. Tears stung her eyes. She tried not to scratch, which only made her obsess harder.

"What's wrong?" Timothy touched her wrist. He used a spare fob that Helen had stuck in his coat pocket to let them into the front door. Christmas music played over the speakers, the ubiquitous sounds of the season doing nothing to replace Rachel's bleak mood with good cheer.

She looked at the ground. The inside of her nose burned now. This could not be happening, not yet. She was supposed to have a chance to fight it off. Had she failed already?

"Talk to me, Rachel."

She shook her head, muted by her own personal horror. The roots of her hair were for sure alive, squirming. It was like lice, but worse. She knew what was coming. Growing. Birthing. She'd been so stupid to agree to the experiment. Stupid, broke, and gullible. Now, she'd never be the same. Never be able to fall for a wonderful man like Timothy. Not really, because she'd hurt him eventually. "Give me your hat," she hissed through her teeth. "Mine isn't big enough."

There were a good dozen people milling about the apartment lobby, entering and leaving the restaurant. People everywhere, merry and bright, men, women, and children laughing and chatting and carrying shopping bags. Scarves draped necks. So many chunky knitted mittens.

A fake fire burned in a glass case. A seven-foot Christmas tree, erected by the sliding doors, greeted visitors. The people didn't look like anything but potential victims. Happy faces ready to deteriorate into screaming, panicked messes at the first sight of her true self.

Timothy's sable-colored eyes saw right through her. "It's not happening again, Rachel. We have time. You don't have to be scared."

A trio of elementary-aged kids raced through the vestibule, one hauling a sled dripping with melting snow. All the holiday happiness spit in Rachel's face. "Give me your fucking hat before someone dies," she snapped, and tore the stocking cap from his head.

The music might as well have stopped with a screech for how fast the mood plummeted. People stopped and stared. Parents grabbed their children and steered them away from Rachel.

"It's okay." Timothy wrapped her in a hug, shielding her from the judgmental eyes, and steered her into an unoccupied elevator.

"I'm sorry." It came out a whimper. She pulled his hat below her brows, then her eyes, hiding from his perception of her as she turned away. The hat was saturated with his delicious scent of spice and outdoors. She'd had too much fun at the rink. She'd let her guard down and triggered the mutation by being overly happy. "I messed up. I slipped up. I got lazy, which gave them some inroad to return." Water wobbled in her vision. "We were supposed to have three days."

"Breathe." Timothy cradled the back of her head in one of his hands and rested her face against his shoulder. "In and out. You're okay."

"I'm not okay, and neither are you. This is the furthest possible thing from being okay."

"Let me see." The lights on the bubbled numbers glowed in numerical order. They had a few more floors before they were back at Helen's. "Even if you're changing, there's no way it's too far gone yet."

She pulled off her hat.

He examined her gently, with both eyes and fingers. She closed her eyes, indulging the treat of his touch. His slow and meticulous hands tugged on the strands that hadn't been tugged enough and left alone the ones that'd gotten pulled too much. "There's nothing here but you. I promise."

The itching had stopped. It was all in her head. She felt so foolish. "I'm going crazy."

"You aren't crazy, you're stressed. Which is understandable. What's the last good movie you watched?"

"What a random question." It wasn't. He was trying to get her mind off the obvious. Which was both thoughtful and clever. Lighting a candle versus cursing the darkness. "I watched the weirdest, most random movie on Netflix the other day. It was called *Horse Girl.*"

"What did you like about it? Are you a horse girl?" The elevator stopped on Helen's floor.

"I mean, yeah. I'm from the rural Midwest, so horses were a big part of my childhood. Four-H. Farms. But the movie got to me on a deeper level."

He listened, those dark eyes patiently holding space for her. "Go on."

"The protagonist was this woman who never fit in anywhere. Then odd things start happening to her. Her dreams merge with reality until she can't tell the difference anymore. She's trying to figure out if her dreams are randomly appearing in her real life, or if she's manifesting them somehow, or if she's losing her mind so badly, she'd confused the order of dreams and waking life."

"As in, she might be dreaming of things she saw during the day but is getting the order wrong?"

"Exactly." They made their way down Helen's hallway. Rachel supposed there was still a lot of unknown when it came to the mind and dreams. Which one created the other, or even if dreams existed in some universe or dimension outside of the mind of the dreamer. These days, anything seemed possible, and her consciousness had already expanded beyond her wildest imagination. "Life imitating art, or vice versa."

"How does it end?"

"The movie?" she joked, "Or existence as we know it?"

Timothy laughed. The generosity of his high spirits in turn lightened hers. He said, "Let's stick with the movie."

"She walks into a clearing with her favorite horse and is abducted by an alien ship."

"Random."

"I told you." Helen's door, festooned with a red and white wreath, marked the end of their journey. "I used to believe in aliens. Now I think they're—I don't know. Shifters, maybe. Or some kind of Other One."

"Except neither uses spacecraft."

"True." She knocked on Helen's door. No answer. "She must still be asleep."

"Oh, shit." Timothy pointed to a spot below the door handle.

Rachel immediately saw what he was talking about. When she'd knocked, the door had opened ajar. Helen hadn't fully closed it. Odd.

Timothy stepped in front of Rachel, urging her behind him. He pushed the door open and called out Helen's name.

The first sight in the living room slammed into Rachel's face, a terrible trespass seared onto her eyeballs. Helen floated upside down, belly-up, her eyes open and lifeless. She stared right at Rachel, dead-gazed, unseeing.

Below, on the floor, sat Rachel's book. It turned 180 degrees, independent of any guiding hand. Helen moved with the book, her body flipping until her head pointed at the window and her feet dangled at the opposite end.

"Wake up." Rachel ran to her sister witch and shook her legs, her arms. Rubbed her cheeks. Nothing was happening. Except, she had a terrible feeling something was happening. A bad thing, an awful thing, was underway. "Helen, can you hear me? Blink once if you can hear me. Give me a sign. A signal. Anything." She tried to pull Helen down, but an opposing force counteracted gravity. Invisible hands held tight.

Timothy shouted, "Watch the window, watch the window!"

Rachel snapped her gaze to the wall of glass. In her preoccupation with reviving Helen, she hadn't even noticed that the upper part of one of the windows had been cranked open to reveal a three-foot wedge of a gap. An icy breeze slipped in to chill the room and freeze her soul.

She ran to close it, but it was too late. A sick acceptance took hold.

She fit the pieces together, fumbling with the metal crank even as she braced herself for what was about to happen. Her worst fear came true a second later. Helen's body ripped through the air like she'd been shot from a cannon, sliding right past Rachel and through the window gap. There, she dangled in the frigid midair, barefoot and pajama-clad, seventeen stories high. Shit!

Her lifeless body floated fifty feet away from the building, easily.

"Get my book." There was no other way. She had to act fast. Blood whooshed in her ears. Her vision tunneled to Helen, hanging embryonic in the amniotic fluid of empty air. Snow had begun to fall in flurries, dusting the helpless witch's hair and clothes. "We'll figure something out on the fly."

Timothy scooped up the book. "She could drop her at any second just to hurt us. Think of a backup plan in case she falls. A trampoline. Mattresses on the ground."

She grabbed her book out of his hands and pawed through chunks of pages until she landed on her section. "You're thinking and heart are in the right place, but she could just as easily throw her against one of those buildings out there. This is a test. This is it." She cut him a knowing glance.

"The rope from the ashes."

"Except I don't have any idea what that fucking shit means." Adrenaline fried her nerve endings and short-circuited her prefrontal cortex. Chaos had lodged its hooks. She fought to stay composed, level-headed. Freaking out would do a massive disservice to Helen. Her hands shook as she flipped through pages. "Symbolic. What if it's symbolic, or figurative? The ashes represent destruction, residue, remains. The rope is regeneration. Recycling. New out of old."

"Ashes also result from fire. A byproduct, a remainder as you said."

"We have to draw upon the fire element to make ashes. Burn something down and use my chaos to reconstitute the debris into a useful tool. Fire magic, then chaos."

"Fire is adjacent to chaos. So you're in luck. If we use me in partner work, I can access air and set off the chain reaction."

As usual, Timothy was on top of his game. Hyper-competent as always, and a good companion to have on board. "Been studying the chain reaction?"

"It's in my best interest to familiarize myself in case I can be of service."

She grabbed his hand and claimed a tight hold. "I'm so glad you're here."

"I'm glad I'm here, too, and I'm glad you're in charge. I have the utmost faith in your ability." His brown eyes burned with conviction. His support grounded her and took the edge off her anxiety.

"This had better work." Helen's life was in her hands. Tragedy of a lost life notwithstanding, her death would have grave consequences. Losing a witch would mean breaking the coven circle, ruining their chance at stopping the prophecy.

Timothy nodded once. He understood what she meant, the stakes, without her having to say.

Following a bit more perusing, Rachel locked in on a chaos magic spell allowing for matter to be transmuted into different types of substance. Chaos was all about disorder and entropy, breaking down order to upend expectations. What was taken for granted could be made to no longer apply. Laws of physics? Never heard of them.

She sucked in a thin breath through her teeth and held on tight to Timothy.

"You've got this." He squeezed her, the warmth and strength in his fingers enough to clear the junk out of her head and get her calm and purposeful.

"We've got this." Rachel dove in. "Sister Folly, I, a chaos born, humbly call upon your assistance." It turned her stomach to hail her adversary and antagonist, but this was an angst she'd have to accept. Her elemental overseer was the most tyrannical of the six, and the most capricious, but she had to be approached with reverence all the same. "My sister is imperiled, and I require unconventional means to save her." Holding her breath, she glanced at Timothy.

He nodded, then closed his eyes, employing a meditation to help with the partner work. "I've keyed into air," he said. "Render an object to reach her, and the air magic will float it."

"Has to be from fire to get the ashes." What if she could serve a dual purpose? Burn down something no longer needed. Release what no longer served her into the cleansing flames of regeneration.

A phoenix would rise from those ashes. New, and stronger than before.

A light of eureka flashed. "My snakes."

"I'm not sure I follow."

"I'm transmuting them. Freeing them. Allowing them to morph into something better, something helpful. It's the symbolic aspects of fire and chaos. Fire to consume the old in the process of combustion. The ashes represent the mutation. What's been produced by the chemical reaction."

"The result. Potential. Possibility."

"Exactly. The ashes are the rope." She flipped another several pages and found a spell she could improvise on. A chaos spell to merge her inner and outer states, to transfer one sort of matter into another form. Perfect for her purposes. "To save my sister, I require a rope. The material for this rope will come from the scales of my appendages, those who have shared my body. They no longer serve me, nor I them. Free them, release them, burning to ash the resentment and sorrow their presence has caused. In their place, make a rope. A mighty serpent, loyal and fierce, who will rescue my sister from her travail."

Timothy arched one eyebrow. "Did you just conjure yourself a familiar?"

She covered her mouth with her fingers. "I'm not sure. Maybe? It was kind of a spontaneous thing." All magic was. Chaos magic doubly so. A witch had to go for it and roll with the punches.

Rachel's head jerked back, the force shocking her. Pain and pressure stung her scalp, like someone was pulling her hair, hard.

"Hang on!" Timothy shouted, but it was too late.

Rachel flew out of his grip, dragged, pulled—control over her own body was totally gone. Her heels skidded across the floor before the tug yanked her off her feet. Footing gone, she flailed in midair and hit the ceiling with a dull, painful thud. She scrabbled for purchase against emptiness.

Her vision blurred, dizziness and nausea compounding the disorientation, but she caught sight of Timothy running down the apartment hallway. He returned with a stepladder and unfolded it with a snap.

"Hold on to me." He lifted his arms, and she gripped his wrists.

All her energy was focused on trying not to puke despite the flips turning her stomach over, but she saw his face twist into a rictus of horror.

"What's happening?" she gritted out, spots speckling her vision, pain searing her scalp. She didn't want to speculate on what Timothy was seeing and didn't want to know, but at the same time had to find out.

"Stay calm. Stay calm and breathe. Remember your spell. What you visualized. What you wanted to accomplish."

She was in agony, sick and hurting, and concentrating on anything but her misery was near impossible. But she buckled down and tuned in to the intention of her spell. Her goal was to transform her snakes into an agent of value, an asset, and a means to save Helen.

What saving her would entail, the form or outcome her effort would take, those specifics were out of her control. Her job was to let the chaos magic work.

Gripping Timothy for dear life, she powered through another bright burst of pain. The skin on her face stretched so hard she was sure it would rip. Her hair had to be all gone by now, torn from the root. Her skull was cracking under pressure. She was sure of it. She screamed until her head was clear, all thoughts burned away by the purifying mysteries of pain. Rachel screamed and screamed, her palms slick against Timothy's firm grip, until her throat was raw.

Blissfully, miraculously, the agony left her body in a clean snap. She gasped, ecstatic at the influx of cool relief. Pressure had left her face and head, a giant splinter removed to leave only a wondrous release. She was still reeling when whatever was holding her let go, sending her crashing.

Timothy somehow caught her without falling off the stepladder. He eased both of them to the ground where he cradled and rocked her, murmuring soothing words while she recovered from her ordeal enough to take stock.

He banded her in his arms. She clutched the sides of his shirt. "Did it work?" The words came out slurred after great labor. Her mouth was molasses, her tongue too big, her brain not caught up.

He stroked her sweaty hair. "Take a breath. Keep breathing. Give yourself a few minutes to recover. I don't want you to get a shock."

His tone was calm and soothing, but the content of what he said disturbed her. "What do you mean, a shock?"

"It worked," he said softly. "You're amazing. The spell worked. She's going to be okay, and so are you."

She had to see. Not to hear an explanation, but to see with her own eyes. She staggered to her feet. The instant she got upright, her head swum. She spaced out, slurping thin breaths, and stumbled. Timothy caught her before she fell. She planted her hands on a soft piece of furniture. "Damn." Standing upright had triggered a miserable, sickening headache sinking iron teeth into her temples and battering her eyeballs. "Nothing beats a person up quite like chaos magic."

"You should lie down. Rest for an hour."

"No. I need to see." She pried her eyes open, straining to pin down her grip on the physical world.

Finally, after much effort and encouraging self-talk, she was able to look out the windows without fainting, vomiting, or zoning out in a catatonic stupor.

What she saw out there, though, nearly knocked her flat with shock.

Helen was still floating, but now she was supported. A serpent the size of an airplane, its scales a rich indigo glimmering with a sleek, violet shimmer in the winter sun, cradled Helen in the center of its coil.

A mewl escaped Rachel's lips. The creature was magnificent. Regal. Imbued with mystique. And she'd seen dragons. But this dark phoenix, this rope from the ashes, was even more special.

Seeming to catch her gawking, the serpent turned its head to face Rachel dead-on, its ice-blue eyes igniting in twin flames.

THIRTEEN

NOW THEY HAD AN EVEN BIGGER PROBLEM ON THEIR HANDS. A problem the size of a jet, its scales as shiny as latex, a ribbon of nightfall amid starless dusk. Timothy considered himself a problem solver, but this one might be a doozy.

Could people see the creature if they looked up? What then?

"We don't know yet it if it's an ally or enemy." Timothy pulled Rachel into a hug. They had to stay calm. The serpent's gaze was fixed on him, a look both coldly detached and targeting in its awareness. "Or what it wants."

Like a magic carpet, the new entity floated towards the apartment. The rope of midnight got larger and larger, heart-stopping large, before settling to hover by the window. Helen still appeared to be unconscious, her eyes closed, her face peaceful. She rested in the center of its coil.

The beast angled itself flush against the open window, scales the size of dinner plates pressed against glass. A flex of its massive muscles, and Helen slid down the chute of flesh until her legs dangled through the opening. Rachel rushed over, caught her, and urged her to collapse on the couch.

In a blink, the giant snake unfurled, aiming one last piercing, blue-eyed stare into the windows. It shot skyward like a firecracker, shrinking with the rise in altitude until it was no longer visible.

Rachel sat beside Helen on the patchwork couch and shook her gently, rousing her. "We made the serpent with our partner spell. Like a familiar baby."

Timothy stopped craning his neck to the sky and walked over to the witches. "Have you ever heard of anything similar happening before?"

"No. Cynthia brought Buddy back from the Other Place, but I've never heard of a familiar being conjured or created here." Cynthia, the air witch, had been gifted with her precious dragon familiar during a visit to the Other Place. Gifted by Folly, even, though of course there had been strings attached. Cynthia had figured out how to break them.

The visitor wasn't malevolent. They would have learned of any ill intent fast. "The bad news is, if beings like the serpent are moving back and forth, the portal is nowhere near closed. Meaning Scarab is hard at work as we speak. The good news, and I hope I'm not jumping to a conclusion, is I think we passed the test."

"Rope from the ashes." Rachel ran a hand through her hair. "So far, so good. I'm guessing we transferred my snakes into whatever we saw a bit ago. Moved matter and energy around. Chaos magic at its finest."

Helen stirred, moaning a pained sound. Timothy ran to the kitchen, poured her a glass of water from the fridge, and returned to lift it to her mouth. "You're safe. You're home."

"I want to go back," she groaned. She tried to sit up too fast, bumping into his arm and splashing the water. "I was there. Send me back."

"Easy." Rachel held her shoulders, urging her to stay put. "Take a minute to adjust."

"I'm fine." Her eyes snapped open. "You guys did it. You merged the timelines. Why did you pull me out? Did you just un-merge them?"

He wasn't sure. But Helen's skepticism seemed to have evaporated on her journey, so he counted a change of heart as a win. "Where were you?"

She shook her head like she was clearing out the last of the cobwebs. "I started out in my recurring dream. Just like always, same clothes and everything. Towards the end, when I start to wake up from it, I went lucid instead. I went to a magic store and met a witch. She gave me a book, which looked almost exactly like the one you cart around." Helen pointed to Rachel's book on the coffee table. "I met Brian completely randomly. Like you said, we're connected. Then I did a money spell from it to help out my business. Somehow, he got pulled into the spell in a bad way. I was trying to explain this to him when I ended up on this couch again. He's in danger. We all are. I have to get back."

Timothy and Rachel looked at each other. "Did a serpent factor in?" he asked. "Or a dragon?"

"There was a dream within a dream." Helen slumped forward and massaged her forehead. "The witch I met appeared to me as a snake. Layers and layers. So many dimensions. She told me I needed to use my book to reverse the spell." She looked him dead in the eye. "I have to get back there and work before someone gets hurt."

"Do you remember what element you worked with?" Rachel rubbed Helen's back.

"Spirit," she whispered. "Just like you said. I never should have doubted you guys. I've always known I was different, but I've been so stubborn. I needed to see something concrete and irrefutable with my own eyes. Fuck! We've wasted so much time already."

"It's going to be okay." Timothy wasn't sure he believed Rachel's reassurance, but it was important she offered it. "We can send you back to the other timeline permanently. But I need to know you're fully committed. Once we do this, there's no guarantee we can call you back. Frankly, I don't think we'd be comfortable undoing that once the wheels are in motion. Are you sure? This is your choice?"

"I've never been more sure of anything in my life. This is my destiny. What I was put here to do. When the dream changed, you guys, it was like a religious experience." Tears rolled down her face. "Suddenly my life had meaning. Purpose. Colors were more vivid. My heart was open." She swirled a hand in front of her chest. "I felt this buzzing sensation, deep inside. This presence of an energy belonging to me, or was with me, yet external at the same time." After a broken sob, she caught her breath. "My lifeblood had returned after being dormant for years. I was finally alive."

"You're feeling the magic," Rachel said. "I've felt it too. The awakening."

"It's not for the faint of heart," Timothy said. "This path. You won't always be in control. The battles will feel too big. And there's no going back, like Rachel said."

"I'm not worried." She didn't sound concerned. Not one drop of hesitation stained her tone. "The other timeline, or dimension, or whatever, is where I'm meant to be. The track where I flow. This place here..." She twirled her finger in a circle above her head. "Is like purgatory. I've felt like this forever. Like I'm always adjacent to the meaning of life. On the outside looking in. It's hard to describe..." she trailed off, biting her bottom lip.

Timothy knew exactly what she'd meant. He'd felt the same way until the shifting had found him. To a lesser extent, he'd stayed stuck until his hitchhiking journey in search of a similar meaning, purpose, and direction had brought him to Peru. "Like there's a sheet of water separating you and your experiences, and if you could just push through it, connect with what was beyond it, everything would finally click and make sense?"

"Yes," she whispered, her eyes wet and red. "There's joy on the other side of the wall. Contentment. Even if it isn't always easy to be there. The challenges are worth it. They'll be worth it. The right kind of challenges. Inspiring ones."

Rachel glanced at him in a way conveying a clear, profound understanding. "She's describing what happens when the timelines merge. When someone moves into alignment with where they're supposed to be. We've both been through it, but we didn't recognize the shift for what it was."

He nodded, convinced. "Okay. Let's give it a shot. Helen, is there anything you need to take care of before we get started?"

"No. Everyone I care about is in the other timeline. Get me out of this one. I can't be here for one more day." She sniffled, then eked out a soft laugh. "I've got shit to do there. Here, I'm spinning my wheels."

Rachel spoke first. "Fair enough. We'll sit in a circle and hold hands. This way, we can draw from every element in the chain to maximize our efficacy." She slid the coffee table off an area rug and took her place, the book in the center.

"Works for me." Helen sat down, her back straight, her face set in a determined cast.

Timothy was still concerned about the snake, but it wasn't productive to hold them up based on one loose end. Helen was ready. Getting her ready was the goal of this trip, and it was time to close the loop while she was eager.

Rachel leafed and settled on a spell to send a whole person to a different plane of reality. She explained where Helen needed to go, and how she had to reunite with her book and complete a life-or-death mission.

Helen closed her eyes and looked to the ceiling, her face calm and raptured. The effect was almost chilling, her total surrender in the wake of so much doubt, but Timothy trusted they had the situation as under control as it would ever be. He trusted Rachel. Her competence, her expertise, her leadership. He caressed Rachel's hand while she talked through the spell, awash in respect and adoration for her. He'd never thought much about having a partner, an equal by his side to lead the community in Peru. Now, though, the notion pleased him.

The future nature of their relationship, however, was not a topic for the present moment.

Once Rachel finished speaking, a phosphorescent shimmer seemed to leak from Helen's pores until she was covered head to toe in a second skin, glimmering with an oil spill of colors. The hues of chaos magic, sparkling black and deep purple, were especially pronounced. The effect was gorgeous. Magic, alive, and acting in accordance with their wishes. At least, he hoped.

"Stay with it," Rachel said. "Concentrate on where you were. Where you want to be, and the particular events after your dream changed from the usual script to the new content. That's the heart of the matter. The good stuff, the juice, the new timeline."

Helen's form began to blur, her features running together as the magical sheen thickened, enveloping her until she was little more than a glowing blob. "I'll wake up seated across from my witch mentor and go from there. See you on the other side." Her voice was faint, little more than an echo, and then she was gone.

The sparkle cloud shrunk, gathering, its density increasing as its overall size compacted. A clear crystal remained in its place. Rachel picked up the rock. "It keeps finding me one way or another." She turned it over in her hand, worrying the inside of her cheek. "I hope she's okay. How will we know if she's okay if we can't communicate with her?"

"We have to trust." He stroked the inside of Rachel's wrist. "This is what we were brought here to do. We'll see her on the other side, like she said. We did our best. You did amazing. We'll be reunited. I know it." He had to project confidence. Confidence was his thing.

"You're right." She let out a hard sigh. "I say we go back to the forums. Try to get a better idea of what Scarab is up to before we plan our next move."

"Agree. We need all the info we can get on how to close the portal. Once we do, they shouldn't be able to touch us anymore. If we cut their connection to the chaos magic, it's over, and we win."

"Yeah. Sounds right. Their final ritual is what feeds *her* enough to finalize the hologram prophecy. It's a huge feedback loop. If we choke off their supply and stop them cold, we've got leverage. Let's get back to Peru and ensure everyone is safe and that this portal is closed."

There was no one else he'd rather be working with to put this issue to rest. Timothy led them back to Helen's office and booted up the computer.

Rachel grabbed an extra chair and settled in beside him. "What do you figure happens to this space when she links in with the new reality? Does it become an abandoned apartment? A different place altogether?"

"From what I've been able to determine, the old reality shifts to accommodate the existence of the new. So this place will alter itself to basically delete Helen. The specifics aren't as cut and dried." A twinge pulled his heart while he brought up the familiar website. According to his research, he'd been written out of his former reality in Utah as if he'd never lived there. His parents had been going about their daily routine, he imagined, and in a flash lost all recollection of how they'd ever had a son named Timothy. Same with his old friends and beloved teachers.

There was a melancholy aspect to it all, touching upon the frailty and impermanence of existence. Like Helen's dream world, real and beautiful and so wanted, only to slip through one's fingers and fade away.

"You okay?" She craned her neck to get a better look at his face.

"I'm good." He snapped out of his moody reverie of bygone bonds and typed the site name into the search bar. "This life of ours is a strange way to live. It hits me now and again. What's lost. What we lose. Though I suppose existence in general isn't much different. It's fleeting."

"You went and got all philosophical." She rested her head against his shoulder, the gesture tender enough to turn their moment into an intimate one.

He pretended to type. Past the panes of Helen's office window, he could see into one of the rooms of a neighboring apartment building. Glowing in a soft white aura, a Christmas tree supplied the only light source. Windows into the lives of others reminded him of alternate dimensions.

In either case, he had no idea what was going on in those neighbors' heads, how their perspective was unfolding. Timothy laughed at his brooding detour into heady topics. "I always get this way a bit during the holidays. Nostalgia for a time that never was mixed with the memories I have of my past. This year it's amplified."

"I can't imagine why." She fidgeted with a loose thread on his shirt. "I have to say, I wouldn't go back to normal life if given the choice. Normal is overrated."

Rachel was a mysterious person in many respects, one whose motives often remained opaque or at least eluded him. Their companionship had become a push-pull where he nudged forward and retreated when he sensed he'd crossed a line, taking her cues in whatever direction. Here, he sensed an opening. She'd been through so much horror and retained her composure, her center. She was so strong. "What was your normal like?"

Her hazel eyes had him locked in. The spell having dissolved, her natural color shone through in all its rich layers of green and amber. "You mean before I was made into a freak and brainwashed into doing the bidding of an evil spirit and her corrupt corporate henchmen?"

"I wouldn't have put it in those exact terms." Endured and survived was more like it.

"We were poor. Happy enough, but with all the stress and tension coming with poverty. Bill collectors calling, random people at the door, etcetera. I grew up in a trailer park with my mom."

"Where was your dad?"

She shrugged. "Half-in, half-out. Mostly out toward the end. Mom's side hustle was as a...sex worker. He cheated on his wife with her, and I was the product of the affair. He tried for a little while, bringing gifts and sending money. The visits and gifts gradually diminished, until one year it stopped. The child support dried up a couple of years later. Around then, Mom got back into drugs." Her sigh carried a buildup of weight. "So yeah. You can imagine that was just as much fun as it sounds."

"How old were you?"

"Twelve when I started taking on more responsibilities Mom couldn't handle anymore. Cooking, cleaning, paying bills. Fending off people who we couldn't afford to pay. College felt like such an escape. A chance to start over fresh. I got my mom into a supportive living situation, rehab. By some miracle, her low-income health insurance covered it. Then I was out of there. I enrolled at the cheapest college that was also the farthest away from my hometown and never looked back."

"That was my early life too. Running. Running and searching for a new beginning."

"I think my idealism about my new life was what led me to the experiment. Idealism and my money trauma. I had loans I didn't want to drag around with me because of course my parents didn't pay anything. Then there was the prospect of being part of a huge, groundbreaking innovation. It sounds silly in hindsight, but I think I was looking for any opportunity to escape my small life and expand my horizons. This seemed like a way to get outside of myself and join a larger mission. For the good of the research, for scientific progress. Boy, was I misguided."

"You're too hard on yourself." Castoff light from adjacent buildings twinkled beyond the windows, mixing with the layer of snow and holiday magic. The two of them were warm and safe in their cocoon, even if only in illusion, ensconced in the private abode of someone who had taken leave from their plane of existence in search of grander dreams. He felt the magic in the air, the invisible miracle field surrounding them. Catching a mystical affect made the craziness of his life mostly worth it.

"You were thinking bold and expansive. Beyond yourself and how to make a difference. How admirable."

After moving away from him a couple of inches, she spun in her office chair. "You and your positive spins." She eyed his computer screen. "You think we'll win?"

There was a difficult question with no clear answer. "I don't know. But we're going to try. We aren't giving up. I know that much."

"You know what?" Following one more complete turn, she stopped and faced him.

Even though the chilling effect of the Medusa gaze had vacated Rachel's stare, he nonetheless surrendered to her eye contact and the poise her look carried.

He'd never met someone as calm as Rachel, as composed, with such immersive depths hidden behind a reserved nature. He wanted to drown in her, get lost, lose himself. "What?"

Perhaps her power wasn't completely gone, or the experiment had augmented some natural gift. Wordlessly listening, he waited for her to answer. Timothy didn't always need to talk with Rachel to have a conversation with her. He could simply hold space.

She said, "There's no one else I'd rather be stuck with in this than you."

Quite the compliment. The maze of madness they staggered through threatened to subsume them at every turn, the obstacles jagged and the pits bottomless. But together, they would hold each other up. Together, they would not only endure, but they would also prevail. If he got to work. He wrapped Rachel's hands in his larger ones. "I won't let you down." He meant it. He had to deliver on his promise.

"I know," she whispered, her pretty eyes damp.

Before getting back to business, Timothy leaned in and pressed a slow kiss to Rachel's soft lips. The kiss sealed their pact. Solidified his word. The kiss was a promise and a vow. When he broke the press of their lips, he cupped her chin in his thumb and forefinger, holding her entirely with only his fingers and eyes. He'd be strong for her. Stronger and more capable than he'd ever been. "Let's get back to work and see what these bad guys are up to, so we stay one step ahead."

"One step ahead until the end." She spoke with such confidence. Her conviction posed a challenge. "You and me."

Timothy would work his body, mind, and spirit to ash to make her proclamation come true. First, a deep dive into the rabbit hole labyrinth of the message boards.

FOURTEEN

AFTER FOUR HOURS OF RESEARCHING, RACHEL'S EYES BURNED, HER lids heavy. Even though visiting this space was a necessary evil, she never wanted to look at these message boards again. "Be right back," she told Timothy, rubbing her tired eyes with her whole palm. "I need a break from this."

"I understand." He swiveled in his office chair to meet her gaze. "I'll be here."

"Please do. I can't handle another person dissolving into oblivion. Especially you."

He rose to his feet. "Helen isn't gone. We'll see her again. After we stop this ritual, we'll find her." After gesturing to the screen, he cupped Rachel's cheek. "I promise."

Don't make promises you can't keep. Since he was trying to be strong and supportive, she bit her tongue. There wasn't any point in being mean to Timothy, and to do so would make her feel guilty and awful. He was her ally, and she cared about him. Feelings notwithstanding, circumstances sucked, and she was ready for them to change. "Thank you."

"I can tell you're wavering. Unsure. Try to keep the faith. For all of us."

"I need eye drops." She turned away from him and walked to the hallway bathroom.

It was all too much to bear. Helen's enraptured, emotional vanishing. The snakes giving way to one massive serpent slipping away like another ephemeral wisp. The darkness they'd uncovered on the message board, which she wasn't prepared to think about yet. Sinister rituals in shady rooms, hidden from public view, the thought of them rendered doubly nefarious by a cloaking veil of mystery. Everyone and everything was an apparition now, brief and fleeting.

She locked herself in the bathroom, sat on the toilet, and hunched forward. A deep yet ragged breath got her semi-centered, her mind temporarily freed from the crawling paranoia of the message boards, where little information was trustworthy, but the dubious nature made it no less scary. Some meditative belly breathing cleared her mind, but the stress rushed in fast to fill the void.

Even her peace was now a ghost of a ghost, seconds of tranquility unfurling in wisps so thin she'd never grasp them. Helen's comment about the clear, wobbling wall standing in the way of calm made more sense now. Relief liked to languish out of reach like a tease. "Eye drops." She muttered the reminder out loud to hear her own voice.

It was weird hanging around in Helen's apartment when she was gone, having left as she had. Had Rachel screwed up the spell? Killed her? Sent her to the wrong dimension, the wrong body?

Helen had placed a red, cinnamon scented candle on the toilet tank. She'd hung a trio of miniature wreaths on one wall and laid down a bathmat in the shape of a smiling, red-nosed Rudolph. Rachel choked up. The small aesthetic details reminding her of Helen's personality, individuality, had a haunting, chilling effect. She couldn't take this anymore. Life needed to get back to normal.

The thought of hanging around in a dead, suffering, or missing person's space made her sick. The tears stung. She flung open the medicine cabinet. Over-the-counter pain meds, skincare products, a few jars of essential oil and other all-natural remedies. She found a tiny bottle of eye drops near the back and squeezed the remaining liquid onto her eyeballs. The fluid soothed her fatigue.

With a sigh, she shut the door.

Helen stood right behind her. Her image was watery, half-translucent, but it was definitely her. The expression on her face was too neutral to read.

Rachel gasped. "Are you okay?" She turned around and reached for her sister witch, but once she wasn't looking in the mirror anymore, Helen was gone. For all she knew, she'd hallucinated. She had to get out of this apartment, even if the next destination was worse. The specter over her head loomed too large.

Back in the office, Timothy was taking notes in one of Helen's spiral bound journals.

"Doesn't it feel like a violation to handle her things?" With Helen in limbo, the sight of her possessions being re-appropriated bothered Rachel, even if their use was for an important end.

"She'd have wanted this." Timothy wrote a bit more, his stare volleying between the page and the screen. "She started her journaling project. I'm filling in the gaps to keep the flow moving." With a sigh, he shut the book. "I know this is tough. Painful. But try to hang on a little longer. Remember how ready she was to merge? How much she wanted it?"

"I need some assurance, you know?" She glanced over his shoulder at the post he was reading, those terrible words. "I have to know the merge was successful. I need to know she's okay."

"You will get reassurance. We will. But first, we have to stop this ritual."

Their next task was laid out before them in a somber series of typed lines from reliable posters, the information cross-checked for as much accuracy and verifiable truth as could be guaranteed.

Ex-Scarab informants, operating behind the shield of internet anonymity, had reported the location of the Ballad of Capricorn—the keystone ritual on the winter solstice that would detonate the wall between worlds and allow Folly's magic to flow freely.

With the portal to Peru compromised, Other Ones would invade the earthside world unfettered, killing shifters en masse to serve Folly's sacrificial goal. In turn, Scarab would leech off this energetic feeding frenzy and absorb the power they craved. Their experiments would become unstoppable, and they'd reap the benefits of the completion of the hologram prophecy through their nefarious innovations in magic-infused science and technology. The company was nothing but a bunch of ravenous parasites feeding.

"We need to go to them." Timothy didn't sound pleased, but he came off as certain.

"The thought of going back there is a nightmare. Not that I remember being there in the first place." She rubbed a dead hollowness at the center of her chest. "Except somewhere in my body remembers my captivity. Being used in rituals. Having my mind wiped."

"I'd go alone if I could, to save you from the trauma." She believed him. "But I need you. Your magic. Your input. I'm so, so sorry. The last thing I want is to enter that hellish place. Especially considering the misery you must've endured there. And what Julian and Taylor told me about what they witnessed."

One minor saving grace was Taylor and Julian's experience. When they'd infiltrated the bunker to save their kidnapped daughter, they had found and rescued Rachel as well. They'd shared their account of how she'd been trotted out in the middle of a ritual and displayed as a showpiece.

It gave Rachel a measure of cold comfort to have some idea of what had happened to her, and not happened to her, when she'd been brainwashed under Scarab control and used as a magical asset for their insidious goals.

"I want to help," she said, meaning it. She was burnt out, exhausted and fried, but she wanted desperately to help. To make contributions that mattered. "Next step, Florida theme park, yeah?"

He enveloped her in an embrace and swayed her in a gentle rocking motion. "It doesn't have to be tonight. We can go tomorrow and still have time to stop the ritual." She'd grown accustomed to his warm hugs but had to guard against dependence on them. She wasn't entitled to his soothing. She had battles to fight.

"Let's go." Taking a step back, she broke away and laid her hands on his upper arms. Her role was to face him as an equal, a comrade-in-arms. Not to lean on him for emotional support. "Tonight, let's go. We can use chaos magic to get to a hotel and pay for it. I don't want to be here anymore. All I'm doing is thinking about Helen, worrying about where she went and what's happened to her. It isn't healthy. A change of scenery will help. And some productive action."

"You're sure you're ready?"

"I'm ready."

"Fighter." He brushed a kiss to her forehead. "I'll call Julian and get any last pieces of information we might need. Then we'll go save everyone we love."

His high spirit was infectious. Contagious. "Kickass." She held out her fist for a bump.

With a half-cocked grin, he knocked his knuckles against hers. "Kick ass and take names."

The playful gesture, fist bumps more the purview of buddies than lovers, both pleased and confused her, stirring up ruminations of if they were just friends, or more than friends, and if what had happened between them had been exclusively sex.

If they'd talk about it eventually, well, she didn't have the foresight to predict. Feelings weren't at the top of the agenda right now, though, so she screwed her head on straight before she thought any more about screwing Timothy again and if it really was just screwing or meant more or—*enough*.

Practical matters pushed her outside of her head, and she went to the office closet. A red canvas messenger bag sat on the ground. Rachel murmured a silent word of gratitude to Helen before slinging the bag across her body. She stuffed her book inside. "We'll need some food and water. A roll of toilet paper. Two days' worth of stuff is enough."

No doubt he grasped the subtext. More than two days in there and they'd be dead anyway. Everyone would. The clock was ticking. "There's a store in the lobby."

"I have kind of a weird request."

"Anything."

She laughed with appreciation at his willingness to agree before she'd even said the words. "You never cease to amaze me."

"I detect a touch of sarcasm in there, but I'll take the compliment." He wagged his finger.

"As you should," she said.

"What was your request?" His eyes danced with intrigue.

"Can we do the spell by the ice rink? It has to be closed by now. There won't be many witnesses. And if there are, who cares? They won't be able to stop us."

At the rink, they'd shared a tender moment. A sweet escape. A brief vacation to each other, with each other, where they were just two people on a date enjoying the pleasure of one another's company. It may have been a fantasy, but she hoped to soak up some of those residual good vibes, metaphorically stick them in her borrowed messenger bag, and call upon them for strength when their ordeal at the bunker became too much to bear. Magical thinking? Sure. But why not? Nothing was off limits anymore.

He didn't ask for clarification. With his expression, the way he looked at her, he understood. Perhaps not her every thought and step of reasoning, but enough of the context to not have to question her. Theirs was a moment of synergy. Synthesis. The power of the unspoken, the empathetic wavelength, the good faith effort to bridge the gulf between one mind and another. He made this a practice undertaken with Zen-like dedication. She was so grateful.

"Let's go," he said.

✳

A FRESH, LAZY SNOW DRIFTED DOWN IN SCATTERED FLAKES, SPARKLING in the illumination of streetlights.

Peace fell on the night along with new snow, the quiet coldness of a sleepy winter weeknight making Rachel pensive. The sky was starless. A whiff of burning wood perfumed the air.

Timothy took her gloved hand in his own. Helen had a bunch of extra stuff. It felt weird to take it, but Helen would have wanted them to have adequate supplies. It wasn't like she was dead. "Can you read my mind?" She squeezed his fingers.

"No. I can pick up on subtle changes to a person's emotional state, but I wouldn't call it telepathy. Why do you ask?"

"You're so attuned. It's like you pick up on how I'm feeling and know how to respond." Their footprints left soft indentations in the dust of white. Years ago, before her world imploded, Rachel felt a pleasant type of alone on nights like this. Solitary, but comforted by the notion that she wasn't alone in the universe. Someone, or something, was watching over her. That was the closest she'd ever come to a spiritual awakening. She'd been sure the presence was benevolent, or at least neutral.

Now, she wasn't sure of anything.

"Look." He pointed skyward.

Miles away, light years away, a luminescent streak shot upward in a sparkling trail. The end petered out first, going dim, before the head of the glittery object blinked out. "I want to take solace in whatever we just saw and believe it was more than a natural phenomenon." It was no shooting star. Completely different behavior pattern. "But right now, it's so hard to maintain a perspective of everything happening for a reason, and to trust there's some kind of order or even inherent goodness at play." She sighed, her breath melting as vapor into air. "I'm hung up on the impermanence of everything. The precariousness of existence." She puffed out another exhale and watched the dissolution. "How all that is solid melts into air. I think some philosopher I read in college wrote a similar line."

They moved along in deliberate, careful steps, Timothy subtly leading her. "I think we're noticing the chaos magic at work. It's insidious, from what I've been able to determine. Devious. Covert. Gets in your head and fills it with thoughts of entropy and nihilism."

He had a point. "Which makes me easier to control."

"Or at least more aligned with your element. Less likely to ask questions or challenge its fundamental tenets. So yeah, more stirred into the fold. Less of a wild card."

A gray tabby scurried across their path. They'd walked past the turn to get to the skating rink, wandering now. The allure hadn't held. She wasn't feeling nostalgic vibes anymore.

"I feel like this magic is making me crazy. I second guess myself, my thoughts." She laughed without much humor. "My element is the worst one. The scariest one. The hardest to master or even understand. Hard not to feel like I got the short end of the stick compared to the witches who got something cool like spirit or fire. Sorry if I'm whining."

"I don't think you are. People to vent to are in short supply in this life."

"You're right. Thanks for listening," she said.

"I take it we've nixed the ice skating rink?" Timothy looked over his shoulder.

The streets were so calm, coated in white frost that itself seemed to have a magic property of stilling the atmosphere, slowing down activity, and driving everyone indoors. Wandering the city at this exact moment was like soaking in the first moments of awe after waking up from a coma to a post-apocalyptic situation. Reverence for the silence. No fear yet, the zombies undisturbed. "Let's do the frozen lake instead."

"Take this journey full circle. I like the symbolism."

"Yeah, it feels like a way to honor Helen by closing the loop on her old life. Maybe if we end our chapter in Minneapolis here, her story will pick up in the alternate timeline where she goes to the magic store and gets her book."

Rerouting to end up by the lake, they walked down a side street intersecting with the one Light & Enlightened was on. Rachel spotted the structure out of the corner of her eye and choked up.

"You'll see her again," he said. "The spell worked. Have faith in yourself. At the risk of going preachy, I think that's part of the chaos magic. Setting it on a course with your mind, your intention. Making it serve you through a belief in things working out as they're supposed to."

"It's just hard because I've never been a spiritual kind of thinker." She brushed away a tear with a gloved finger. The cloth smelled like Helen's incense and skin. "Or believer. I've always been a skeptic. Someone with a scientific mind, even though I wasn't a scientist. Becoming this new me has really required a leap of faith."

There was a light on in the yoga studio. Was Helen's business partner there? Was she worried? Did she sense something was wrong, different, or was she clueless? Or had Helen been deleted from her reality like a file scrubbed from a cosmic computer?

A crosswalk flashed white, and they passed through an intersection. Beyond was the lake, a black disc sprinkled with dust sparkling in otherwise unseen moonlight. Off far away, a dog barked, its low *woof* echoing.

Timothy said, "I know you can do it. Believe me, I've been there. And this path isn't for the faint of heart. It's like we're just trying to live our lives and situation after situation is thrown in our faces, one after the other, challenging us to question and upend every truth we've taken for granted."

She felt so much affection for him. For whatever else she was going through, Rachel was blessed with the company of someone who got her. Who saw her weird world through her eyes. A kindred spirit. She wasn't alone. Whether or not any benevolent (or at least benign) spirits had her back was debatable. But she had one companion walking the path with her. The universe had granted her a partner for her journey.

She looked up at him, his face, the slope of his jawline. Timothy was both strength and softness, an anchor and an empathetic ear. Her heart was overflowing. She had to stop herself from uttering some serious words to permanently change the nature of their relationship. Besides, the bond she felt forming could be simply a result of their shared stress and trauma. Such a theory sounded psychologically valid. Instead of pouring her soul and feelings into his lap, which might accomplish nothing but making him uncomfortable and render their partnership awkward, she chose a milder expression of fondness. "I'm really glad you're here."

They made their way onto the ice. It was slipperier than before; the coat of snow having done a number on underfoot traction. Still, she knew she wouldn't fall. Not with Timothy to catch her, literally and figuratively. A baby step into some kind of faith, but she'd take whatever gifts she was offered.

"This is where I'll stay until the job is complete." His words alone, their assuredness, carried her. They shuffled halfway onto the ice. In any other context, she would have felt nervous, unsure of what dangers lay below her feet. Instead, she'd never felt more surefooted. He continued, "I won't let you down. I won't desert you. I'm here, and I'll protect you until we're all safe."

Her monkey mind was tempted to interpret his declaration as one of obligation or duty, the burden of an alpha, but she shut down the impulse to overthink. Right now, she needed to take his claim at face value and allow it to nourish her weary spirit, so she did. She let him in. "Thank you."

Another ten feet of paces landed them dead center. Once their task was looming, imminent, the weight of her spell book pulled on the strap of Helen's messenger bag, causing the heavy load to bump against her hip.

They stopped their shuffle to the center of this eerie, cold world within a world. The city was tiny beyond, their domain desolate and arctic.

"I believe in you." He took her face in both of his hands and held her like this, the fabric of the gloves tickling her skin. "When you don't believe in yourself, remember you have me to pick up the pieces."

She breathed. Nodded. She was cold, but not alone. It was time to embark on the next phase of their journey. Rachel opened the bag, plastic clicking against plastic when she undid the buckles. She wedged the book free. It was so damn heavy in her hands.

There wasn't quite enough light to read by, but she got the sense it didn't matter. The intention to work with the book was enough. Reading the actual incantations was largely symbolic.

Nonetheless, in honor of symbolic meaning, Rachel opened the book to the chaos section and started in on an incantation to deliver them to their enemy combatants so they might fulfil their destiny.

She'd barely pushed the final word from her lips when a sickening crack split her eardrums. Dread dragged her low before the solid material below her soles gave way and caved in. Gravity plunged her into a frigid, breathless hell.

FIFTEEN

SCREAMS RICOCHETED IN TIMOTHY'S EARDRUMS. THE REST OF HIS senses were gone. All he had were the screams. Only screams to accompany him while he floated in outer space, where nobody could hear the screams. Or they could hear, but they didn't care.

I'm in hell. It wasn't a hot place, no lakes of fire or scorching pokers. Hell was an icy, senseless tundra of loveless screams.

The screams were hers.

That one realization snapped him out of his despairing mind and into his fighting instinct.

"Hold on," Timothy shouted, unclear if his speech breached his lips or stayed in the cacophonous underworld inside his head. "I'm here." He stuck out his hand, or at least his brain sent his body the signal to complete the action. "Hold on to me. You aren't alone. I'm here with you."

Rachel gasped. Gurgled. Moaned. But the awful screams stopped. He felt pressure against his fingers and clutched as tightly as he could. "I've got you. We're here."

"Where the fuck is here?" Her speech was hoarse from the screaming, the scratchy rasp making his throat hurt in empathy. "Can you see?"

"Not yet." Some spatial awareness had returned to his body since he could feel her grip. She was his lifeline, and he hers. He scrambled for purchase, fought for footing, trying to discern if he was standing, lying, sitting, or what. No equilibrium. His inner ear offered no stabilizing. Balance was a sense he'd taken for granted until it was gone. The more Timothy tuned into the precise nature of what his body was feeling, the precise characteristics of the unmoored sensation, the more familiarity crept in. He'd been this way before, just not in this exact place. "This happens when I shift sometimes. My connection to my body and the outside world goes into freefall. There's a limbo period. You have to ride it out until it's over. Ride it out with me, Rachel, hang on."

"Welcome to pure chaos," Folly crooned from somewhere in the nowhere. "Get used to it, because it's just getting started."

"She's here with us," Rachel said, grim. "She spoke to me."

"Same. She's in both of our heads. We can't get distracted. We have to stay in the mission." To stay focused, they had to exit the liminal state and connect with their environment. He had some experience with this from shifting, and, with any luck, had advice to offer Rachel. "Take deep breaths. Ground yourself in your body by doing a scan from your toes to your scalp. Feel each part and send your breath into it. As you do so, identify any other senses you have with you. If you can smell. The touch of my hand. Floaters or specks of light in the corner of your eye."

"Okay." She voiced her agreement with a note of confidence despite the weak sound of her voice.

He brought her hand to where he imagined his face to be and searched for her scent. The fragrance of her skin, fruity and floral and tender, was his first anchor. He breathed her in while doing the body scan exercise. Finally, finally, pale yellow auras glowed in the edges of his vision. Hard ground supported him on his left side. His mouth tasted awful, bitter. But he was coming back. With Rachel. "Do you have any grounding yet?"

"Yeah. Sort of."

"Talk to me. What do you see?" He could smell the space now in addition to Rachel. Musty, like old clothes in a vintage shop. He was too queasy to open his eyes fully, his stomach both turbulent and knotted, but he was aware enough to see flickers of dim light.

"There's stuff everywhere. I can't tell what it is. We're somewhere cluttered. Oh, shit, I'm going to be sick." She retched. Heaved. The sound was awful, pained, but nothing came out.

"It's okay." He wasn't convinced of this, not at all, but right now, comforting Rachel came first. He pulled her close while she coughed. "Keep describing what you see, hear, smell, feel. It'll bring you back faster."

"I'm on the floor. There's an overhead lighting fixture. A cluster of three bulbs hanging from cords. I thought they were stars or planets at first, like we were in space." She hacked again. "And things are pretty fucking far afield from okay."

Her sarcastic wit startled a laugh out of him. "Shame on me for thinking I could patronize you, even if my intentions were good." His vision, though blurry, was over halfway back in his command. Rachel lay curled, fetal, in his arms. Her complexion was sallow, greenish. They were both seated. Racks of clothes loomed all around them.

"Well, the good news, if there is any, is your shifter tips seemed to help. I guess your initial instincts about how I could harness the ability to shift were correct."

He didn't need the validation or ego stroke, but he was thankful he'd been able to help Rachel recover and wasn't wildly off base with his initial theory. "We're symbiotic in some way. My shifting, your magic. If we can keep feeding each other, back and forth in a give and take, hopefully we'll have some added protection."

"Yeah, hopefully." She craned her neck, looking around. "Because what in the crazy dark magic is going on? Is this some new place in the backrooms or Other Place or whatever we're calling it?"

At last, he could see normally and open his eyes without surrendering to a dizzy spell or bout of nausea. He could see where she'd drawn the backrooms conclusion. The room they sat in had a warehouse feel, with high ceilings crossed by exposed pipes and fat, puffy vents.

The walls were taupe, painted for industrial blandness instead of aesthetic. Despite being packed with clothing racks, stackable so they stretched halfway to the ceiling, the space felt cavernous and fit for echoes. The clothes were mismatched and not organized by any discernable order. A flashy quality to the items on the racks gave him an uneasy, foreboding feeling, but he couldn't put his finger on it.

Rachel staggered to her feet, Timothy following suit as fast as he could in case she stumbled and needed to be caught. Fortunately, she stabilized in a couple of seconds. Her eyes were wild. He felt her distress. "I've been here before." She said it like she was spitting out poison.

"Can you elaborate?" Though tempting to ascribe a positive quality to her familiarity—she might be able to navigate—he knew better than to make any assumptions.

She walked to a rack and pawed through hangers. Metal scraped against metal. Fabrics flew by in a blur of blue lace, pink leather, sanguine velvet, polyester the color of a tequila sunrise. "Not here, here. But close. Close to these costumes." With a certain aggression, she yanked a hooded, bloodred robe off the rack. "She's fucking with us. Trying to scramble my mind and re-traumatize me." She shoved the robe back in place. "I can't let it work. I have to fight." Her face went spacey. "The déjà vu." Suddenly faraway, her pitch dropped in register. "The déjà vu happening right now is unbelievable. If I'm even accurately describing what this is. I feel like I'm not real. Not here. Like a character in a movie."

Timothy cupped her chin in his hand, forcing her glazed eyes to meet his. "Rachel. You're here, now, with me. Stay present. Don't slip away. To beat this thing, we have to remain lucid. We'll connect the dots, I promise. But don't zone out on me. Losing our minds is what she wants. It's a trap."

Sharpness returned to her expression; the slack quality replaced by keen awareness. He let out a breath and moved his hand to her shoulder where he offered caresses of support.

"I was here for a ritual," she said. "Brought here. Captured. I was used in the ritual. The first one. The Song of Virgo. They wore these robes." She jiggled the frock on the hook. "I escaped. Taylor saved me and brought me to Peru. I knew those facts before because I was told them, but now I know it happened in a more real way." After releasing a long groan, Rachel rubbed her temple. "So much of it was wiped from my mind. I only remember fits and starts. I woke up in a pod with Taylor, then I went to Peru. Before, it's fragments. Fuzzy."

A red tint tinged the whites of her eyes. She swayed on her feet even as she clutched a knuckle-whitening grip on the red robe. "I need to be strong for the community." Her voice broke. She swallowed. "I'm having a hard time being strong. My mind was torn apart. Here. So much happened here, and none of it was good. I feel it in my body. I'm so weary."

Compassion exploded his heart into broken pieces. Rachel had been through so much. Deception, betrayal, the forgotten trauma of this ritual. And now she was back in the den of atrocity, facing pressure to be strong when she'd barely had a chance to heal.

"Come here." He swept her into himself. As weird as the clothing room was, and as charged with bad, diluted memories, it gave them a moment of relative isolation and peace. "You don't have to be strong right now. At least not every minute. Just breathe and be."

Her exhalations exited in ragged bursts, but at least the length increased. She pressed the side of her face into his chest. Her fingertips dug into his back like she wanted to hold on tight and never let go. He didn't blame her. He'd rather not go spiraling into outer space, another dimension, a frigid pool of blackness—ever again.

They both knew they had no choice. They could not quit until the mission was completed. These words didn't need to be spoken out loud. They could be communicated through touch, though, in a moment of closeness. Stolen handfuls of silence, solitude, and each other were all they had right now.

"This fucking place." A harsh laugh chased her words. "I never wanted to see the inside of these walls again."

He had an idea. Rachel had already suffered too much, endured more than one ever should. "Go back. We can send you back. To Peru."

Her eyes popped open wide. "You aren't serious."

"I am. I've worked with you enough to wield your magic. We both know it's transferable. I can do it. You go home and rest. Take care of the rest of the coven. I can beat this thing." As an alpha, it was his duty to step in when others needed to tap out. It was his duty to shoulder the load, and to do so with grace. He could do his duty in this instance. He could. He'd have to, because Rachel was too precious to put at risk anymore.

"Absolutely not." Her steely hazel gaze said it all.

"Rachel." He pressed the pad of his thumb against her lower lip, trying not to notice the fullness, or how her flesh yielded beneath his touch.

She stepped back. "The subject is closed. I stay. I fight. I can and I will close this loop once and for all so no one else has to suffer." She swallowed hard and steeled her backbone. "Neither of us should be alone. We're in this together. You and me. Side-by-side."

Timothy wasn't sure what came over him next. He was tempted to name the feeling as a spiritual overtaking akin to possession, but he'd learned not to use that term with colloquial lightness. The only surety he had was how he and Rachel were, in fact, in this together, even though he wasn't always sure what "this" was.

Madness. Magic. Chaos. A perpetual upside-down where nothing was what it seemed, and, the instant he grasped the rules, the game master flipped the board. Upending was the point. Stability and predictability were null and void. Why not roll with it?

He pulled Rachel flush against his front and kissed her, hard, on the lips. This kiss was not tender, or sweet, or even one of desperation in the midst of bleak sorrow.

He claimed her, took her, the one constant in an ever-changing world of slipping shadows and shaky ground. He'd never had a fated mate like Julian did, or he'd been looking in the wrong places. He'd cynically pretended to trash the entire concept of fated mates when he'd really been lonely all along. He'd assumed his mate, *if* he had one, would have to be a shifter, but perhaps the concept of shifter was more fluid than he'd assumed.

Rachel couldn't alter her form into another creature at will, or she hadn't unlocked the skill, but she had the special stuff in her. The magic made them different. What if, in a primal, eternal way, she and shifters were the same?

Or what if he was overthinking it, and he wanted her more than his next breath, and having her was simply what would be? Either way, he surrendered to his urge.

Her mouth softened to his, her lips parting to accept what was next. He slid his tongue into the warm space she presented, his entry firm but not forceful. She kissed him back, sensually at first, licking and playing.

Emboldened, she crushed her mouth into his. Her tongue shot out to stroke the inside of him. A moan escaped her lips, rumbling with a vibration in the back of his throat. With only a kiss, they were one again.

The moan was what did him in. Pushed him to the next level. He was already half-hard from the kiss, but under her ministrations and sounds, he stiffened to full readiness. Her hands wandered under his shirt, exploring skin and muscle. She ground her pelvis against his cock.

Scents of her excitement and sweat plus her delicate baseline fragrance mixed with the musk of the clothing room to concoct a strange, foreign, almost taboo excitement. Their affair was forged in outlandishness and had been from the beginning. No dates or standard courtship. Their latest location was paradoxically perfect even as the space itself generated a sense of so much wrong. Timothy embraced contradiction along with Rachel. He embraced the chaos.

She pulled her lips away a millimeter. Her mouth was red and swollen, her eyes glazed at half-mast. "Make me forget." Her hot breath tickled his chin. "Make me forget how much I hate this place. Give me new, better memories. Let's change the goddamn energy here once and for all."

"You're sure?" He ran the backs of his fingertips down one of her velvet cheeks. He'd never take advantage of Rachel in a moment of vulnerability or tumult. "Because I need to know you're sure. Positive. Not one iota of doubt, Rachel. Impulsive is fine but give me assurance you want this."

Yes, they'd had sex before. But this felt different. More charged. Higher stakes. Like the moment was only about the two of them, as raw and exposed as frayed nerves rubbing together.

"Here and now." She fisted two handfuls of his shirt and yanked him close with a surprising force, stoking his arousal to new peaks. Her strength was formidable. "Don't be gentle, either. Fuck the bad vibes out of me. Cause an earthquake. They want a ritual? Let's give them a ritual."

"Fuck." He groaned. The blood rushed from his head and pooled below his belt. She was hot and ready, waiting. He wasn't going to wait anymore. She was right. Their act would be one of rebellion. Resistance.

Rewriting the codes of reality, changing the rules with a special, electric sort of magic like nothing else.

Wild, animal, and lost to the craving, Timothy flipped Rachel around. This wasn't going to be pretty or sweet. She'd already indicated what she wanted, and he was ready to give it.

She gripped the metal bar of the rack. Metal scraped against metal with a shrill whine as she shoved coats and tuxedos out of the way to make space for her hands.

Her back arched, her round ass presented in its full, round, jean-clad glory. Chestnut waves tumbled below her shoulders. She was a gift, a prize presented to him.

Stars danced in his eyes. Instinct swallowed him whole. He reached around her waist, unbuttoned her pants, and pulled them along with her underwear to her knees.

She gasped. "Yes. Hard and fast. Like an animal."

She didn't mean 'animal' literally, though he could certainly channel the energy of his inner beast to satisfy her craving.

He stroked and squeezed her globes, her pale flesh quivering under the command of his brown hands. He could take her. Mate her. Bond her in his human form. Or at least he'd sure try.

With his thumbs, he parted her cheeks, allowing his right thumb to trace a lazy trail down her crack before dipping into the pink pocket of her wetness.

Thrusting her backside into his hand, she let out a soft cry.

He continued his play, swirling his thumb inside of her before pulling out and dragging it forward to rub her clit. She moaned, thrust. She liked his technique.

In the interest of shocking her senses a bit, and keeping her on her toes, he reached forward and buried his left hand in her hair. His mouth watered. His erection throbbed against his fly. He clenched a tight handful, close to the scalp, and pulled her head back far enough to where his lips closed in on her ear.

Her eyes were wide open, startled, even, tracking his actions behind her. Her lips, red and glistening. "You're mine," he whispered in her ear, issuing a complete and total declaration of truth. "How does that sound? Are you ready to be mine, Rachel?"

Her body was saying yes from head to toe, but he needed her words to back up those physical cues. He required her full, complete, and total acquiescence to square the circle.

"I'm yours." He'd never heard anyone speak with more conviction, those words of hers hissed with near harshness through broken breath. "Make me yours right now. Here. Take this place away from them and give it to me."

All he could offer in reply was a grunt. Verbal ability had left him. Keeping the grip on her hair, Timothy ripped at his button and fly with his free hand, jamming his fingers into his boxers.

He freed his cock, finding it harder than he'd ever seen the damn thing, and pressed against her entrance. She was soft, damp, and ready, welcoming him with full receptivity. He used his first and middle fingers to open her outer labia and target her clit. She was ready there, too, swollen.

Using a circular motion, he stroked her, speeding up or slowing down with the gyrations of her pelvis and the speed of her panting. Her clit pulsed under his finger pads. Her moans came closer and closer together. She was on the brink.

Above them, there was a noise he failed to place, and his ears were trained. A light object, likely small and even hollow, struck the upper-level floor with a pat. It clicked a rhythmic path, skittering in a succession of taps before petering out. Activity was happening. They might get interrupted. Time was scant, his heartbeat feral.

Timothy butted the head of his cock against Rachel's opening. Her body welcomed him, swallowing up his length. Enveloped in tingling warmth, the hug of her, he pushed in and out, drowning his troubles in the haven of her body.

She must've been lost to him too, so gone she hadn't even registered the intrusive sound as far as he could tell. If the rolling item produced any more sound, wet skin slapping soon drowned it out, those personal and shameless noises enveloping them both.

He could smell her tang and sweat along with his own musk. Frantic, he thrust, matching the movements of her pistoning ass. Plunge after plunge, each chased by a grunt or curse. His, hers, their voices merged.

"Yes," she gritted out as a spasm seized her clit.

Her pleasure augmented his own. Bliss rose to crazy need, and he went fast, brutal, all the refined parts of himself submerged and gone. Four more dips and he broke into euphoric relief, pulling out just in time to stifle his final cry against who or whatever might be with them in the building. Part of him, a daring, defiant part, didn't even care. Let them challenge. Let them try.

He caught his breath and sanity, using the hand that'd gripped her hair to smooth the locks. She'd barely had time to turn and face him when the creak of a door opening stopped them both cold.

SIXTEEN

A CHEMICAL COCKTAIL FLOODED RACHEL'S BLOODSTREAM BEFORE she'd had a chance to think. Bursts of adrenaline made her hands shake as she fumbled with the snap on her jeans, the dusty odor of the clothing nauseating her. Climactic aftershocks rolled through her system, mixing unhealthily with the stress hormones. Why couldn't she catch a break?

It was happening again. Starting up again. They were going to catch her. Get her. Erase her mind and put her snakes back in her scalp and subject her to more sick experiments and rituals. Her stomach dissolved into a cramping mess of acid. Her vision sharpened, scanning for danger. She stayed on high alert for every creak, squeak, or voice even as she seemed to float outside of her body.

As if reading her mind, Timothy banded his arms around her chest. He laid a palm over her breastbone. The unbearable rabbit skitter that'd fired up the instant she'd heard the creak of hinges slowed. He had a way with her in every sense. He knew her body and read her so well. She relaxed into him, as much as she was able to relax, grateful for his presence and support.

Once halfway out of panic mode, her brain switched back on. Who had opened the door, and which door had they opened? Maybe the movement had been far away, and her hyper-vigilant reaction had tricked her. Trauma sucked and lied.

But then, an unfamiliar female voice spoke, crisp and businesslike. "I'll double check with my team, but I'm nearly positive nobody has caught her poking around here in months. The security cameras haven't picked up any sign of the truck, either. Until further notice, let's assume our little Nancy Drew has moved on."

Nearby, a door shut with a snick. A man talked next. "Okay, fine, but we can't rest on our laurels. Not with the asset escaping after Song of Virgo and those intruders stealing the baby. We can't risk the main event being polluted or compromised in any way. All contingencies must be accounted for. The area has to be swept, and full security protocols instituted."

Her pulse and heart returned to overdrive mode. These two were referring to the stilted ritual where Rachel escaped and Taylor and Julian saved baby Luna. Their victory hadn't been the end of Scarab's scheming, of course. Now Rachel was responsible for stopping what was next. Somehow. She squeezed the messenger bag between her feet, the bulk of her book supplying some assurance. She had a weapon. She had means.

"In general, I agree. Full security is a smart precaution," the woman said. "But we don't want to lose the forest for the trees here and get paranoid. Nobody else is here to interfere. We should focus our attention and energy into rehearsing the order of the ritual. The executive leadership team values aesthetics. Perfection. This launch had better be beautiful and breathtaking and all that shit, because my performance review is coming up and I need to hit 'exceeds expectations' to have a chance at securing a spot in the C-suite next quarter. We can circle back to your concerns tomorrow before the rehearsal, but I'd like to close the loop on this topic by EOB today."

"Fine," the guy said. "One more sweep of the perimeter. We'll touch base in the A.M."

"Finish the sweep yourself. I have a high-priority client deliverable to finish."

The literally demonic, soulless cabal used the same jargon as any mega corporation. Checked out.

Two sets of footsteps made their way to the end of the costume room. The door shut behind them. They were gone. Rachel let out a breath and a gust of relief. "There can't be security cameras in here. Otherwise, we would have been caught already."

"My sources tell me they use flying drones for security," Timothy said. "Cheaper and more effective than fixed cameras, which are relatively easy to disable."

"Meaning we could be spotted at any second if someone sends a drone in here."

"Bingo. They can open doors and windows with relative ease. We should never assume we're safe or under the radar."

"Believe me, I wasn't." She wracked her brain for the next steps. "Megan found this place a few years ago and was doing investigations for her paranormal show. She didn't really get anywhere, but Megan is who they were talking about."

A muscle in his jaw tensed. He looked to the left, visual evidence of the gears in his brain turning. "Julian and Taylor wore disguises to infiltrate the ritual. I'm hesitant to copy their approach, though, because I worry they might be on the lookout for anyone suspected of hiding under a costume. I'm not sure we could fool them twice."

A spark flared in her mind. "We don't have to disguise ourselves. Not identically, not if we're lucky. The second door in here is our best bet. Let's go."

"What are you thinking?"

"Come on." She walked out from behind the clothing rack. "I'll show you."

Taylor had mentioned a small personnel room in this space where Scarab employees kept photo evidence of Megan's investigations, though they hadn't been able to catch her. Whether the cubby held any answers or solutions remained to be seen, but it was a next step where Rachel could at least explore her idea.

He checked their backs. The main room was larger than she'd assumed at first and well-stocked with costumes. Scarab had to have a massive labor force, a large operation, which was not a good sign. Some of the costumes were likely deployed for the theme park above ground, but still. She and Timothy were massively outnumbered.

The sub-room was locked: no give from the bronze doorknob.

He sprang into action without missing a beat. "Check the bag. I can work with a paper clip or hairpin, but a credit card is best."

Rachel rummaged in the messenger tote. Nothing at first except old receipts and sticks of gum in paper wrappers. But then, jackpot. Her heart soared. An expired health savings account card at the bottom of one of the inner pouches. Same weight as a credit card. Thank God. She handed the piece of plastic to Timothy.

In a single, swift motion, he slid the card between the door and the jamb. A twist, a bend, and the lock gave way to his efforts with a snap. Much more efficient than going the magical route with its trial-and-error uncertainties.

"Nice skill," she said.

"It's handy at least. Can't say I envisioned having to use it in this exact situation, however."

"I don't think any of us did." She turned the knob gently in case any other Scarab staff were looming.

Little more than a janitorial closet, the nook was unlit and smelled of citrus air freshener covering up a stale stench. Rachel flipped the light switch with the same dour swiftness one would use to rip off a sticky bandage, anticipating a flash of pain.

A cheap desk rested against one wall, taking up most of the room. A chunky desktop monitor from a few decades ago sat on the surface, flanked by a few paper clips, some coins, and blank index cards.

He swept the paper clips into his palm, then pocket. Rachel smiled at him. "Industrious," she said.

He poked a key on the computer keyboard and swirled an unpadded mouse. The machine groaned and clunked; its warmup process as labored as expected.

"This is the office they were using to gather and record information on Megan." He pointed to the long wall facing the door.

Black and white photos, grainy as if taken with a surveillance camera, plastered taupe cinderblock. Megan aiming a camera inside a dumpster, her red hair messy. Megan's truck driving away down a wide access road. Megan crouched, peering into a window of what looked like a warehouse. The pictures were interesting because they showed other parts of what were presumably the building's layout, but otherwise pretty useless.

"There has to be something in here to help us." A file cabinet sat opposite the desk. The first drawer she pulled made a tinny nails on chalkboard noise, making her squirm. Inside were old yellowed papers. Upon further inspection, they proved worthless. Or she lacked the context to derive value from them. "I'm so tired of these spells."

"I understand." Timothy rifled through a Bankers Box on the floor. More papers he didn't appear to be interested in. "But it might be our only option. Hang on a little while longer. We can try a disguise spell. Or even invisibility."

His zeal to up the ante with chaos magic concerned her. Conventional wisdom held that the coven daughters' magic had an addictive property to be monitored with vigilance. Magic use required mindful, conscientious moderation to be successful without hurting the practitioner. Any tilt toward irresponsibility in usage could compromise their minds and make them vulnerable to possession. "Let's see if we can find an everyday solution first." She looked him square in the eye. "Trust me. I know it seems like spells are the easy way out, but the bill will come due. We probably already owe more than we're aware."

"Okay." He paused from flipping through a legal pad to give her his full attention. From his tone and expression, it was clear he was taking her seriously. "I trust you there. You're the expert. Any ideas?"

Two of the large desk drawers were empty save for a plastic fork, a candy wrapper, and some chicken scratch notes scribbled on scraps of paper. As hesitant as she was to use magic as a go-to, a lazy first resort, they might not have any other choice. "I wish we could both shift into spiders or butterflies or something." She searched another drawer and discovered only a plastic bag and several sheets of blank computer paper. "Be literal flies on the wall. Is that a thing, swapping out one animal element for another? If so, we could at least spy. Arm ourselves with information without risking being caught. Plan."

"No. Someone's animal element is set from birth, at least the evidence points there. Before birth, even. It's ancestral. If there's a way to transform to different animal elements, I haven't figured out what that is." He stood on the folding chair by the desk and ran his hands along the seam between the wall and ceiling. "There could be a secret compartment in here. A safe or hidden panel. From the way those two were talking, this room matters."

The computer had booted up and now asked for a password. Her hunch was anything valuable was contained within the machine, and they had no clues how to get access. She was about to give up when she tugged open the final drawer, the slim one in the middle.

Huzzah! Her prizes beamed up at her like gold bricks. "Timothy. Look. Holy shit. These are perfect." Spilling out of a manila envelope was a cluster of employee IDs. Some were bundled by a rubber band and stamped with a pink Post-It with the word "termed" scrawled on the front. Others were loose.

She held up a wad of the badges and cards, proud as a winner flaunting a trophy. Some dangled from lanyards, others were magnetized or outfitted with a pin to be clipped to a shirt. The ones with photos on the front were duds; there was no way she and Timothy could remotely pass for the people pictured. The IDs in the "termed" bundle were tricky, too, in case anyone recognized the name of the former employee who wasn't supposed to be there anymore.

The greatest potential lay in the batch of generic badges. These were marked "trainee," "contractor," "vendor," "support," and even "regional director." From the looks of things, Scarab's turnover rate was high enough to where they didn't always bother to assign names and faces to some of their roles. Figured. Anyone with a conscience likely didn't last long in the employ of these fiends.

Glowing with triumph, Rachel held a "management liaison" badge in the air. The white card dangled from a rainbow lanyard with some flair buttons pinned to the cloth material. *Slay the day*, *she/her*, *boss babe*. "Ready to go to work for the original devil corporation?"

Timothy grabbed the "regional director" one and pinned it to his shirt. "So what, we just walk around and fish for information we can use?"

"You got a better idea?" She slung the "management liaison" credential around her neck, figuring she and Timothy had both made smart choices.

Vendors and contractors would be expected to have, or at least speak about, tangible content. Support staff might have to demonstrate skills. Management and directors, on the other hand, had a better chance of skating by on bullshit. Rachel had worked in offices. She could circle back, close the loop, touch base, and break people out of silos—talk all the standard, empty corporate talk.

"You're brave." His eyes sparkled. He looked the part of a regional director, projecting authority.

"Or completely insane." She poked around the room some more before giving up. The badges were the big score. "But I need a break from this magic. We both do. It can overtake you if you aren't careful. There are other ways to beat this thing, and we can break out spells if we get stuck."

"A good old-fashioned test of wits. Fuck it. I'm in."

She laughed. High spirits were good for morale. There wasn't any benefit to being dour and morose. They had to be light on their feet, nimble, and positive in their thinking. "Let's go find this meeting and see if we can throw a wrench into the plans."

Like always, Timothy set off first, taking a couple of steps ahead to claim the lead and protect her in the process. As they blazed past the clothing racks, he stuck his arm out from his body, shielding her with his limb. The gesture was so automatic it seemed subconscious. Like he wasn't even aware he was doing it.

Warmth spread through her chest even as she pushed out a scoff and caught up to walk beside him. "You don't have to guard me. I'm not a damsel in distress."

"Of course not." He reclaimed his slight lead and curled his fingers around the doorknob. His gaze was firm and knowing. "But you are more valuable than I am. You're the key to saving the world as we know it. I'm just the bodyguard."

Hardly true. But she'd rather fish around in his feelings than affirm his status. Timothy's humility was more than a little affected, which made it even sexier. He carried himself with just a touch of arrogance, enough to command respect but not so much that he was insufferable. The man was a golden mean of ego and modesty. "Here I was thinking you were hanging out with me because you liked me."

"Do you really have to question how much I like you?" he winked.

And damn, the man had a killer wink. Smooth and unassuming, cheeky, without a hint of smarm.

"I was just checking in. It's challenging to maintain a situationship while stalking an underground lair in search of diabolical supervillains to thwart."

"They aren't supervillains." He opened the door. "Don't give them too much credit. They're power-hungry fools who'll be brought down by their own psychotic obsession. We've got this."

With their path laid out in front of them, her jitters returned. She'd been using banter to stall. "In the bag. Thanks for the pep talk, Regional Director." His tough talk hadn't neutralized her nerves, but she appreciated his efforts all the same. Timothy's calm, unwavering power was contagious.

"You hardly needed it, Management Liaison. You're a force to be reckoned with."

After acknowledging him with a quick squeeze on his forearm, they got back in character and set off. The hallway itself was nothing special. Gray cinderblock walls, dim lighting, air faintly tinged with mold. Concrete floor. Generous width, so at least lack of claustrophobia lined their otherwise dreadful ordeal in a veneer of silver. No security cameras, at least no visible ones. Not a window in sight. The atmosphere strongly suggested they were in a basement. Or sub-basement. Sub-sub-sub-basement, rubbing shoulders with the borders of hell. A shiver ran up her backbone. A plan would be nice, but they lacked the luxury.

Farther off, voices travelled toward them. Male and female. Faint echoes. She couldn't make out the words. With a shared glance, she and Timothy agreed to follow the sound.

They marched in tandem, passing closed doors in pursuit of the talkers. Despite how much she strained her ears, the content of their speech eluded her. Timothy, going from his scrunched brow, didn't look any more clued in than she.

After a few more turns down identical hallways, they kept track of the voices but didn't feel any closer. An anomaly in the monotony made Rachel stop and take notice. They'd passed a large window, clear glass, providing full view of what looked like a laboratory. No effort at discretion was made. Nobody wanted to hide the contents of the lab. They were there to be shown off, so why not look?

She glanced at Timothy to get his attention before peering in. She had to cover her mouth to stifle a gasp, though nothing should shock her anymore. The sterile room with its sparkly clean linoleum floor was lined on three sides with enclosures, aquariums. In them lived creatures.

The largest ones were about the size of a housecat but in no way mammalian. Chunky and fat, they had gray, scaly skin, twin legions of stubby legs fit for a centipede, and proportionally small heads with beady, lifeless, black eyes.

The faces had a broad, dull quality belonging to an insect. Restless, they stalked their cages. Back and forth, back and forth. Each tank was outfitted with a water bottle filled with red liquid. A smaller creature, a kitten to the cats, mouthed the metal end of its bottle. Red drops sprayed its lips. The beast seemed to balloon before her eyes, growing to the size of a football as it slurped.

One of the things ceased its pacing and looked to the window, seeming to perceive her. A black, forked tongue shot from its wide mouth. Then it opened wide enough to display two rows of pointy teeth.

Rachel had heard stories of these genetically engineered abominations. They were called Pollyannas and used as some kind of biological energy weapon. They could attack physically, too, and do a lot of damage in a short amount of time. But their real power lay in their psychic ability.

"Cover your ears," Rachel said.

Timothy was already handing her a pair of earplugs. Evidently, he'd heard the stories, too.

She shoved the soft plastic plugs in her ears as he did the same.

Fixed in its monstrous pose, gaping, the Pollyanna's entire body shook. The air seemed to vibrate as it trembled, every molecule in the vicinity lost to its malevolent, silent scream.

Even though the earplugs helped block the attack, Rachel felt woozy and nauseated, off-kilter, as if the howl had invaded her blood cells and bone marrow. She hated to think how the scream would have affected her unfiltered.

A mousy woman in a white lab coat emerged from a back room, her hands full of some wire-stuffed piece of electronic equipment. She set her gizmos on a metal table. She wore a headset with bulky, foam-ringed circles sealing off her ears. Scowling, she dashed across the laboratory and pulled a black curtain across the window. The Pollyanna shut up.

The woman joined Timothy and Rachel in the hallway and shut the door to the lab, tugging her headset down to rest around her neck. She did not look pleased. "I don't know how many times you corporate types need to be reminded, but my workspace isn't a zoo where you can stop by to gawk at your leisure. I leave the curtain open because the Pollyannas need external visual stimulation to thrive, not to enhance anyone's viewing pleasure."

Rachel popped out her earplugs. Her eardrums still ached from the residual ring of the scream. Even though this woman didn't look happy to see them, they might be able to squeeze her for valuable information. Flattery could be the ticket. "I'm so sorry. I was just admiring your work. The Pollyannas have come a long way in design sophistication since we last visited. I'm Jane." Rachel stuck out her hand. "Management Liaison for Scarab regional headquarters. This is my colleague Roger, the new Regional Director."

The scientist crossed her arms over her petite chest. "Turnover's as rapid as ever, I see. I'd be surprised if both of you are around for next year's Song of Virgo."

"You might be right." Timothy withdrew his hand after it became apparent the handshake offer had been rebuked. "And we're so sorry to disturb your work. But we'll put in a good word for you because, as Jane said, we're amazed at how far the Pollyannas have come."

The tiniest smirk of pride crossed the severe little woman's face. "As you know, these will be our front-line warriors in the Ballad of Capricorn, which will help us preserve the Other Ones for the soul harvesting and sacrificial bout. Fewer Other Ones sacrificed means greater odds of success."

"Absolutely," Rachel said, fighting to keep the contempt out of her tone. "Can you point us in the direction of the all-hands executive meeting? We decided to give ourselves a self-guided tour of these incredible facilities and seem to have gotten a bit turned around."

The woman stared for a few seconds, her resting face giving nothing.

Whether she was utterly fooled or forming suspicion was impossible to determine with certainty. "You'll really put in a good word for my research? Because I'm operating on a shoestring budget down here and moving mountains with crumbs. I could use a grant for new equipment. Or several grants."

"My job is to ease the flow of progress," Timothy said, in full embodiment of his corporate persona. "I am here to support you and the other brilliant people who make this operation possible."

Her smile spread as if to say 'you aren't so bad after all.' The scientist pointed straight ahead. "Turn left, and you'll see two sets of elevators. The executive suites are on the sixth floor, which is two levels underground. I'm assuming that's where you want to be."

"Thank you," Rachel said. She and Timothy took off walking. She couldn't wait to get out of earshot of those mutant freaks in case one screeched again.

"Don't even think about trying to stop what we've started." The scientist's threat was an icicle bullet to Rachel's heart. "Witch," she hissed. "You're both going to die down here."

Rachel turned around to face her aggressor, and Timothy grabbed her arm, but the scientist wasn't standing in the hallway anymore. The window to the lab had vanished as if it had never been there at all, and only more of those gray cinderblocks remained, sectioned off into rows of dead eyes.

SEVENTEEN

TIMOTHY WAS BEGINNING TO IDENTIFY WITH THE HORSE GIRL RACHEL had mentioned, even though he'd never seen the movie. Dreams and daydreams, though, had begun to merge with reality until nothing but the thinnest slip divided the two.

His memories were beginning to slip through his fingers, watery remnants, while he clutched at a futile attempt to capture the ocean. Matter always returned to the source. The notion of the individual mind was fiction, folly.

Horses. Though they were historically part of his culture, he didn't even particularly like horses. They were spooky and aloof and unsettled him with their uneasy combination of potent strength and delicate emotionality. Too much beast, if you asked him.

Whatever had happened moments ago wasn't good. In fact, it was bad, but his grip had surrendered. The details had eluded him, left him. They'd passed an important checkpoint, seen something meaningful, and connected with another person. But now, his recollection was gone. This fucking place was eating his mind, swallowing it whole. The hellhole had to be teeming with nefarious magic. He had to get his bearings. Be strong for Rachel and everyone else. Guard. Protect. Lead.

He anchored himself by connecting with his senses. At least he still had those five trusty pillars of connection to the physical world, however unwelcome his world had become. He breathed in to the count of three and exhaled to four, the rusty, stale smell of the basement filling his nostrils. Their footfalls clicked in tandem as they marched down the drab, underground hallway. The overhead lighting was a nauseating shade of yellow, this particular facet of the environment made more unpalatable by the stream of tepid, recycled air hissing through the system. Passing a water fountain reminded him of his dry mouth, but fuck if he was going to ingest anything down here. All they had to do for now was make it to elevators.

He canted his head to find Rachel studying him, her expression troubled. "Did you see what I saw?"

"Not sure." He was telling the truth. Not wanting to freak her out, he'd better keep it vague. "Tell me your version of events."

"The scientist and the entire lab disappearing." Now she looked jarred. "If we're seeing different things, we have a problem. It means they're altering our realities to make them different. Or there isn't one stable version of reality both of us share."

His stomach sunk. He had no memory of a scientist or a lab. Which didn't mean they hadn't been there. Her theory on why their accounts would differ was certainly possible. Anything was. All bets were off. "If so, it's likely a divide-and-conquer strategy. A tactic to sow division and distrust between us by removing our shared experience."

She stopped and put her hands on his shoulders. "You aren't crazy, and neither am I. We must remember that until the very end. We have to trust ourselves and each other. At all costs."

"There's a protection spell to shield against this type of thing. To tie our minds together with a single thread. I ran across a description of it while I was researching."

"The last thing I want to do is cast a spell down here. There's too much chaos magic in the field as it is. According to my book, oversaturation can cause spells to backfire."

"There might be another way. If we concentrate, it's possible we can mind meld without an incantation. To help us stay consistent." Which was the point of tapping into her chaos magic all along. To leverage her power for mutual protection. While he understood her reluctance to keep mining the murky depths of spell work, it wasn't like they enjoyed a plethora of options.

A small group of chattering voices, unseen and around ten feet away, cut off their conversation. In mutual understanding of the need to look assimilated and unsuspicious, Timothy and Rachel restarted their walk at the same moment. Though they didn't always agree about how or when to use magic, or in what circumstances, but they were a team when it came to self-preservation instincts.

As one moving unit, they turned a corner. There were the elevators. Two, one on each side of the hall. Four people stood by one set of black doors. A man in a white half-zip pullover pushed an already lit button. The Scarab logo, a beetle with its pinchers lifted above its head, was emblazoned near the breast pocket. The bug held the outline of a hexagon.

A different guy, underfed and baggy, gave Timothy an unsmiling once-over. His branded apparel was a too-large button up in the same white color with identical logo placement. "You're here for the leadership conference, I presume?" He did not sound pleased by his assumption.

"Correct." Rachel extended a hand. Nobody mirrored her gesture to shake. "Erin Beasley, liaison to managerial relations and quality control."

A lady who looked fresh out of college sucked her teeth. She had black hair and a bullish septum ring. A Scarab logo pin was affixed cockeyed to the label of her pink blazer. "Is your liaison-ing with managerial relations what caused the latest cuts to our retirement accounts?"

The one who'd impatiently pushed the button replied with a sharp laugh. "And now they're here to figure out how to raise our health insurance premiums, right?"

"It's layoff season, that's why they're here." The second woman, gray roots sprouting at the base of red curls, rolled her eyes. "I'm honestly fine with getting cut." A few faded coffee stains blemished her company-issued polo. "Fire me. I dare you. If they fire us, we get to collect unemployment and sue. Carly sued last year and won."

A few murmurs of affirmation supported her statement.

One of the elevator doors dinged open. "That's the way to your evil overlord convention," said the guy whose clothes didn't fit.

"You don't know the half of it." Rachel made her way to the doors.

"Do they use level twenty-five for anything other than conspiring on how to screw over the average worker?" The graying woman's glare could have melted glass. "Tell your overlords the health insurance they offer sucks balls. My husband had to go to the E.R. last year. The bill was ten-thousand dollars *after* insurance."

Inevitably, the conspiracies perpetrated on level twenty-five went much deeper than fleecing the little guy out of hard-earned money. Timothy was grateful to the baggy man for unwittingly giving up his and Rachel's destination.

"Fucking fire me too. Go for it." The pierced woman looked on defiantly. "You people will have to work to get rid of me. I'm not going to make your job easier by quitting. The dirty work is up to you, sweetie. I'm gonna wipe my hard drive and delete a shitload of files on the way out the door too."

"On the contrary, you should quit as soon as possible." The things Timothy had read on the message board haunted his nightmares, both sleeping and waking. These people had already decided they knew who he was and didn't like him, so chances were that they wouldn't listen. But he'd still try. "You don't know the half of what goes on in these meetings. Or maybe you do, and you think it won't affect you. But it will. And the effects will be worse than you think. My advice to you is run. Right now. Literally run out the exit doors and never look back. Change your names, move, and get as far away from this place and these people as you can. Don't stick around to see what retaliation looks like."

To an audience of stunned, pale faces, he stepped into the elevator. "Goodbye and good luck."

The doors closed. "Always nice to meet new colleagues." Rachel's quip lightened the heavy mood some, but not much. He appreciated her attempt. Bubbles blinked yellow as the elevator ascended, each rise in the floor elevating the level of dread. "Do you think they sacrifice employees once they've outlasted their use?"

"There were a lot of old badges in the desk drawer." A small speck of discoloration stained the corner of his. He told himself the unusual russet color was paint. "Nothing would surprise me anymore. Nothing at all."

"I confess, the whole not having a game plan thing doesn't feel great." She shifted from one foot to the other. Chewed her fingernail. The bubbles continued their relentless onslaught. Eighteen. Twenty.

He reached for her, but she pulled away. Her reluctance to accept comfort hurt some, but he understood. She didn't want to be vulnerable in this place. They had to stay strong. "We're well equipped. Based on my research, we might even have the means to contact the rest of the coven and possibly Julian. Sort of like a psychic lifeline."

She raised her eyebrows and parted her lips as if to speak, but before she had a chance, the elevator stopped on floor twenty-three.

Rachel played with her hair as tension tightened her chest. Her patience was minimal. She wanted to get the ordeal over with.

The doors opened. The first sight of the incoming company sent a fist of revulsion into Timothy's gut. The sight was worse than the smell, and the smell wasn't great—a murky stew of coppery, meaty odors mixed with disinfectant.

A buff, balding man in a lab coat pushed a plastic cart into the elevator, his load driving a hideous wedge between Timothy and Rachel. The cart was piled high with the bodies of monstrous creatures, the bodies as round as giant pill bugs but covered in delicate scales. Each had more legs than a centipede.

The sight of the carcasses, limp and lifeless with rolling black tongues and vacant beads for eyes, sent Timothy into a strange flashback. He'd seen these creatures before, stout and gray with an unnatural, hybridized look. Here. He and Rachel had walked past a lab and witnessed a roomful of them, then they'd disappeared. Scarab didn't want them to know about these things, so they'd wiped their memory of them. Which meant they were important. This new person and his bodies had broken the program. Timothy had to remember. They were key.

"Sorry, I know this stinks." The Pollyanna (that's what they were called! His memories were in there) undertaker adjusted the blue surgical mask he wore. "I wish we could still burn the expired ones like we did in the old days. But apparently the genetic material is precious for tests and cloning." He pulled two masks from his coat pocket and offered one to Timothy and Rachel.

Timothy shook his head. The smell would help burn the image into his memory. Rachel had the green hue of someone who was about to be sick, but she also waved away the offer. She was on the same wavelength, no doubt. The elevator rose to twenty-five, then stopped. Flesh jigged on the cart. Timothy's guts bundled into a wad of revulsion. He couldn't take much more of this, but his needs and wishes didn't factor in anymore. He had to figure out what the agenda was with these Pollyannas.

"How's the cloning project going?" Timothy subtly touched his badge. As hoped, his gesture drew their companion's eyes to where the word "Director" was printed. With any luck, invoking his fake authority would send their companion, who'd opened with a fawning apology, into full deference mode. "My colleague and I have heard great things about the progress. Exciting things."

Rachel smiled thinly. Her face was both pinched and bloated, like she was holding her breath. Timothy liked to think he was doing the talking and breathing for both of them so she could have a break. Protecting her however he could, even if his effort was small.

The doors opened to what was already the nicest space they'd been in since arrival, and he'd barely snatched a preview. The air smelled like clean linen and citrus, an about face from the stench of death, which mostly succeeded in underscoring the horror by way of incongruity. Vinyl flooring with a wooden look separated their elevator from three more.

"Thanks, man." The guy reached back into his pocket and pulled out a business card. Timothy accepted the token to flatter him. "I've been on the genetic engineering team for a few years now. Hoping to make principal investigator." His gray eyes lit up. "It would be so cool to get a promotion ahead of the Archon project." His tone was wistful as he unsubtly dropped his hint. He backed out of the elevator with his terrible bounty in tow, unaffected, like he'd done this many times.

"We have a bit before our meeting." Rachel exited the elevator next. "Why don't you tell us more about your work? We can walk and talk."

Timothy's heart swelled with pride. What a smart way to gain intel under the cover of legitimacy. This researcher was primed to talk, and Rachel had struck at the perfect moment. There was nobody else Timothy would rather be slogging through this nightmare with.

He catalogued his surroundings as he stepped into the foyer, hyper-vigilant as ever in case they had to attempt a quick escape.

Hallways on either side were painted a light and soothing green. A few pieces of wall art hung in a neat row, colorful close-ups of digitally photographed flowers. Scarab's strategy was sickly intelligent. Hide their rot under a veneer of nature imagery dressed in pleasant color schemes. Outwardly, they showcased the best of science, donning a costume to disguise an infected underbelly.

Their new companion led the way, taking them down one of the hallways. Halfway down, one side of the corridor split off and opened into a nest of conference rooms. Lots of glass gave full views of Power Point presentations and suited up busybodies scurrying about. Timothy didn't spot a single window.

He began to wonder if the building was cloaked somehow, hidden from external view. Wasn't there supposed to be a theme park above the costume shop? Or was the terrain unstable and ever-changing?

"Are you listening?" The scientist looked back, pushing his cart of death. His tone had soured.

"Of course," Timothy said. "Continue."

"Basically, as I was saying, the work has reached an exciting new phase. We're moving away from reliance on these guys—" He patted a dead Pollyanna with a gloved hand. "—And toward projects blending strictly biological material like them with extra-dimensional helpers."

"Right, helpers." Rachel's brief comment did a lot of heavy lifting to invite the scientist to say more.

He took the bait. "Yeah, we use similar jargon in the labs. Not sure what you call these resources over in the big offices." He swirled his hand in the general direction of a conference room packed with tables, each spot occupied by a person and a laptop. "The whole idea is, they're helping to expedite this prophecy, or reimagining of the physical world, whatever you want to call it. But they're also helping guys like me make a name for themselves. Because if everything goes off without a hitch, my name will be attached to the innovations making the big shebang possible. My life's work, you know? My legacy." He sighed and rounded another corner.

Life's work indeed. In all the darkness, Timothy had lost sight of how most ordinary people were motivated by banal drives. The desire for money, recognition, notoriety. These employees weren't cosmically evil, just evil in how they were going along with things for personal gain. "Let's see this workspace of yours," Timothy said.

The halls had changed to an aesthetic both more drab and comparatively sterile in this wing of the twenty-fifth floor, a mélange of white walls, colorless tile, and stainless-steel doors. Their escort pulled a ring of keys out from under his coat and unlocked one of the doors.

Timothy and Rachel looked at each other as if to simultaneously gird their collective loins. They weren't likely to see anything pleasant in the impending room.

As always, at least they had each other.

Inside lay what looked to be a cross between a lab and a morgue. Metal slabs were lined up in the middle, each accompanied by a wheeled cart outfitted with a basin and a hose. Trays of sharp, shiny tools gleamed under fluorescent lighting.

The scientist wheeled the bodies to the far corner of the room, grunting as he yanked open the door to what looked like a massive freezer. Cloudy puffs billowed out, swallowing the guy and his corpses. "Be right back," he said. "Have a look around at these top-notch facilities." He propped the door open with his foot until he got the cart inside. "I do my best work in here." The door shut behind him.

Rachel made a beeline to one of the trays and pilfered a scalpel, which she stuck in her messenger bag. She repeated the process with several other trays, taking a different pointy tool from each. Someone would have to look closely to catch what was missing from the extensive collections. "It's this research," she whispered, snagging a box cutter. "The key. I'm sure of it. We have to stop the experiments to stop the rest of the operation."

"How do you figure?" He snapped a few photos from his watch in case any of the pictures caught a code, number, or any other clue proving valuable down the line.

"My memories are coming back. The snakes prevented me from being fully lucid. That's my theory. They kept me in a kind of stupor, a brain fog. A poison in their bodies leaked into my brain, and with the toxin gone, I remember again. It's all coming back. When I was trapped down in the dungeon before, they had even bigger monsters locked in energetic prisons. Holographic shapes."

A clunk sounded off in the freezer. Both Timothy and Rachel jerked their heads in the direction of the sound, but when the scientist didn't immediately emerge, she resumed talking.

Her rate of speech increased along with the urgency of her whisper. "That's what they were doing down there. Casting spells to release the archons from their energetic prisons. They called them Titans, too, used the terms interchangeably." She gasped for air. Her pupils dilated. "When I escaped, when Taylor and Julian saved me, it fucked everything up. My magic was supposed to get them out of their cages once and for all, to tear the veil off and clear their passage into our normal physical world. But the end goal didn't happen because I ended up in Peru. Now, they've circled back to these Pollyannas somehow to use them to free the archons. We have to figure out how so we can stop them."

He held her hand. He believed her. "You're right. It's good we got into this lab. I think being around those things triggered your memories. Being here is bringing them back. As awful as it is, it's constructive. All we have to do is stay the course, gather information, and figure out how to deploy it."

She nodded. Her breathing was choppy. Her chest rose and fell.

The scientist exited the freezer empty handed. "You guys cool?"

"Not as cool as you," Timothy returned.

"Ha." He pointed a finger gun. "Seriously, though, you like my workspace? You impressed?" He walked to a metal desk, hunched over a computer, and pecked some keys.

"Absolutely," Timothy said. "The work you're doing is outstanding. I'll make sure to recommend you for more funding and a promotion. Thanks again for the overview of the exciting initiatives taking place here. We tend to lose sight of the boots on the ground contributions when we're holed up in our silos."

He laughed. This one had a chilling effect and wasn't inviting. Timothy decided not to lay on any more praise. Maybe he'd overkilled it.

"We'd better get going," Rachel said. Her voice had the smallest shake; one a stranger wouldn't have caught. The vibe had changed. Deteriorated, though he couldn't pinpoint how. Maybe Timothy was just getting paranoid. A hellscape like this would have a chilling effect on anyone sane. "Our meeting starts in a few minutes. Like my colleague said, we'll make sure to let everyone know how impressed we were by this tour."

Wordlessly, the scientist stood tall and walked toward them.

Timothy's arm and leg muscles clenched, his fight instincts kicking in even before his brain registered how things had gone wrong. He smelled a musty, sharp cocktail of adrenaline, testosterone, and danger. The air vibrated all around. He could take this guy. Especially if he shifted.

The scientist jammed a hand under his coat. When he pulled it out, he held a black gun.

Timothy lunged for the weapon, but he wasn't fast enough. With a dancer's quick grace, the scientist jumped backward and to the side, out of range. He pointed the semiautomatic pistol at Rachel's head.

"Cut the shit. I know who you are, girly pop. And we aren't letting go of you again." He waved his gun at Timothy before returning the aim to Rachel. "Both of you, in the freezer. You love the Pollyannas so much? Here's your chance to spend some quality time with them."

EIGHTEEN

RACHEL THRUST HER HANDS UP IN THE UNIVERSAL POSTURE OF "DON'T shoot." Her heart was an ice cube in her throat. She looked into the narrow vortex of the gun's barrel, then past it to the fat, rubber-clad hand clenching the handle. Her vision wobbled, on the verge of doubling.

The room smelled both fleshy and rotten while at once over-cleaned. She had to figure out a solution. The easiest route was to transmute the gun with her magic. Melt it, transform it into a flower or banana. She'd done similar with the receipts. Casting spells here wasn't ideal, but they'd face the consequences later.

"Back up," snarled the man in the lab coat. "Into the freezer. I see how your eyes are glazed over. I know what you're thinking about. You'd better stop."

She took two slow steps back, her concentration never breaking. The edges of the gun were blurring, softening now as she aimed the full force of her magic into its particles. She had a grip, a handle. She just needed to finish the job and play it cool.

Except before she was able to finish the effort, her magic fizzled out. All that remained was a fuzzy blob of purple and black, hovering near the ceiling where all it managed to do was barely change the color of the paint. Her spell had been subverted.

"I'm backing up." A chill hit her from behind, making the back of her neck hairs stand. A whizzing sound came from the belly of the humid, icy pit. Bumps burst onto her skin. It sure was cold in there, too cold. Too cold to last long. "I'm going in the freezer. But before I do, I want you to know I have something of value to you. Something that'll be lost forever if I die. A precious substance. You could bottle it if you experimented on me more. You could sell it. That's what you and everyone who works here want, right? To suck the magic out of me?"

"You think we didn't try that already?" He curled his upper lip into a sneer. "The point of the snakes, sweetheart, was to serve as extraction tools. You're useless when it comes to extracting magic. Worthless." The man's grimace morphed into a slimy smile. He swayed his head, as if reconsidering his own words. "You were worthless as an experiment while alive, that is. Once we aren't bound by the constraints of keeping you breathing, we might see more potential for you. Dead girls are hot. Might be fun all the way around."

Timothy had been silent by her side—until now. The sentinel erupted. He let go of the most ear-shattering howl, human but not quite, a battle cry of such magnitude that her bones shook with the reverberations of the primal scream.

He lunged at their aggressor, hurling his body into the other man's before tackling him to the ground with a dull thud of flesh against bone. Timothy grunted. The scientist swore. Rubber squeaked against flooring as the lab coat man, on the bottom, struggled to regain his footing.

A tangle of limbs flailing in quick, jerky movements made it difficult to discern who had the upper hand until Timothy's fingers closed around the gun.

Timothy balled a fist, reared his arm back, and slammed a punch into the guy's jaw. The resulting wet, horrible crunch let her know things were broken. His head fell limp to the side. His jaw hung cockeyed and dislocated.

The center of his face was reduced to red ruin, crimson and crushed where his nose had been. Dark rivulets flowed from each nostril before dripping as bright blooms onto the surgically white floor. Flecks of cherry sprayed his coat. His chest moved up and down, which both relieved and annoyed her. Timothy hadn't taken a human life, which was good, but vital signs meant the nefarious scientist would eventually be their problem once again.

"Let's put him in the freezer and prop the door open," Rachel said. "He'll survive in there until he wakes up. His unconsciousness will buy us some time at least. His comment about my experiment was interesting. It's possible that if we can infiltrate the work they're doing here, we'll learn enough to subvert the ritual. And pick up some tactics for wrapping up the timeline merge while we're at it."

Timothy stuck the gun into the back pocket of his slacks. "How do we make it look like we're supposed to be there? Do we just walk in? Which brings me to another question." He walked to the desk and gave it a closer inspection. "How do we find out where the Medusa experiments are taking place? This building is a labyrinth, and nothing is as it seems." He flipped through a thin book or manual, then set it back down where he found it.

They could attempt to transform their clothes, but using magic in here was proven to be unreliable. The power players had scrambled the signal. They were a step ahead of Rachel. She and Timothy would have to get old school.

She crouched by the fallen researcher and pulled on his arm. Repositioning his body was hard, as he was a big man reduced to dead weight, but after grunting her way through a few attempts, she'd yanked him into a half-seated slump. "Help me get him out of his coat." She slid the starchy white fabric over his shoulders, wincing when a seam ripped. The sleeve stuck near his elbow. Already, the plan didn't bode well.

Timothy joined her in a squat and worked with the other arm, wiggling until the sleeve came free and the unconscious man's appendage flopped at his side.

The fallen enemy let out a soft cough. His outbreath sputtered free in a hiss. They didn't have endless time. Luckily, Timothy got the lab coat off and worked the length out from under the guy's seat. He held the garment in the air. "You want to do the honors or should I?"

"It would be great if they had spares in here." She laid the scientist on his back once again. He'd stay out longer if he lay flat in the natural resting pose. "Two, ideally, so neither of us had to wear a lab coat with blood on it." After getting on her feet, she scouted out the lab some more. A pile of cardboard boxes looked promising as a potential stash of supplies, but they contained only plastic syringes and tubing. "Any luck?" She glanced over her shoulder, past the unconscious interloper, to where Timothy had opened a door to a small room.

"No, just a janitorial closet. I'll wear the one we have. It's better if I'm the lightning rod. If I draw any hostility, you're free to concentrate on your magic if you have to."

"I keep telling you, you don't have to play my bodyguard anymore." She turned to the portion of the room devoted to rows of chrome drawers lining an entire wall. The morgue. Being in this space gave her a primal, icky sense of unease, even though the feeling wasn't rational. Anything kept behind those gray squares was dead. "We're in this together. Equals of equal value."

"Please." His footfalls landed softly on the ground, his presence comforting even though she wasn't looking at him. This place was dead last on her list of destinations she'd like to visit alone. Hell was a close second. "We've been over this. If we lose me, the community appoints a new alpha. Julian, obviously. If we lose you, well, we lose everything."

"No pressure. And don't sell yourself short. We'd all be lost without you." Her, especially. Winning this war while losing Timothy would be the definition of a Pyrrhic victory. "We both get out alive. No exceptions."

A thump from within one of the drawers cut short their banter. Though the noise was relatively nonviolent, about as forceful as a paperback falling to the floor, her viscera and muscles initiated lockdown. Nothing should be moving in there.

She tried to ignore what she'd heard and continued looking for coats, though her heartbeat had launched into rabbit mode. The morgue part of the room contained a sink with a compartment underneath (only cleaning supplies), three autopsy slabs, and a cabinet full of examination tools. No coats. The sound of Timothy moving around in the far corner of the lab kept her centered enough to where she didn't run out of the room screaming, but not so calm she lost sight of her desire to forget about clean lab coats and beat feet to the exit. "We tried. We can get by with the badges until we find another location that looks promising for uniforms." Admitting defeat brought relief. Time to go before the half-dead Pollyanna flopped into the door again or the psycho mad scientist woke up.

A second thump, and this one had more force to it, like a burly shoulder-check against the metal door. Her throat closed around her breath. She raced in the direction of the center of the room. "Let's go."

She hadn't made it more than a few fast steps when a third thump, more like a slam, crashed into the door of the morgue compartment. Emitting a throaty, pained battle screech, out vaulted a Pollyanna—a big one.

Larger than a pit bull, the abomination had seen better days. A diagonal, crusty gash split its broad head diagonally. The skin of its back looked burn-scarred, or chemical burned. A pale rope of twisted welts snaked from neck to tailbone. A few of its legs dangled as if broken, useless. But it wasn't fucking dead, which was all that mattered.

Midair, the Pollyanna flailed, and Rachel hoped it would die before it hit the ground. No luck. It landed on the floor awkwardly, on its side, and yelled again before righting itself. Nostrils or sensory pits at the side of its head flared. The forked tongue stabbed the air. Though imbalanced from bad legs, it bolted into a sprint, the pits opening and closing like gills, the tongue lapping greedily at invisible tastes.

"Timothy, shoot! Fire!" She chased the fiend, keeping it in her line of sight, its chunky, round backside dragged forward by a mess of legs in various stages of functionality. "It's coming for you, be ready!"

Despite the Pollyanna's injuries, it was too fast, lurching around the corner a few feet ahead of Rachel.

She was terrified the monster would attack Timothy until she caught up to it. A terrible sight stopped her dead cold in horror.

The creature had claimed what it *really* wanted, and it wasn't Timothy.

Bile rocketed up her throat to poison her tongue.

Her gag reflex shoved vomit to the forefront.

She covered her nose and mouth, dizzy from a sight she could never un-see.

The Pollyanna plunged its red, pointy teeth into a bloody cavity where the researcher man's face had been. Blood sprayed everywhere in arcs and globs, flying from the wreckage and the carnivore's stained jaws before splattering on the walls, floor, ceiling. The dead man's body twitched and shook under the force of its attacker, his lifeless flesh as limp as a rag doll's fabric.

Before she could puke or faint, Timothy was facing her down, holding her in place by the shoulders. With him in front, she wasn't able to see the carnage, but the heinous sounds of an unwholesome feeding frenzy cancelled out the lack of visual input. "Breathe," he whispered. "You have to. Three deep breaths until you know you're able to stand up without falling. Your first job is to breathe."

She sucked in a jagged breath and let it go, using her mouth only to block the smell. "You have to shoot it," she bit out. Squelching and snorts assaulted her ears.

"No point. It's doubled in size. It's the blood. It's like a super fuel for them."

Right. She'd remembered Eve saying something similar about the Pollyannas. They had a vampire nature, which she'd hoped she'd never have to witness like her sister witch had.

"We have to run, then." The sounds, the smells. Her body screamed for escape. But she had to think. "How distracted is it?"

Timothy's nostrils flared. His Adam's apple bobbed. "Very. It won't leave a big meal behind. Let's go."

Together, they broke into a run and got the fuck out. She looked back and wished she hadn't, but at least her final glimpse confirmed Timothy's assurance that the beast was consumed by its carnivorous feast.

They power-walked down the hallway. Adrenaline wore off to leave her with a sharp headache and a dull pain in her chest. "Someone will be over there any minute to investigate." Passing bathrooms, she heard a toilet flush. Voices came from inside. Elsewhere on the floor, a door opened and shut. Employees were everywhere. One would run across the scene. Worse, whichever unlucky soul stumbled upon the incident was at risk for being next on the menu. "Which is not only bad for us, but for whoever comes face-to-face with that thing."

"You're right. We have to warn them somehow without giving ourselves up."

Now he was talking. Her brain was out of shock and ready to cook. Still on the move, ten feet away from the bathrooms now, they passed an eye wash contraption and a couple of other stations mounted to the wall. One was a red emergency box. Inside was an axe. "You think if I broke the glass an alarm would sound?"

"Not sure. But that one will definitely set it off." Beside the axe was a fire alarm. Beside it, an intercom.

"I say we use both." Somewhere on the floor, Rachel heard human voices chatting in a relaxed manner. They had to act. Now.

She wrapped her fist in a section of the lab coat and whacked the side of her hand into the glass box. The material shattered with a shrill yet satisfying crack, splintering into big pieces. They crashed to the ground. She grabbed the axe and pulled the fire alarm.

Little did she know, pulling the fire alarm would cause the overhead lights to blink on and off in a dizzying strobe effect. The alarm blared, shrill and relentless, its bleats interspersed with a robotic male voice. The drone repeated one word: *emergency*.

No turning back now.

Timothy got on the intercom. "Breach in the lab on twenty-five. Man down. Fatality. Assailant at large. Vacate floor twenty-five at once. Clear the area as fast as possible. No one is to approach until threat is contained."

The message was received. Casual chatter turned to gasps and whimpers. Then fast footsteps. Running. A commotion poured out of the bathroom, people openly fretting about whether this was real or a hoax.

The good news was, if this plan went off, she and Timothy would have the twenty-fifth floor to themselves. As long as they stayed a step ahead of the bloodthirsty mutant, they'd be able to explore, get what they needed, and get out.

She moved them away from the intercom and other stations, and they race-walked in the opposite direction of the lab. Individuals and small groups passed them, their faces trippy and surreal in the strobe lighting. Nobody paid much attention to other inhabitants. "We need my file," she shouted over the alarm. "If we can get to those papers, I'll be able to figure out exactly how they were using me. My role in the rituals, including this big one. Once I have my file in my hands, I can do some real work to disentangle my chaos magic from the progress of this prophecy."

"Good thought, but then what?" He poked his head in a hastily abandoned boardroom and resumed his march. "We can't use magic in here. How do we merge the timelines and get home?"

She had a hunch. An inkling, an inclination. "I don't think I need to use magic per se to merge. All I have to do is make an intentional choice to break the matrix, to step outside of the loop and set the course of events on a different track. That's the benefit of chaos magic. It exists independently of incantations. It's woven deeply into the fabric of reality, of the universe as we know it. It's just kind of *there*. Like quantum physics."

"Waiting," Timothy said, gazing at her with a look of awe, "for you to take over. That's always been the case. The magic is dormant in the field until its master exerts her will over it. Once you can take control, *you* guide the timelines. And the prophecy. You determine whether or not this ritual happens. You control the fate of the prophecy itself."

"Exactly. It's like I have a manifestation superpower. The law of attraction cranked up to level eleven. Fuck, I hope I'm right. Because I don't have any more ideas."

"You're right." By now, they'd made their way to an open seating area where rounded loveseats flanked coffee tables and electronic charging stations. A phone, two coffees, one laptop, and a half-eaten sandwich had all been abandoned in haste. "Your book said as much. All you need are your own conscious choices and the power of your intention to shape your world."

"My world." Rachel stayed with the notion for a second, both scary and comforting, one that left her feeling, paradoxically, both powerful and tiny. "My inheritance. My destiny. Not hers. Not Scarab's. Not anymore. Mine."

"There's one last test. We return to the site of your experimentation and reroute your timeline."

"To one where this prophecy was never even conceived of, let alone set into motion. To one where I already was the elemental sister of chaos. To one where she never even existed." She felt the truth in her bones, cells, atoms. They'd hit the bull's eye.

"Our mistake all along was assuming she ever had control and ever wielded the power she claimed to. By recognizing her how she wanted to be seen, we fed her. Gave her the power. Gave it away. Consented to taking it away from you. But we fell prey to a fraud."

They stopped by a vending machine. The alarm kept yelling, but the external mayhem seemed inconsequential compared to the revelation their brainstorming had brought about. "It was me all along. Always me. I just let myself get tricked into giving my power away. I've had the wool pulled over my eyes for so long. That's what she was trying to show me with the eyeball under the building. Perception is reality. These guys..." she waved her hand in the air to signal Scarab in general. "Are little more than ticks. Pests who have no idea what they're really doing. She's going along with them because they prop up the illusion of her power."

"It was you all along." He squeezed both of her hands in a gesture of either assurance or tentative victory, she couldn't quite say. But his touch grounded her and had never felt more right.

He was her rock. Not just the bodyguard of her body. Of her spirit. Her magic. Her truth.

"Thank you." She thanked him for so much, those two words far too comprehensive to refer to one mere action or gesture.

The alarm was relentless. The lights had ceased their strobe throb and gone dim, which she appreciated. Less disorienting and more of a potential cover of darkness. She hadn't seen a person in several minutes. For their sake, she hoped they'd all vacated and not ended up as a bloody snack. Another incentive to hurry was that the alarm overpowered other sounds. If the Pollyanna was stalking them, they wouldn't necessarily know it.

The rooms were turning out to be useless dead ends. Administrative offices decorated with plants and cluttered with trash. Locked doors. A lactation room. Three soulless, corporate conference rooms in a row.

The alarm beat at her brains, making her edgy and irritable. They were never going to find the file at this rate. If she really was equipped to be the elemental sister of chaos, wouldn't completing a relatively simple task like locating an object be easier?

She thought she'd found a promising lead in another lab until the space turned out to be empty, functionally abandoned. "Maybe we can find someone and ask a few well-crafted questions to point us in the right direction." She opened and closed an empty drawer. "Or maybe asking questions would be giving us away. Shit. Fuck."

Her head and stomach hurt. She was tired and getting nowhere, going in circles. Maybe she'd been tricked again or had tricked herself. Maybe she was failing a test, coming up short, not good enough.

Maybe Folly had built a mousetrap out of Rachel's thoughts and theories and her own hubris had led her into the snare and now her mistakes were symbolic ciphers representing—gah! She was going crazy. Folly probably loved the prospect of mental decay.

"Rachel." Timothy spoke her name in a way that got her hopes up, but she knew better than to jump to a conclusion that he'd found anything good. Wary, exhausted, she turned to face him.

The door he'd opened wasn't just another janitorial closet or junk room. The door led to a tiny closet with a trapdoor in the floor. Timothy crouched and pulled the handle. Bright light spilled upward, illuminating a steel staircase heading down.

NINETEEN

WHEN NOTHING IS WHAT IT SEEMS, AND EXPECTATIONS ARE consistently turned on their heads, the brain and body enter a sort of secondary Zen state. Timothy's system did.

What was the point of being scared, worried, or even aggressively confrontational? Reality as he'd known it no longer held purchase.

He supposed he should have accepted long ago the prospect of the world containing multitudes of mystery, stretching far beyond the bounds of reason and extended into an endless cosmos of nonsense.

The first time he shifted his shape, his body stretching, tearing, merging as his fractured mind had convinced its many fragments that he'd gone insane or died and gone to hell.

The first time he witnessed others changing their form.

The first portal he travelled through.

The first time he saw color energy burst from a person's fingertips.

You never forget your first, and there had been a lot of firsts. Each time, the laws of physics had been broken before his eyes and not been put back together.

Perhaps paranormal impossibilities were cumulative. With each new rupture of the known, the possible, the tear gaped wider to let in an ever-expanding range of unfathomable phenomenon. The veil was Swiss cheese at this point.

But enough philosophizing. He had a clandestine room, one whose features made no sense spatially in the layout of the dark magic prison, to investigate.

With each step, he had to stoop more, the downward tunnel compressing him in claustrophobia. The bottom of the steps still wasn't visible. The stairs seemed to be subtly veering left. Perhaps the hidden space wasn't the result of magical conjuring, just a secret room stashed behind the walls. He wasn't sure which possibility was creepier.

"Ever seen *Being John Malkovich*?" Rachel asked.

There was a blast from the past. "They find a portal into John Malkovich's mind inside some weird building, right?"

"Basically." Her voice comforted him, as did the random pop culture reference whose point was no doubt about to emerge. "A portal in a weird building with a secret floor all squished so you have to crouch. It's like this. A floor within a floor."

"You think we'll beat this thing by overtaking John Malkovich and puppeting his possessed body?" He could see the proverbial light at the end of the tunnel now. Perhaps Rachel had conjured the glimmer.

The stairs bottomed out to open to flooring. The tunnel they were in was too narrow at the opening for him to tell what lay beyond. An earlier version of him would have been distressed, but he remained nonplussed. He'd gotten used to living in the moment and expecting the unexpected. Kept him fresh and on his toes. Exhilarated, even. A strange urge to laugh bubbled in his throat.

"Possibly," Rachel said. "Or who knows? Maybe we're about to find a portal into my mind, and we jump in there and transport both of our conscious minds into the version of me still existing in Peru. Another version of reality exists in the quantum field, so why not?"

"What do we do once we're there?" He wasn't seriously entertaining this possibility. But it was fun to talk about. Light, senseless chatter with Rachel shed light on the absurdity of their predicament was therapeutic, and kept his mind off darker possibilities.

"I dunno, fight for control of the host? Learn to share my physical form as all three of us, two mes and one you?"

Timothy couldn't take it anymore. The portrait she'd painted was too ridiculous, and yet—why not? Laughter burst from his throat and wouldn't stop coming. "Sorry," he choked out, his belly aching. "I'm not laughing at you, and I realize I shouldn't be laughing at all."

Except she was laughing too, full and beautiful in an unbridled stream. "I mean, what the fuck, right? How is this real life? How?"

He stopped and turned around.

She giggled into her elbow, her eyes glittering, her face a mask of mischief and befuddled amusement. She joined him on his step, where they hugged and embraced, surrendering to the moment, the situation, their togetherness in it all.

Their bodies knew when to stop, a subtle flow of chemical cues and invisible energies uniting them with a cord of steel. His abdominal muscles ached in the best way. He gazed into Rachel's eyes. "I love you."

Tears made her pretty eyes misty and red. "I never thought...I never thought this would be possible again." She choked up.

"What?" He caressed her cheek.

"To look into someone's eyes, your eyes, and feel anything but dread that I'd accidentally hurt you. I didn't think I'd ever be able to lose myself to a moment like this ever again." She pulled his hand to her lips and kissed his palm. "Do you know how many times I've looked at your eyebrows out of fear and reflex? I've finally let go. And I love you too. You've never once given up on me. Even when it stopped being your duty."

"You've always been more to me than a duty. Since the first moment. The very beginning. From the first moment I saw you in the jungle, I knew you were special and had to be protected at all costs. You've brought me to life again, Rachel Harris. You're the one." He brought up his other hand to cradle her face in both palms. "My mate."

"I never believed in fate before. Or destiny." Leaning forward, she pressed her forehead into his, the tender intimacy medicinal. "Until now. There is nobody else I'd rather careen through space-time with than you."

"Let's save the world and go home."

She entwined her fingers with his, the lattice of their flesh sealing a bond forged in chaos. They'd be each other's anchor. Rope. Lifeline. Together, feet moving in tandem, they marched down the remaining few steps.

Before him were six doors. Each door's knob was the symbol for one of the elements. Various triangles and a swirled circle for spirit were laid out in a patient row. The dastardly handprint squiggle waited at the end of the line. Their choice had to be strategic. He had a feeling they'd only have one chance.

"Picking chaos seems too obvious," she said. "A trick. A trap."

"Possibly." None of the doors had any other distinguishing features. They were all a bright, unblemished crystalline white. "We could choose spirit, since we merged Helen."

"If we follow the logic, though, we'll have to go through each one individually and merge each witch onto the new timeline. At first, I thought we'd have to do that, but now I'm not so sure. That option could be a trap sprung for our thinking to make us believe we have to go through them one-by-one so we waste our time and energy."

"What does your intuition say?" He touched his stomach. "Deep down below?"

She walked to the chaos door. "This is me. My path. Even though it seems too on-the-nose to pick the chaos door, I don't think we do ourselves any favors by overthinking either. What if, to merge, I have to take control myself? To walk through my own door?"

Part of protecting Rachel was protecting her process, her spirit, not just her physical body. He had to know when to back up and listen. If he did right by Rachel, he did right by his community, regardless of outcome. "Lead the way. I trust your judgment."

Still grasping his hand, she reached for the door. After clutching the twisted knob, she looked over her shoulder. "Hold on to me, okay? Whatever happens, please don't let go."

He'd hold onto Rachel and never let go, just like she'd said. Full stop. No negotiations. They were a pair now. Bonded mates. His fate hadn't worked out exactly how he'd anticipated, but the machinations of fate were hardly predictable. Most importantly, he'd never have it any other way. "I won't let you go, Rachel. It's you and me."

She tipped her chin down once and opened the door.

At first, a bunch of nothing underwhelmed him. The room was white all over, a blank and empty space about the size of a high school gym.

Their hands clasped, they walked to the center. "I remember a space like this." Her voice echoed off the walls. "When I was trapped by Scarab before." Her eyelids fluttered closed. She pressed two fingers to her temple.

"Are you okay?" Timothy asked. Her forehead had creased to an appearance of pain. "What are you feeling? Experiencing?"

"Someone or something..." she stammered, then fell into him but regained her footing. "Is after my mind. It's her. I feel the evil all around us. This is a staging area. A conjuring area. Where realities are made."

He was about to ask for clarification when Folly's voice rolled in to fill the pale cube. "Categories," she purred. "Friend. Foe. Ally. Enemy. Good. Evil. Has it ever occurred to you that these designations are arbitrary? The labels your kind assigns to relationships are entirely subjective."

"How can you even begin to suggest you're anything but our enemy?" Timothy held Rachel close. She'd zoned out and was swaying and muttering incoherently. "You've tried to kill our friends. You flooded our world with evil. You've collaborated with the worst people in the world to turn the universe into something horrific, and all for personal gain for you and them. How can you claim any of our assumptions are arbitrary? What have you ever done to be a force of positivity?"

"There you go again with your blather about friends, evil, good, and bad. Bold of you to assume I care about this company. These Scarab thugs and their freak show experiments are pawns. I need the two of you to think outside the box. Outside of this box, if you want to bring about your desired outcomes. Your talk of manifesting and painting your own realities is starting to sound like a bunch of empty air. Your spirit witch was similar." She chuckled with smug satisfaction, like she knew a secret. "You are both so, so close to getting the point. I warned you. I prepared you. I told you what to expect. Yet you look, but you don't see. Witches." She scoffed. "Shifters. All the same. Blinded by the dumbing down of your hearts. I thought you were different. Better."

"You can't manifest in physical form anymore," Rachel gritted out.

"That's correct, isn't it? You can't assume a corporeal shape, and now you're losing the ability to possess the minds of the witches. As we grow stronger together, you grow weaker. You're dying, and your last ditch effort is to try to spin my brain in circles so I go insane and fold in on myself. The tests. Tricks. The giant snake. Luring me back here. So much misdirection, right? Red herrings everywhere for me to fixate on until I lose my mind?"

"We've already beaten you." Timothy acted as a bulwark to keep Rachel upright, but he struggled more by the second. Her balance was going downhill fast. "You've already lost. Rachel, babe, I need you to listen to me. Listen to me closely and do exactly as I say."

Her eyes were glassy and distant, her complexion gray. She sagged in his arms, battling to stay on her feet. "She's got her hooks in me," she slurred. "In my mind. She's concentrated her efforts into not just possessing me but erasing me."

"Nothing left of you," Folly whispered in the blankness. "Except space for me."

Rachel staggered forward before lurching to her knees. She wailed. Then, a horrific thing happened and made Timothy's heart sink. A raised rash of brown bumps flared on her neck. Her lower half melted into an oily pool. Gunk spread across the pearly flooring.

"My body," Rachel screamed, "she's breaking me down from the outside in." Her speech slurred like she was drunk. "Feeding on my matter." A rattle sprouted near her wrist. A section of one of her arms morphed into a scaled bulge of muscle. "She's latched onto the magic dormant in my DNA from the experiment and is leveraging it somehow."

Folly spoke, "Scarab was good for giving me a toehold into one of you witches through their tinkering. We are bound by an umbilical cord in a way that you and your sisters are not. Surrender, my child. You are mine, and I am yours. Return to Mother and let her take away the pain. Float in the embryonic fluid of chaos and entropy once again. It'll burn, but only for a moment. Soon you'll feel nothing at all. Forever."

Rachel had gone boneless. Her pretty face had blurred to a mushy, grotesque shape. She kept screaming, resisting, but her voice came out drowned in horrible gurgling sounds. One of her hands had changed into a serpent's head.

"So much glorious chaos," Folly sighed. "Everywhere, all at once. You're a veritable buffet of chaos magic, my darling daughter. A feast to sustain even the bottomless black hole."

"We can still beat her." Timothy didn't know if Rachel could still hear him, or process his words, but he was damn sure going to try. "Push one last time. I know you can do it. Manifest the timeline changing. Go back through your mind and locate the experiment. The experiment was the first moment that made you vulnerable. The snakes. Go back to the experiment and stop it. This room is a crossroads in your story. The junction of past, present, and future. The quantum realm. Infinite possibility. Whatever you want to call it. Take control. It's our last chance. Now."

Her nod was weak, a single bob of her now-malformed head, but she did it.

Rachel screeched, the last vestiges of a battle cry, so loud her voice rang from the walls.

It was as if her voice had always been there, eternal, an original voice to move all other voices.

Her cry sucked the air out of Timothy's lungs. He wouldn't have had it any other way. The wetness of his own tears stained his cheeks. It had to happen like this. Fate was predestined. Awful yet holy.

What remained of her exploded into ash, fat particles glimmering with the blackened, purple iridescence of her magic. He caught one flake in his palm and kissed it. His tears wet her and merged with what was left of her. He swore he saw a reflective pool in the remnant, an oil spill of darkness and color opening a mirror into both his soul and hers.

The two of them entwined into an infinity loop. "I love you, Rachel Harris. I've always loved you, even before I knew you. Before I knew me. Please come back to me in some form or fashion. Some time line, some reality. Look into my eyes and return to me. I see you."

The ashes rained down on him like glitter, dusting his shoulders and the floor at his feet. He liked to think Rachel was communicating with him through those shredded remnants. All he had were her ashes, yet those scraps assured him.

He dropped to his knees and gathered her remains in his palms. She dissolved into miniscule flecks, then nothing at all but for the electric charge of her memory pulsing in the bones of their ancestors. "Before space and time and all that has ever existed or will exist, I've loved you."

He had to clutch the hope. Somewhere, in some dimension or potential reality, enough of her was left to hear him.

TWENTY

A SEARING STAB OF PAIN JOLTED RACHEL'S INNERMOST DEPTHS. THE agony transcended body pain. Soul pain. Hell-pain. A violation most wicked and diabolical. A scream shook her through and through, but didn't make a sound.

She had to vocalize her distress. With a labored push, she forced air out of her lungs. Her gasp was a pathetic squeak, but she breathed. Fuck yes, she breathed.

Next came her eyes. They snapped right open to face a scene that clobbered her with even more shock than the initial agony piercing her neck. Pierced her neck acutely and radiated down her spine. At least she was able to locate the source.

Two masked figures hovered over her. Hospital masks, blue cloth tied around the ears with white ties. Scrubs. Clear plastic hairnets. A bright light shined in her face, the lamp contraption hanging from the ceiling.

Through the misery, her mind caught up. Hospital. She was hurt. In the middle of a procedure. She'd woken up during the operation.

"Not enough anesthesia," she tried to say, but an obstruction in her throat made her effort at speech clumsy and unsuccessful.

She looked at her chest. Tubing snaked over her midsection. She was wearing a hospital gown. But if she was in surgery, why weren't the doctors actively working? There was no open cavity or screen separating her from them.

Something wasn't right. She reached up to pull the gag from her mouth, but her hands didn't cooperate. She looked. Her wrists were bound to her gurney with leather cuffs.

Panic overthrew her rational faculties. She thrashed, jerked, flailing both arms and legs in futility. Correction. Not futile on the legs front. Those weren't tied down, and they were all she had.

The doctors, or whatever they were, scrambled to restrain her legs. But the short and round one on the right was too slow.

Rachel fired off a kick and smashed her foot into a soft belly. The medical person staggered backward, wheezing in high-pitched whines, and lost their footing. They fell into a glass cabinet and hit their head on a panel. The impact was hard enough to crack the glass. The person slumped to a seat on the floor.

There wasn't any time to waste, no moves to waste. The second person didn't even bother to check on their fallen comrade. They charged Rachel, growling a curse, and fumbled underneath the lower half of the cot.

When their gloved hands emerged, they held a length of black material that looked like a rope or belt. "Should've done this from the start. Dignity, my ass. Safety first." The voice was feminine. A good sign that emboldened Rachel. Feminine usually meant smaller and less muscle mass—a fairer fight.

She lacked the luxury to strategize in the immanent fight, so she resorted to the first resort and only weapon at her disposal.

As the woman stretched the rope into a length of slack, her gaze surveying the lower half of the gurney, Rachel hurled her full force into her opponent. This had better work, because the resulting commotion would no doubt get attention and send backup running.

Her lower half got airtime off the cot, enough leverage to kick the woman twice in her center mass and send her to the ground with a dull thud. The lady let out a yell, but her scream didn't last.

The momentum of the impact upended the gurney. Metal clattered against metal, and a sickening scrape screeched across the floor as the wheels fought for traction. Before Rachel knew it, she was hurdling forward, strapped in and out of control. She crashed onto the doctor with a thump that knocked out her wind but left her on top of the other person. All things considered, a good position to be in.

Sucking wind, arms bound and useless, she slithered her way up her adversary's body until they were face-to-face. The cot was forged onto her back like a metal backpack. She smelled this stranger's skin, felt the pressure of flesh-on-flesh. There was fear in her combatant's dark blue eyes.

The added weight of the cot served as an advantage. The woman couldn't push her off with the extra burden in tow, and she might have been hurt from the fall.

Rachel twisted her upper body until her forearm bore down on the woman's nose and mouth. The enemy moaned, jerked, and slapped Rachel's head hard enough to make her ears ring. Kicking her heels against the linoleum, the woman aimed for a body part and missed. None of her strikes were to any avail.

"Untie me and don't you dare scream again." Rachel's words came out muffled and raw, the tube choking her, but this chick got the gist. Rachel pushed down harder for emphasis. She had the right angle, so the woman wasn't able to open up and bite. Messy, dirty combat, but it was what she had. "Untie me right now. You better not freak out, or I'll smother you." She had no idea if the pressure she was exerting was sufficient to induce suffocation, but judging by the woman's scared animal expression, the threat was good enough to work. A bluff was adequate in this case.

The woman kicked again but only managed to tangle their legs together. A whine popped out from deep in her throat. She jawed at Rachel's arm but didn't sink in her teeth. The mask worked to Rachel's advantage.

Two more slaps at Rachel's arms and face proved more annoying than painful or destabilizing. The stink of undignified sweat, perfume, and hospital antiseptic flooded Rachel's nostrils and turned her stomach, but she held on to her leverage, shoving the entirety of her weight into this ugly scuffle.

Finally, finally, the woman went slack. She growled. Her forehead knotted. After what felt like an eternity, she threaded her hand through their pressed bodies and unbuckled one of Rachel's cuffs.

Relief flooded her from wrist to shoulder. She hadn't realized how tight the clamp was until the pressure was lifted. "The other one," she rasped.

Cinch gave way to slack, and Rachel was free. She dismounted her rival, crawling backward to disengage as quickly as possible. With a shrug, she ditched the cot. The stupid thing crashed to the floor, the cacophony of impact ringing in her ears.

Once on her knees, she yanked the tubing from her throat. Her gag reflex rebelled, the urge to retch charging upward. Scraping pain chased the impulse. This was the worst thing ever. Once the tubing was out, and there was a lot of it, she threw the plastic to the ground and wiped her mouth.

"Tell me everything." She didn't recognize her own hoarse, beaten voice. Her tongue tasted like shit. This doctor person, or whatever the fuck she was, whimpered in the fetal position. "Why am I here? What have you done to me?"

This was the first time it occurred to Rachel, in a striking hit of clarity and terror, that she had no memories. Of anything. Of the event preceding her unceremonious awakening. She remembered her name. Her name was all she had. The rest of her memories were lost to the mysteries of a bottomless black hole.

"You weren't supposed to wake up," moaned the scrub-clad person, still curled into herself. "This is all wrong. You were supposed to be out until the procedure was finished."

"Yeah, well, I've always marched to the beat of my own drum." She dragged herself to her feet. The sole saving grace of this madness was that her legs worked. In the adrenaline of the fight, she'd forgotten about the pain in her spine. It was returning as an ache, a tender pulse. "What did you do to me? What is this?" She pawed at the nape of her neck. There was a port or insertion back there: chunky plastic that was sore to the touch.

"Leave it," the doctor snapped. She'd propped herself on her elbows. "We have no idea what the consequences will be if we abort mid-procedure."

"What procedure? And who is we?" The third person was still knocked out in the corner. The only door in the room, windowless and thick looking, was shut. An alarm hadn't been triggered. They would have known by now. "I'm not here because of an accident, am I?"

The woman was now upright. She was fitter than Rachel initially assumed. Strong leg muscles. She'd assumed an aggressive stance: legs wide, shoulders broadened, arms out wide. The scuffle might not be over.

Rachel looked around for something to arm herself. The room wasn't a regular hospital room. The surroundings were lab-like and barren. The cabinet the other staffer had crashed into was full of steel instruments glimmering menacingly in the halogen light.

No nurse's call button, no oxygen or screen for vitals, no chairs for visitors, no blood pressure cuff. Nothing normal.

Fuck it. Time to break this clown matrix. She yanked out the port at the back of her neck in a single, hard pull. Pain smarted, and the lady rushed her while shouting a protest, but Rachel didn't care. She threw the hunk of plastic to the ground. "You want me to reinsert your precious port? Start talking."

Her unwelcome companion didn't have a chance to explain before Rachel's world went upside down. A foreign sensation of bleeding out, but more primal, sucked her into a daze. She slapped her palm against the back of her neck. She had to stop the leakage. Her soul was oozing out through the damn spot right under her hairline. "What did you do to me?"

She staggered backward, tripping over the upended cot. A sharp pain near her ankle made her suck in air. White blotches blotted out her vision. Her heart fluttered. Her breath wasn't right. She slumped against the wall, her emotions spinning in a maelstrom of anger, frustration, helplessness, and shame. Her butt plunked on the ground. In front of her, her legs swung uselessly at dead space.

The other person limped to Rachel, injured from the fracas, but she still held an advantage. Rachel was so woozy and dissociated, she barely inhabited her body anymore.

"Are you going to listen to me or beat my ass some more?" The woman squatted in front of Rachel and pulled her mask below her chin. Red welts and scratches marred her smooth complexion. She looked young, in her twenties.

"I'll listen." It was a trick question, or at least a rhetorical one, as Rachel so obviously wasn't in a position to engage in any more ass-beating. But it behooved her to listen if this woman was talking.

The woman went to the discarded port and scooped it off the floor. She handed it to Rachel. "Put this back in."

"How? I can't see back there well enough to insert a tube. I've never even drawn blood."

She thrust the gadget in Rachel's hand. "Trust me. It's custom tailored to sync up with your blood. Your DNA. Almost like a magnet. Place the device back there, and it will find you."

No part of the explanation made Rachel keen to obey. Yet her toehold on reality, what was left of it, slipped away by the second. Her eyesight had deteriorated to blurs of light and color shapes. Her breath came out in ragged hisses. Her pulse had a panicky and frantic quality.

So spacey. A thread, thin and frayed. She was a leaky sieve. Swiss cheese. On the verge. "What if I don't want to sync up with this piece of shit?" Shoving the words out was a herculean struggle where each one weighed as much as a bowling ball in her mouth.

"Then you'll be dead in five minutes. I don't really care. We have other experiments lined up, so you're expendable. However, if you both value your life and would like an explanation, I'd listen."

"Why are you helping me? Why should I trust you?"

She shrugged. "Trust me or don't. Again, I don't really care." A flicker of compassion went off in her eyes. Not pity or contempt. A human recognition of shared vulnerability, and enough to give Rachel pause. "I was in your spot once. Well, not exactly, because I was never brave enough to try to break out. But yeah, I started out as an experiment. Paid my dues. Worked my way up until I was on the Scarab payroll."

She snatched the stupid port before she drained away any more and stuck the damn thing against her skin. Right away, she regained enough of her bearings to feel halfway normal. "What the fuck is the Scarab payroll? And an experiment? You're gonna have to explain." She'd regained enough of her strength to fight more, at least she figured. But she'd rather know what was happening to her, especially because she was apparently an amnesiac.

"My supervisors are going to be in here in five minutes to check on the procedure. Ten, if you're lucky. If they show up, they'll restrain you again and absolutely believe my explanation of how you attacked me. Which is true. So we can either do story time and risk you being apprehended here, or I can hand over your file and point you in the direction of the most reliable escape route. You still might get caught and picked up by Scarab security, but at least you'll have a head start." She stared at Rachel, blinked once, and went back to staring.

"What the hell is Scarab?"

"Do you believe in black magic?"

She froze over. The room had an even more sinister quality than she'd initially noticed, sterile and nondescript, vaguely medical but not in a legitimate way. "No."

"You might want to start. Don't mess with the port again until you know more." She walked to the cabinet where the other guy was still knocked out. In a series of delicate movements, she reached in and pulled out an object small enough to fit in her palm. Next, she went to the computer in the corner.

Rachel watched with interest as her shadowy companion worked, pulling a thumb drive from a drawer and inserting the data stick. A box popped up on the screen, and they both looked, though Rachel wasn't able to make out anything of note.

The woman in scrubs tapped her foot. She wore white clogs, the popular brand with holes on the top. No charms. "There," she muttered after a minute and pulled out the thumb drive. After pressing the silver stick into Rachel's palm, she showed the other item she'd collected. A roll of gauzy medical tape. "Keep your hand in place until I'm finished."

Squeezing the data stick like the thing was a lifeline, Rachel let the tech spool four loops of the soft, sticky material around her throat. She cinched it up so tight it felt like a collar. Clearly, she was serious about the port staying put. Now Rachel knew why. "Who are you?"

"Doesn't matter, like I said. I'm a nobody who owed a debt, and Scarab offered to pay me to take part in an experiment as long as I didn't ask questions. Desperation got me here in the first place. Same story with you, right?"

Déjà vu rippled through Rachel along with the stifled yet frantic sensation of forgotten knowledge clawing below the surface of her conscious awareness and struggling to break free. The woman was right. She owed money. Debt. She'd ended up in this place, or the place that'd been a precursor to the place where she currently sat, thanks to these debts. A trickle of a recollection seeped in through a small hole. She had to break the dam. "There are answers on here?" She held up the drive.

"Your entire file. Now here's what to do. Open the window and climb out. Luckily for you, we're on the ground floor. This place is isolated as fuck for obvious reasons. Isolated is good, though, because there are trees everywhere. A lot of woods to the south of us. Your best bet is to make a mad dash for them. The security cameras might pick you up, but the guards are lazy and underpaid, and it's dinnertime right now, so they're distracted. If you make it to the woods, follow the creek to the south and east. The path will lead to a highway after a few miles. From there, you can hitchhike and hope someone who isn't psycho picks you up."

Rachel's throat closed up. The odds as the woman had laid them out were long, and bad. She wasn't dumb. She was shooting a long shot. "What if I don't make it to the woods?"

She shrugged. "Then I'll see you back here in an hour or so, and this experiment will proceed. I'd say you wouldn't like the results, but they'll take your mind away, so you'll be as good as dead. Not sentient anymore, at least. A walking, talking vegetable."

Rachel swallowed. "I'll make a run for it." There were a lot of moving parts, and a good chance she'd wind up eaten by wild animals or dismembered in a ditch, but she had nothing to lose.

The woman patted her on the shoulder. "Good luck. I hope you get to safety and have a chance to review your dossier. Promise me something, okay?"

Rachel nodded.

"If you make it, expose these fuckers to the world. It'll all make sense after you look over your file." Her eyes went red and wet, teary, yet at the same time they lit up with indignation. "They need to burn for crimes against humanity."

"Okay." Rachel had no idea what they were talking about anymore, but her clock was ticking, and the time to escape was now. "I'll do my best. Promise."

"Give me a hand." The medical lady walked to the room's lone window, and Rachel followed.

The heavy-duty window required both of their full effort to shove open, as did the double storm windows behind it. A burst of cool air brought relief in both the fresh air and the teasing promise of freedom. In the distance, patchy, poorly tended grass gave way to a wooded area dense with trees and brush. The sun cast a mellow glaze over the treetops. It had to be low in the sky by now. Late afternoon. Not an abundance of daylight left. The trees still had their leaves, but the air was crisp. September? Judging by the current temperature, a cold night lay ahead.

She had no identification. No substantive memories. No shoes. No sustenance, no blanket. No water, except for the promise of the creek in the woods. She had a bad feeling.

As she looked into the distance, a haunting remnant floated to the forefront of her mind. Old dream imagery, perhaps. Yet much more unsettling. Like a forgotten vestige of a past life, coming home. "I've been here before. With a man. Does a giant eyeball mean anything to you? A huge eye under the foundation of this building?"

"You're delirious from dehydration." She handed Rachel a tumbler with a handle and her white clogs. The mug held at least thirty-two ounces and was half-full of water. "I wish I had more to give you. Now hurry. If you stay on track and are decent with directions, you'll be able to get to the road before dark."

Rachel curled her fingers around the mug's handle, taking solace in its sturdiness. She slid her feet into the clogs. "Thank you."

Rachel slung her lower half out of the window and lowered a few feet until her soles hit the ground. Her heart slammed. Adrenaline fueled her, making her tunnel-visioned and crackly.

A quick scan of the fence, and she keyed in on the weak spot. No time to doubt or second guess. Rachel dashed to the fence and wiggled her body through the gash in the chain links. The fabric of her gown snagged on spikes of ragged metal, ripping a hole near her side, but she worked the material free. Then, she herself was free, and she bolted into the woods as fast as her feet would fly.

TWENTY-ONE

Wherever Rachel was, darkness came early.

Though light remained, she could feel the encroach of night, a wild and cold specter that both seeped up from the ground and pushed down past the knot of branches twisting against a gray sky. A knobby expanse of brown fingers grasped for her; their reach thrust out for miles ahead. The woods seemed eternal.

Her neck hair stood tall. Each breeze cut right through her flimsy gown and sent violating prods under the hem. Where *was* she? She didn't have enough knowledge of botany or trees to place her surroundings based on the vegetation scraping her legs, snapping under her feet, and snaring her clothing only to ricochet and land stings on her cheeks.

Quiet. A little too quiet. So quiet she was close to bugging out while hacking her way through green and brown, brown and green, some branch or log or lump of dirt pulling, tripping, or startling her with every step.

To her left, a cluster of turgid mushrooms bloomed from a tree trunk, fish-belly white tumors erupting against dull bark. An alien slug of a hornet's nest loomed gray and angry on the neighboring tree. She saw holes in the ground and didn't want to think about what had burrowed into them.

Her ankle ached from the stumble over the cot. Her stomach growled, mocking her amidst the rest of the noises taunting her in her struggle. Could she eat anything she encountered here? Those mushrooms? She had no survival skills. All she had was her will, dumb yet stubborn, so she plodded along, clutching a death grip on her tumbler.

The rancid-sweet reek of decay blasted her nose as she trudged along on an un-trod, non-trail that so obviously hadn't been seen by feet. Forget about mile markers or trail symbols out here. She tried not to see what her nose had caught but saw anyway. A raccoon or possum, once, now scraps of hide patched over vertebrae and a ghastly death smile of bone and teeth.

Her eyes watered. Her heart weighed a thousand pounds. A black swarm buzzed above the carcass, its carrion song hammering inside her skull as she slugged past. Several flies followed her, hissing in her ears. She swatted her head, smacking herself, an ugly grunt leaving her lips. Mandibles bit at her lips. Teeny legs tickled her face.

She stepped in shit. The smell gave it away at once. In horror, she looked. Dog-sized pile, but nobody would walk a dog back here. Wolf? Mountain lion? The geography eluded her. No idea of the local fauna.

She was no Girl Scout. Never had been. She was going to die.

"Fuck me." All she had was the sun to help with direction. The bright blotch seeped through the treetops, setting in the west like always, assuring her, at least, that she was going the right way. Problem was, she wouldn't have its help for much longer.

Then it'd be dark. And that'd be it. So she clomped faster, in her shitty white clogs, her legs itchy, because moving forward was all she could do. In the thicket, the brush rustled. A twig snapped, echoing. The activity set off a flurry of sounds, crunches and cracks giving way as living things moved.

She wasn't alone. Not at all.

Deep in the bowels of the woods, one of her unseen living companions growled.

She froze. Pelvic muscles deep inside leapt. Her heart in her throat, her pulse beating in her eardrums, she stood alert.

The animal growled again. Closer? Farther? She couldn't tell, which made it worse. She started her march back up, her stomps both pitiful and defiant. Brown bears, you were supposed to play dead. Black bears, fight back. Big cats, throw sticks and rocks but don't crouch. She'd try. She'd fucking try.

A tiny living thing scampered across her path. Fried and jittery from the growl, she jumped, a gasp escaping her lips. Only once she'd freaked did her brain catch up. A chipmunk, tawny and bushy tailed. She'd spooked over a chipmunk. Rachel laughed at herself and kept moving.

The sun was retiring. The air was definitely colder. An owl hooted. She swallowed a lump, and the motion made her realize how dry her mouth was. She sucked on the tumbler straw, rationing. The last thing she wanted to do was run out of water. A close second in the undesirable race was to have to squat and pee, lowering her privates onto any number of wild things able to harm her.

She passed a small valley filled with yellow flowers, which would have been pretty in some other situation. Her legs ached. A jelly feeling had set in. The ankle wasn't self-correcting either, the pain having returned since the post-animal scare adrenaline had worn off.

Rachel stepped over a fallen log filled with shiny gray bugs. She kicked a beer can riddled with buckshot, wondering if the sign of human life was good or bad. Often, people were worse predators than animals with fur.

Her fair-weather friend in the sky assured her she was going in the right direction, so at least she had some guidance. The path had started to feel more like a real trail, pressed down and even compared to what she'd been treading before now, though wishful thinking was surely a possibility.

A streak of tan, large and alive, dashed past in her peripheral vision. She jerked her head to catch a glimpse but was too late. The phantom may have been a sinister mirage, too, her frazzled mind springing cruel tricks as she scanned for death around every corner.

A deer, a deer. It had to be a deer. Doe, a deer, a female deer. Better yet, Bambi, wide eyed and innocent. A spotted faun on shaky legs running to mama.

Not a mountain lion or cougar stalking her.

Those lived in California and Utah, and this place was not there.

There were no big cats here.

Right?

And then she saw it.

Unmistakable.

Looking right at her. No mirage.

Relief careened through her. She pressed prayer hands to her lips.

The creek. It was real. The lady hadn't lied or been wrong.

It was a pitiful thing, barely a trickle of dark water piddling along at the bottom of a cavernous, muddy mouth. "Yes!" She treated herself to a small jump of joy before hustling along at the water's edge.

The sad creek was a lifeline, a sliver of hope as thin as the band of water slicing its claim through the glistening dirt. A baby turtle no larger than a silver dollar waddled down the muddy bank.

She identified with the little guy, tiny and all alone in such an unforgiving environment. She watched him until he got in the water and swam. If he could do it, so could she.

Rachel followed the creek. She forced herself not to think any thoughts, to neither fret nor hope. One foot in front of the other. All she needed to do. Her jaw locked up tight. Every part of her ached, smarted, itched, or burned. The time of day definitely qualified as sunset. Perhaps even twilight. She gritted her teeth and tried to jog, but the ankle wasn't cooperating.

The temp dropped again. Now she was cold all over in addition to all the other unpleasantness. She gritted her teeth. Keep. Moving. No thoughts allowed. She had the creek. Creek, creek, creek.

The creek petered out and stopped. Bottomed out into dirt. She crouched despite a bloom of pain near her bad foot. Shit. Fuck. No more creek to follow. What now?

A new sound, more of a seismic tremble in her bones, entered the landscape. She stayed still and tried to place it. A similar noise blew past. It had a whooshing quality. In her gut, she felt okay about this sound, and that was the precise moment when she took note of a break in the trees.

Hope floated her heels and got her hustling. "Please let this be what I think it is."

After staggering her way through a final thatch of irritating, snappy foliage, Rachel broke through the woods and ended up on the other side of the trees.

At the bottom of a hill steep enough to deter even a sledding daredevil, it was there.

The road.

Rachel nearly collapsed in on herself with joy. The road was real, and it was right there. Two lanes. Paved blacktop, power lines above. Highway. Someone would see her.

Clutching her tumbler, she took two baby steps down the grass before the incline got the better of her. Control gave way to gravity, and she stumbled down, her feet moving on their own. The bad ankle wasn't happy with this awkward, careening dance. The only other choice was to roll. Rachel threw herself to the ground, undignified and uncomfortable, the impact snatching her breath.

Her world became a dizzying whirl of blurred light and nausea. She spun and spun, gathering momentum, her distress tempered by how she was headed somewhere she wanted to go. In a strange moment, she wondered if this was what having a baby felt like. Miserable, but tolerable because you got something you wanted out of the deal. She laughed crazed, uncensored joker laughs as she rolled down, giving birth to her new beginning.

She ended up in a crumpled pile on the shoulder. Gravel dug into her hip and shoulder. Stillness was worse than the fall because the world kept spinning. She dragged herself to her hands and knees and retched. A car tore past, the velocity and resulting wake of air pressure nearly knocking her down again.

"Help," she bellowed, but the car was long gone, having either not seen her or ignored her.

Once she'd wrangled a crumb of faith she wouldn't stumble into oncoming traffic, she stood and waved her arms above her head. Two more cars, a yellow moving truck, and a motorcycle all zipped by.

She wasn't even mad the first four ignored her, because with this amount of traffic, the odds were good someone would stop. Now she had to hope the person who picked her up meant no harm.

The first fall of night had set in as a dusky haze. The next handful of cars and trucks had their lights on. She kept shouting and waving her arms to no avail. They probably thought she was a drug addict or escaped prisoner.

Though she wanted to be indignant about the lack of help, Rachel wasn't sure she would have picked herself up either. She had to look horrid, like she'd stabbed an orderly in the jugular with a pilfered pen before breaking out of the maximum-security mental hospital.

A semi barreled toward her like a hulking automotive monster. The driver flashed his lights. She waved her arms above her head until they ached. The semi slowed. "Please, please, please," she shouted, though she obviously had no idea who was driving. This was a leap of faith.

The truck came to a stop about thirty feet ahead. Rachel limped gratefully in the direction of her mysterious, maybe-rescuer, maybe-killer. She was a sad sack. A broken-down piece of meat. Emptied out except for pain and the survival instinct. She might be hobbling to her murderer. She didn't give a fuck anymore.

She'd got herself to the back of the truck and fixed an exhausted, battered stare at the slew of numbers stuck on with decals. Texas license plate, a phone number, other identification she was too spent to memorize. An additional number to call to complain about the driver's road behavior, if needed. An American flag sticker about the size of a credit card glimmered in the dying light thanks to a metallic sheen.

A figure quick-stepped around the back of the rig. He looked to be around thirty, good shape, and wore jeans and a flannel. Short brown hair and dark eyes, Latino or Native American.

He ran to her. "Oh, my God. What happened?"

As soon as she heard the compassion in his voice, saw the empathy in his eyes, she dragged her broken body to his stronger one, collapsed in his arms, and sobbed.

His scent of clean linen, soap, and safety enveloped her. She was drawn to his natural scent, attracted on a visceral level. Trauma might have led her to project safety onto him or any would-be rescuer, sure, but she liked to think her intuition helped her sniff out good people from bad. Lately, all she'd had was faith, so she'd allow it to carry her.

He stroked her hair. The affectionate touch felt so good after the trial in the woods and her scuffle with the clinician. A few seconds passed with cars whipping by. She didn't know what to tell him. How to even begin to describe what happened.

He took the liberty to fill the silence. "Let's get off the road shoulder, okay? If one of these cars loses control, we're in real danger. Are you comfortable to come sit in my truck?"

"Yes," she whispered, grateful for the tender consideration of her comfort zone and self-awareness of his status as a male stranger. Her intuition felt safe, that deeper than deep place in her gut assuring her she was okay. "I need to get off my feet."

"I can tell. Your ankle doesn't look great." The man led her to the passenger side and helped her up a big step, holding her upper arm for support as she worked her way into the front seat while trying to keep as much weight off the ankle as possible.

Her door shut. She pressed her forehead into the dashboard and took three big breaths. The cab of the truck smelled like coffee and pine air freshener. Now would be a good time to reclaim some pieces of herself so she'd be able to tell him something that didn't sound crazy. No such luck recovering her identity, though.

He joined her in the front of the truck, his door closing. "We need to get something on your ankle." He crawled through the middle space by the center console and came out holding a wide blue strip. "This'll tide you over until we can get to a drugstore."

She accepted the material, finding it cold to the touch, and instantly knew what it was and what to do with it. The ice pack ended up on her ankle quickly. She sighed when the icy relief hit her overheated, tender flesh. "Thank you."

"Were you in an accident?" She still heard the concern, for sure, but a sharper note layered in with his deep voice. Suspicion, or confusion.

The shock of seeing her in such distress having worn off, he was likely wondering what the hell had happened to land her in such a hopeless state. With time to think, the gears in his head had to be turning. Turning to prisons and mental wards.

Her own thoughts had veered into dark territory. What if the woman at the facility was lying about Scarab letting her go easy? Lulled into a false sense of security, she was liable to let her guard down. They might be looking for her at this very moment, whoever *they* even were. Scarab.

Another black box. She uncurled her palm and looked at the flash drive. Her whole hand ached from clenching.

He watched her face before his eyes slipped to the data stick. He looked even more confounded and distraught. He pursed his lips. Sighed. "If you're in some kind of trouble, I need to know. I'll help you as best I can without breaking the law or putting your or my wellbeing at risk. I won't abandon you on the side of the road, but I need you to tell me how you got here." He reached for her, cupped her chin between his thumb and forefinger, and lifted her gaze to meet his. The gesture felt natural. His brown eyes were mesmerizing, the kind you couldn't help but get lost in. And lost she got, even if only for a brief escape. He was gorgeous in an approachable and wholesome way. "Deal?"

The longer she looked at him, into him, the fuzzier and more lost she felt. Like she'd known him before, intimately, and shared significant moments with him. How? If he was from her forgotten life, he'd surely remember her. "I have amnesia."

He dropped her chin and wrapped her hand in his larger one. "Do you remember anything? Your name?"

"My name is all I remember." She swallowed. "It's Rachel."

"Good start. I'm Timothy."

The name, the name. Her empty mind was somehow paradoxically overfull of memories, impressions, and feelings without shape or content. The cruelest sort of recollection, imprecise and as amorphous as can be. But she definitely knew him. Had known him. Was he tied to Scarab? Her heartbeat skittered. He might be playing her. Fooling her. Getting ready to ship her right back to the lab, or worse. "I'm certain we know each other somehow or have met before." Wild sounding? Sure. But so were the events that led to them meeting, or re-meeting, or whatever.

"It's the weirdest thing." He stroked the steering wheel. "I feel the same way. When I saw you standing there, I recognized you. But I wasn't able to place how. I'd met you before, though. I've never been more certain."

"Where are you headed?" A bit more investigation might dredge up the tie uniting their pasts or get him to slip and reveal any hidden agendas or covert intentions. He didn't seem like he was hiding anything, but lots of people had good acting skills.

"Texas. Dropping off this load, then I'm staying at my buddy's old house for a few days."

Sounded like there was a new chapter was about to unfold for this guy. "What's next?"

"Then I'll officially be an expatriate. I'm moving to Peru."

She'd never been, yet the imagery of the Amazon rainforest and river splashed into her consciousness as vividly as a watercolor. A bird's-eye view of an ancient water serpent winding through lush, emerald wilds. Jaguars, golden-eyed and cloaked in their finery of spots, stalked the night. Blue butterflies the size of her palm landed on the edge of a canoe. The smell of fish roasted on smoky wooden planks. Her heart cried out for this place she imagined so vividly but had never visited. "Take me with you."

His lips parted. "That doesn't make any sense."

"I know. But so what? I don't have anywhere else to go. The story of my life is supposedly on here." She pinched the flash drive and held it up. "You seem nice, and there's some affinity between us, however faint. I won't put you out. You won't have to support me. I'll do odd jobs to make money. Clean toilets. Walk dogs. Anything under the table. I don't have any identification, money, friends, or family. You're all I've got. I don't want to beg you, but I will."

"I don't want you to beg." He grimaced, looked to the side, and mumbled a curse. "This is so fucked." He stared at her for seconds, squinting, and scratched his head. "Where do I know you from? It's like the core memory is dangling just out of my reach. Not that anything should shock me anymore. Not after what I've seen and experienced."

What an interesting comment. "What do you mean?"

"How much do you believe when it comes to the paranormal? Are you in the strictly practical camp, where nothing can exist that isn't scientifically proven? Or do you fall closer to the other end of the spectrum and keep an open mind toward topics like magic and otherworldly entities?"

Screw small talk. This topic felt juicy, substantial, though she wasn't able to pinpoint yet how. Fingers crossed that some more time spent with handsome Timothy and his practical to paranormal spectrum would crack the code. And that wasn't even scratching the surface of her flash drive, smooth and mysterious between her thumb and forefinger. "How much time do you have to really dig into this subject?"

"We're in West Virginia. It's a long way to Texas. So plenty."

West Virginia. Her home state? Would the contents of the flash drive tell? She wouldn't know until she got to a computer. Hotels with business centers had those, and Timothy was the clearest path to a hotel at the moment. "Someone asked me today if I believed in black magic. I wasn't sure how to answer them at first. But judging by the shit that happened today, I'm inclined to say yes."

"Now we're cooking with gas. Getting real." He fired up the engine, filling the cabin with the hearty roar of the engine. "I have a feeling I can be myself with you. Which is not to say I'm a black magician or warlock or whatever."

"Please don't sacrifice me to the devil." She wasn't actually afraid. Fear had no room to maneuver, anyway. She was fearless. Flying blind. Open to receive and light on her toes.

He pressed down on the pedal and steered the truck back onto the highway. "The truth of my story is both more bizarre and less scary. Buckle up, literally and figuratively. We're going to have an interesting bonding session."

"I have so many questions already."

"Me too." For the first time since they'd met, Timothy smiled. A real, warm, genuine smile with eye crinkles. If she hadn't been so beat, she'd have been certifiably smitten. She still lowkey was. He was kind, caring, and attractive. There were worse traveling companions.

Rachel buckled up, literally and figuratively, and readied herself for the ride and road ahead.

TWENTY-TWO

IN HIS LINE OF WORK, TIMOTHY SPENT A LOT OF TIME ALONE WITH HIS own thoughts. The road got weird at night, too, and slunk into a dreamy land where light surrendered but for the traces of headlamps scratching over an endless, unspooling ribbon.

On many nights, once podcasts and radio songs ceased to appease, he merged with the black tape streaked by its broken white lines, forever and ever, and his thoughts.

A special, numbing blend of purgatory greeted him in these moments.

A type of shifting, in its own way, as he fell in on himself to morph into a different specimen.

His excessive alone time on the road had given him a propensity to mild poeticism, if he did say so himself. He supposed his gift-curse of shifting, what set him apart from others, made him prone to existential ponderings.

Beside him, Rachel gazed out the window. Bits of leaves burrowed into her brown hair. She fidgeted with the flash drive, turning it over and over in mud-spackled hands.

He needed to stop for the night soon, let her get cleaned up and rested. First, fresh clothes, food, and water.

Hotel staff down south would notice a brown man with a scraped-up white woman in tow, especially with her wearing a ratty medical gown and a device taped to the back of her neck. They'd notice alright, and not in a good way.

He himself sure noticed. Cancer drug port? Something to do with her spinal fluid? Did the plastic hunk pinned with gauze at the nape of her neck require changing, tending? Was there a wound to be cleaned? Timothy wasn't a medical person and couldn't say. He couldn't help but wonder, though, how closely her predicament was connected to the cargo in the back of his rig.

He tried not to concern himself much with who he hauled cargo for, as all he cared about was getting his money and kicking off for the night.

But this last job had been too interesting to ignore. The things he'd seen and tried to overlook. What he'd inferred was stashed in those plastic tubs marked "live" in big red letters, now seething in the back of his truck.

Again, though, his job wasn't to think or question, so he'd pretended not to as he'd helped the two burly employees at the warehouse pack the load.

To his right, a blue sign covered in corporate logos flashed iridescent brands in the streetlights. A good rest stop. Plenty of options. "I figure we'll fortify ourselves before we make an attempt at conversation. Or we don't have to talk at all. You've been through enough today."

"Somehow, I doubt any conversation I have with you will be as draining and miserable as the last several hours leading up to this moment." She looked at him sidelong. Rachel had a wild sort of beauty, powerful, with piercing eyes perched atop a nose evoking the intensity of a bald eagle's beak.

Quite a feat how she hadn't lost her sense of humor amid her struggles. She was quite the woman. "I suppose I'll take that as a compliment."

He pulled into the parking lot of a truck stop with a fluorescent blast radius lighting up an entire block. The logo, a meaty cartoon heart, pulsed at the apex of a sign tall enough to lure weary travelers from two exits away. "Be right back. I'll get us some stuff and then proceed to engage you in conversation that hopefully neither drains you nor worsens your misery."

She laughed. It was beautiful. Judging by her state, she likely hadn't laughed innocently in a long while. Worse, she likely didn't remember her last moment of joy. Admittedly, the amnesia piece of what she was going through disturbed him but not enough for him to cast her aside.

"What's so funny?" He guided the truck into a designated parking area for big rigs and killed the engine.

"You. Not funny as in I'm laughing at you, but funny as in witty. Your turns of phrase make me feel effervescent or something. Like my mind is turning on."

If she wasn't so vulnerable, he wouldn't mind turning her on back at the hotel. But they weren't here for sensuality or romance. Circumstances were too serious, too worrisome. He didn't know her. It was impossible to get to know her, really, since she didn't even know herself. There was an ethical line there, and the line made sense intuitively even though he lacked a frame of reference to name it. "I'll buy you a crossword puzzle so you won't have to rely on me for mental stimulation much longer. Trust me, you'll get bored."

Not true, exactly, he was pretty good at talking to women and in general keeping conversations going. But holding her at arm's length was the responsible course of action given her condition. He jumped out of the cab and headed in, double-checking to ensure the doors were locked. He'd be quick in case she panicked, or, worse, someone came looking for her.

The convenience store nearly blinded him with a brightness that instantly blotted out the gloom of night, rendering the space a dreamy fairy land of never-ending consumerism. The place smelled fresher than one might expect, like sugar and a good hard scrubbing. Glistening hot dogs rolled over on their metal warmers, cooking eternally. He'd never seen so many varieties of chips. The aisle of souvenir kitsch helpfully informed him they'd made it to Arkansas.

Video games beeped and shrieked from a corner by the bathrooms, redheaded twins mashing buttons. A lean, grizzled man overflowed a Slurpee cup with red goo oozing over the ring on his forefinger. A middle-aged couple in sweatpants smooched by the soda cooler, an army of Coca-Cola bottles assembling into an adoring audience. Truck stops never ceased to fascinate Timothy in their weird, chaotic, and occasionally touching portraits of humanity at large.

He made haste to the clothing area and slung over his arm two pairs of sweatpants, three t-shirts, a hoodie, and some men's boxers. He threw a trucker hat on top of the pile in case she wanted to cover her hair or hide her identity. After putting the clothes on the un-clerked counter, he stocked up on water, toiletries, over-the-counter meds, and food. He even managed to score a couple of sandwiches and an assortment of fruit.

Finally, he rounded out his finds with several magazines and a newspaper that, upon verification, he confirmed contained a crossword puzzle.

Bags in hand, Timothy booked it back to the truck. Once he'd re-situated himself in the driver's seat, the sight of Rachel unnerved him.

She was biting her nails and looking over her shoulder. Her body was tense, hunched.

"What's wrong?" He started the engine. His stomach dropped. His intuition wasn't happy. A voice deep inside growled that he'd made a mistake, and she was trouble. He pushed it down and engaged her more when she didn't answer right away. "Are you feeling ill? Do we need to do something with the device at the back of your neck? I can run back in if there's anything you need."

"Start the engine." Her directive was terse but not stern. He could smell the sharpness of her fear, feel the quivering energy pulsing out of her in waves.

The truck roared to life under his hand. The hotel sign glowed twenty feet down the road. "Hang on. We'll be inside in ten minutes." Except he felt sick. Things had gone downhill. Tilted. One didn't need a sixth sense to sense the swerve into bad vibes.

"No. Back on the interstate." She cast a furtive glance over her shoulder, then jerked her head back to the forward position like she regretted looking.

"Why?" He steered toward the exit.

"We're being followed. Don't look now, but see the red sedan at gas pump number seven?"

After two beats, he allowed a discreet glance. The car in question sat idle at the spot in question. The hose wasn't attached to the tank. A person sat behind the wheel, but their identifying characteristics weren't visible from Timothy's vantage point. "What about them?"

"They've been behind us for the last fifty miles. They pulled off when we took that bathroom break, and they sat in the parking lot. I was hoping we'd lose them after, but then they showed up here."

Timothy had a handgun and a rifle in the back, good combat skills, and his ability to call up the wolf. He wasn't scared. "So what? If they want a confrontation, they're welcome to bring it on. I'm not handing you over to whoever did this to you. You're safe now, Rachel."

Still, he willed them to stay put at the pump as he veered toward the exit ramp. He didn't want to fight even though he was capable. Perhaps more so, he didn't want to learn the extent of what he'd gotten himself mixed up in. The dark details of what brought Rachel to him, and if they fit with the creatures in the back of his truck, were welcome to stay secret.

The car's headlights blinked on. The driver drove around the pumps, in no hurry, and sure enough ended up behind Timothy. He swallowed a curse and tried not to suck his teeth too hard. He exited onto the interstate, staying on the same route to Austin. The car crept up, following at a safe distance.

Rachel buried her face in her palms. "I want to believe you about being safe."

"So why don't you?" It didn't bode well that their stalker hadn't jumped out and rushed him the first time they'd stopped.

This wasn't a case of hot-blooded anger. This was calculated. Cold. Premeditated. The driver of the red sedan was profiling him, them. They wanted to catch him alone, or at least as unguarded as possible. A surprise attack might be in the cards. Unless they'd phoned in his license plate somewhere and were taking liberties to learn everything possible about him or the trucking company.

Or the weird Scarab, Inc. warehouse where he'd picked up the cargo was all over the stalker's radar.

Rachel said, "I don't think we're dealing with the realm of the mundane anymore. The place where I was held was like a hospital, but not a real one. It was like I'd been captured and taken to a secret lab. They were doing experiments on me. Black magic, or at least that's what a lady there said. I guess it's possible she was lying to scare me, but it didn't sound like it."

Black magic. Throwing such a charged term around didn't spook him much anymore. He'd been accused of such things back in Utah the few times he'd let slip how he'd had the ability to shift his shape. Most people, especially non-Natives, didn't get it and were quick to judge. "People throw those words around to label things they don't understand. Has anything returned from your memories? Do you have any more context of the place where you were held? Why this woman thought black magic was involved? Or what they were doing to you at all?"

"Not really. She told me I'd enrolled myself in an experiment there for money. Which I have the fuzziest, haziest memory of. I must have been transported somehow. Kidnapped. I was so far from home. I never would have travelled so far voluntarily." She looked at him desperately. "I might have people close to me who are worried sick. Who depend on me. Who need me. Fuck! What if I have kids?"

The sedan trailed diligently. This was getting absurd, and Timothy was getting mad. Fucker needed to say their piece or go away. He wasn't about to be intimidated by some childish creeper game pulled from a horror movie. "Maybe whoever is behind us is someone from your past. Or a private investigator. You could have been reported as a missing person. You're an adult, so all they can do is ask you to come home. I'll talk to them."

"What if they put a spell on you? Wipe your mind like they did to me?"

He laid his hand on her shoulder. "I'll handle it." He'd never had any experience with spells or magic so potent as to mind-wipe. Sure, his tribe had holy men and women, plenty of folk who were connected to the mystical and ancestral realms, but he'd never known anyone in possession of anything as heavy-duty as mind control. Nor as dark.

Nor had he ruled out the possibility that Rachel was delusional.

They drove twenty more miles in silence, the sedan his barnacle, before the next sizable town appeared in a maze of light and blue signs. Whoever this was wouldn't fuck with him in such a heavily populated area. Let this shadowy stranger cast a mind control spell or whatever in the parking lot of a La Quinta, where the surroundings were stuffed with witnesses. "We really need to get you to a computer so you can see what's on the drive."

The hope to end all hopes was that the information on the stick would put her mind to rest somehow, even if the nature of the content wasn't pleasant. The best bet at this point, in his estimation, was a dose of clear, mundane reality.

There wasn't a La Quinta, but he got them to a hotel of similar market status. The parking lot was nearly full. There were people everywhere. He guided his rig to the truck lot, which was a bit sparser but still in full view of plenty of lit hotel rooms, the fast food burger joint next door, and some kind of video arcade or bowling alley. Everything was busy. He'd raise hell and subdue this leech in self-defense if he had to. Witnesses aplenty were around to back up his account.

He turned off the engine. The sedan claimed the spot behind him and offed its lights. He reached into the back and grabbed his nine millimeter, the cold steel a comforting heft in his palm. After checking to ensure it was loaded, he stuck the gun in the back of his waistband. "Don't move."

She didn't look the least bit inclined. Timothy got out and stormed over to the sedan. "Get out," he shouted, assuming an aggressive stance with wide arms and legs. The last thing he wanted was a physical confrontation, but he'd accept whatever it took to make this follower go away. "Come on out and face me so we can talk."

The sedan door opened a crack. He kept his hands away from the gun. The gun was a last resort. Mostly, he wanted an explanation. An explanation, then for this goof to fuck off and never return to his or Rachel's life ever again.

A foot exited the car first. Small and sneaker clad. A woman's foot, then her denim-wrapped leg.

Buried muscles unclenched within. Plenty of women fought well, and tons owned and operated guns, but by and large they weren't as prone to violence as men. Timothy didn't mean to stereotype, but he'd learned a few reliable things over the years. Nonetheless, he kept his guard up. This particular woman had some courage, following a stranger in a truck for miles. Likely, her courage was backed by something tangible.

The rest of the woman unfolded from her vehicle.

He couldn't believe his eyes. He blinked twice. Vertigo sucked him in and out. His brain caught up to the shock of seeing a different version of the familiar in time for logic to take over for his dumbfounded trance.

Rachel had an identical twin. Now he got it. The twin had spotted them at the bathroom stop. Rachel had no phone. Her twin's only choice was to follow. "She's safe," Timothy said. "I swear I'm a good guy. I don't know anything about what happened, except I wouldn't have been able to live with myself if I'd left her where I'd found her."

Rachel's twin shook her head. "I know what you're thinking. I don't have a twin sister." The voice was identical. So were her mannerisms. How she talked with her hands, like she was shaping each syllable. Like the original Rachel, she rested slightly more weight on her right side. "I've never been a spiritual person. Not really. I mean, I bought a healing crystal once. Beyond that? Total skeptic. Then guess what? Bam. I see my doppelgänger at a random convenience store while I'm driving to see my actual sister." She took a step closer. Pointed at the back of the truck. "Who, I assure you, looks nothing like my literal fucking clone."

"I don't know what you want me to say. Or do." Timothy was as lost as Rachel and this lady. "What's your name?"

"Rachel."

His insides froze solid. What the hell was happening? An elaborate prank or setup? Yet it made no sense to make him the butt of the joke. Rachel hadn't seen her double yet. He had no idea if it was good or bad for them to meet. If an encounter would clear some things up, practically speaking, or tear apart the fabric of the universe or God knew what.

He lacked any frame of reference. "Do you have any connection to magic or mysticism? Spells? Experiments with outside the box practices beyond the realm of accepted science?"

She narrowed her eyes. "I don't think I ever threw away the healing crystal. And I've read my horoscope before. You mean like that?"

Even her wry, sarcastic sense of humor mirrored Rachel's. "I'll go talk to her. Wait in your car." Here was a conversation he'd never imagined himself to be marching into. There was a chance his shifting had done this, though no spiritual or physical evidence grounded his speculation. He lacked any other guesses as to what forces had so completely shredded the divide between worlds and detonated any predictable sense of order or governance.

Unless one or both of the Rachels were simply lying for whatever twisted, hidden reason his simple man's brain hadn't wrapped itself around.

Operating on the premise that the 'clones' theory was at least partially true, even if only in Rachel #2's mind, Timothy returned to Rachel #1. She startled when she saw him but relaxed into her typical resting state.

He got in and didn't say anything at first. It was hard not to laugh, although the latest development wasn't funny, exactly. Certainly not humorous in a lighthearted way. He found himself playing the role of supporting cast in the theater of the absurd.

"What happened?" Rachel asked, scanning him up and down with an exacting gaze. "You don't look hurt or shaken. Did he try anything?"

"It was a she, and no. She didn't try anything."

"She? I can't believe a woman would follow a strange trucker for miles until he got out and confronted her."

"I couldn't believe it at first either."

"What did she want?"

"Speaking of the unbelievable."

He caught her in an intense stare. "Do you swear to me you've been telling me the entire truth this whole time? No lies, no secrets, nothing held back? Because if you have been, I need you to come clean this second. I can't handle much more of this. I'll take you to a hospital, you don't have to worry about being abandoned, but if you're tricking me somehow, we have to part ways."

"Timothy, stop. Yes, I swear I've been honest with you. Everything I know or remember, so do you. What do you mean, speaking of the unbelievable? What happened with this person?"

If Rachel had a twin and didn't remember, there was a chance seeing her forgotten sibling would jog her memory. If so, however, it would mean the other woman was lying, putting him back at square one when it came to unraveling this knot of madness.

Fuck it. Something had to give, so why not use a clash of clones to serve as the catalyst for a breakthrough? "She looks exactly like you. A double. Every detail, even the subtlest aspects of your body language. Why don't you come on out and see for yourself?"

TWENTY-THREE

STARING INTO HER OWN EYES, THE PUPILS AS LARGE AS POOLS, RACHEL both lost and found herself.

She fought to stay grounded, to stay in her body despite the temptation to tumble headfirst into those bottomless, pitch-black ponds and disappear forever.

She'd fall into the icy depths and travel to frigid and unbounded netherworlds where magic pulsed dark and purple, tied to the dark heart by an umbilical cord and fed with an ancestral blood whose full mysteries were known by no one. Gasping, she'd emerge fish-like, her mouth frozen in an "o" of shock.

All around her, Minnesota on a winter's night hummed along with its usual signs of life. A dog barked in the distance. Perhaps a train whistle blew hello. The rich and toasty scent of logs in a fireplace perfumed black skies, their smoke billowing through bungalow chimneys to offset the dark with white puffs.

The lake had represented her rebirth. Amid Christmas lights and ice skates, she'd merged the timelines. Knocked on the door of a yoga studio and met her sister. Held Timothy's body against hers before riding the dragon through her dreams, down to the twisted river deep in the jungle, and back to her destiny.

Half-gone to there already, Rachel dropped her lids. She had to compose herself before she turned to stone. Or turned the other her to stone. She wasn't sure what that meant, except turning to stone was a concern, a risk.

Besides, she wasn't in Minneapolis, or on a frozen lake, or in a jungle.

She stood in the middle of a parking lot in the south, in a hospital gown and those white clogs smelling faintly of wild animal shit, scrabbling to scratch back from oblivion lost, stolen, or surrendered memories. She was sure that diving into the consciousness of her clone wouldn't accomplish the reattachment of her mind.

"I'm receiving downloads," Rachel said. She'd picked the most apt term to describe the influx of gauzy, surreal imagery flooding her brain. The small, lit-up Christmas tree on a kitchen counter in a high-rise apartment. A woman named Helen. Before, Timothy holding her hand. "A nonstop barrage. Not my memories, exactly, but impressions of them. Their ghosts."

He'd been around to help, before. Not with his truck, but there. Before, when the serpents snapped, and she'd owned a book of spells.

"Fucking excuse me?" her own voice shot back in indignation. "What? Who are you and why do you look exactly like me? Do I have a long-lost twin nobody ever told me about?"

"I can't say for sure." Rachel dragged her lids all the way open and looked at her own eyebrows. She wasn't even sure if this version of herself before her was truly a separate person or a projection, a hologram. Magic was afoot, and not all of it was good. This fact had gelled. "I have amnesia."

"How convenient." The clone eyed the truck over Rachel's shoulder. Timothy had stayed inside to give the two of them some privacy. "Where are you two going? And why are you dressed like a patient? Did you check out of a hospital against medical advice, or what?"

"Sort of. We're headed down south to finish his job, then we're leaving the country. I can tell you as much as I know about what's happening with there being two of us, the forces behind it, but I'm not sure how ready you are to accept the truth. How much your brain can handle."

She raised her eyebrows. "I'm starting to think I need to call my parents and have a really long talk with them about my twin sister who I didn't grow up with. My twin sister who appears to be mentally unsound."

"I wish the explanation were so easy."

"Explanations usually are simple, but we insist on making them more complicated than necessary."

Rachel showed her clone the data stick. "There are answers on here. They aren't going to be feel-good answers. In fact, my guess is they'll blow your entire world apart and make you question everything you thought was consistent or certain. But you're welcome to them. I'd go so far as to say you're entitled to them, as you're a version of me and all. We're going to check into a hotel and start reviewing the contents. Feel free to follow us."

Rachel's double slashed her hand through her hair. A brittle laugh ensued, and she shook her head. "No thanks. Look, I didn't mean to get snappy a minute ago. You're clearly going through a lot. Are you..." she cut a quick glance to the truck and back to Rachel, worry in her eyes. "Are you safe? Do you want me to call the police or an ambulance? I can do it discreetly. He won't know."

"I'm safe, I swear. I want to be here. Timothy's a good guy. He's taking care of me. I promise."

"What happened with the hospital and why did you leave?"

"They were doing experiments on me. Dark ones. Beyond the pale type of stuff. Not standard medical procedures." She sucked in a deep breath. "Evil. Black magic. They said so."

"See, this is where you lose me."

"It's your choice if you want to dip out instead of learning the truth on here." She showed the flash drive again. "Like how it's my choice to stay with Timothy."

"Fair enough. I suppose I'm glad we met. Even though this was the weirdest thing by far that's ever happened to me. I truly wish you the best. Maybe our paths will cross again."

Their resulting hug was stiff and awkward, yet warm at the same time. "Yeah, maybe." Depending on what the fraying, interdimensional network had in store. Rachel would soon see if the flash drive had insights.

As the clone pulled away and walked back to her car, the wind mussed her hair. The lifted pieces came alive in an untamed and ancient way, which Rachel had a hard time putting her finger on. It was almost as if each strand was breathing, twisting with purpose, animated by an instinct separating it from both the elements and the person to whom it was fused.

Before Rachel had more time to ponder the strange vibes of her slightly supernatural witnessing, the stranger who'd been her mirror image was driving away.

She got back in the truck. "I need to see what's on this drive more than ever."

Timothy resumed his drive to the nearest decent hotel. "Didn't she leave?"

"Yeah, why?"

He pointed to the bowling alley next door. A group of three people were walking out. Though each was wearing a different outfit, they were all Rachels.

The initial trio was just the beginning. At the Mexican fast food joint, a Rachel hung out the drive-through window and handed food bags to a Rachel. A third Rachel, this one in a purple uniform and name tag, shuffled out the back door and heaved a full bag of trash into a dumpster.

The Rachels all regarded each other with a casual normalcy suggesting nothing was out of the ordinary. Meaning the laws of the universe had changed since the original clone had confronted Rachel. Change didn't sit well because it implied unpredictability. Rachel gaped at a full-sized Rachel crammed into a stroller and fidgeting with a plastic toy. "We need to get to a hotel business center right now."

"Has anything else come back to you?" Timothy drove them to their hotel of choice.

Once he'd settled in the parking area, she hastily changed into the clothes he'd bought a while back. Upon spotting the food in the bag, her stomach growled. She couldn't remember the last time she'd eaten or which foods she liked and disliked. This made her sad. She missed the everyday elements of her personality as much, if not more, than the burning questions about how she'd ended up on a road trip with a random trucker, tearing a dirty medical gown off her body in a cheap hotel parking lot.

She peeled a banana and finished it in three big bites. "I think I fucked around with magic in the past. Whatever I did led to some chain reaction that got me in really hot water." She set the peel back in the bag. For a fleeting instant, the three strips of flayed yellow flesh had the same sentient quality of her clone's hair. Watching her, eyeless, and perceptive of the environment. She sighed heavily. "What does the notion of magic mean to you?"

"Things aren't always what they seem. Our expectations can upend in ways we've never imagined being possible. Connections and cause and effect are processes with a nuance greatly exceeding the bounds of scientific norms."

She looked at him for a long time, taking in his profile of high cheekbones and a chiseled jaw illuminated by an everyday mystique conveyed by dashboard lights. She felt warm and content inside for the first time in ages. "You're a really thoughtful guy."

He tilted his head a few degrees in her direction. Though he wasn't smiling, he was. "Let's get you inside."

A Rachel checked them in. She acted like nothing was wrong. This version had two full sleeves of arm tattoos popping against her black uniform polo. Her name tag aptly read "Rachel," which somehow felt like a mockery. "I'll need a credit card for incidentals." Fake nails clacked against the computer keys. "Continental breakfast is from six to nine. Two keys?"

Timothy nodded and paid. He'd slung a duffel bag over his shoulder.

"Do you have a business center?" Rachel clutched her flash drive. She hadn't let go of it since she'd acquired it out of fear that if she let it out of her sight, she'd never see it again.

"Right over there." The clerk pointed to a closed door with a sign on it. A swimsuit-clad Rachel walked by, drinking from a can of pop. The clerk added, "Pool closes at nine."

She thought of the eyes of the first Rachel, the near drowning in the tide pool wake of boundaries blurred and gulfs crossed. Would the Rachels all eventually merge, blend, subsume, and fold into one another until they were a hive, a collective of nodal bees obeying the dark-hearted queen? Did the queen still rule in all her folly?

Rachel's heart skipped a beat. She wasn't sure why. "I know who I am," she blurted out.

The clerk looked stunned.

Timothy took control of Rachel's elbow and guided her away. "Thank you," he said to the worker.

As they walked to their room, Rachel's mind half-in and half-elsewhere, she was overcome with the realization she'd been here before. She'd had red hair then, and fire magic. She'd been with a man named Thom who played music professionally. Actually, she'd only checked out of the hotel as the redhead.

She'd checked in as a blonde, an air witch with the power to control the flow of financial currency. She'd had a baby dragon on her shoulder then and been traveling on a motorcycle with a black-haired man who wore a leather jacket and was in possession of a secret book.

Before, she'd shifted her shape into a white wolf. "They put microchips in my body." Rachel rested her forehead against the hallway and stroked the walls. The skin of her palms kept her in the material world even as the rest of her left, journeyed, and linked with the other five. "They experimented on me then too. They tried to take my baby. Twice. I destroyed them with water. A tidal wave. But they came back. They always come back."

God, that was it. She heard herself moan as she rubbed the wall, pressing the front of her body against the wallpaper, desperate for grounding. It felt so good to drift and float, to sync up with her coven sisters (Yes, they were sister witches! Memories were in there after all.) and feel the easy pleasure of becoming a mere thread in a knot of yarn made of many souls. But she had to resist to retain the information. The downloads were coming fast and furious.

She'd met herself when she'd been the other experiment. She'd been in a Scarab chamber where an evil ritual was underway. In those white stone chambers, windowless catacombs, she'd worn a robe and seen things she wasn't supposed to see. Blood sacrifice. Insides on the outside.

She remembered herself, her Rachel self, entranced. She'd had the snake hair, then, the head full of snakes. Her Medusa programming had come to fruition.

The experiment. The secret weapon. The killer gaze. The black goo injected into her, connecting her lineage to that of the Titans who would rise once again, those abominations tapped by the dark-hearted queen to lord and rule, to feast on the life forces of the honeycomb captives.

Rachel's heart beat too fast. Her breath struggled to keep up, coming out in clipped gasps. She heard herself yell as she tried to wake herself up, to put some space between herself and the downloads. "I know who I am!" she screamed, her vision blacking. "I know who I am!"

A two-handed pull peeled her away from the wall in one strong tug, and she was moving again, the other person guiding her to take fast steps. The downloads kept coming.

Before she'd been the other experiment, she'd been Eve, but not the Eve from the garden. Unless it was all the same Eve, at the end of the day, the destination at the end of all roads. She'd been an Eve who worked with the dead, both their bodies and their souls, preparing them simultaneously for their funerals and their trips to the afterlife. She'd been the first of the witches to see a Pollyanna. The Pollyannas were back—with them right now. Another ragged scream erupted. These Pollyannas were dumb but dangerous. They were scary tools.

A door shut. Her bottom made contact with a soft surface. In the next download, she was Helen, who was the most powerful, in a way, even though she was also the gentlest. The one who could travel through space time with relative, seamless ease. The one with the most porous boundary between her bounded self and the metaphysical world. The spirit witch.

"Keep going for a little bit longer," Helen's voice assured. "The timelines are merging. You're doing it. Stick with the plan. I'm in Peru, and I'm safe and sound. We did it. We merged me. I'm here waiting for you. All five of us are here in the circle, holding the line to keep the portal closed. You are doing your assigned part, and you're doing great. Keep moving forward."

Helen's words were comforting but how could Rachel honor her and the other witches when she was dissolving, falling apart, and gripped by entropy? She wasn't bringing anything together. She was too weak.

"It feels like it," Helen said. "But it isn't correct. Push the trains back onto a single track. You can do it."

Rock music filled the room. A band she recognized; a famous song called *Deep Dark Woods*. A burst of fire erupted between Rachel's brows. She screamed and screamed, purging pressure while pushing with all her might to shove all six of the trains onto a single track. The tracks all resisted at first, pushing back so hard her temples pounded in agony, but she kept pushing. Then four resisted, then two. Then all lacked the fortitude to stop her efforts. Folly was no match for Rachel.

Pressure and pain dissolved in a bath of relief. Rachel was marathon-spent. Cleaned out. Exhausted. She melted into the support of the mattress and drifted off.

✳

A BUMP IN THE ROAD JOLTED RACHEL OUT OF HER SLUMBER. SHE snapped to a sitting position, rubbing the groggy fuzz out of her eyes. A full sun of daylight shone beyond Timothy's windshield. Fuzzy dice swung back and forth in a perpetual rhythm, suspended from his rearview mirror. "How long was I out?"

"A few hours." He glanced at her and back at the road. "We'll be there soon. We'll drop the cargo and the truck, spend a night at Julian's old place, then we're off to Peru."

She was going to Peru to connect with her fellow witches. After the trial in Minneapolis where she'd aligned Helen to the right timeline, she and Timothy had set off to uncover the truth of what had happened to her. After they'd infiltrated a Scarab lab, she'd been captured again. They had subjected her to more experiments before she'd escaped, and he'd tracked her down in his truck and rescued her. And here they were. She'd been without her memories for a while. In amnesia. Wait, was that right? How did he get the truck? Some of her memories might have been off, the details mixed up, but she knew she was safe, and the puzzle of her past was slowly piecing itself together.

She was grateful to have snatches of her past back, but the chain of events didn't feel entirely right. There were gaps and parts that didn't make complete sense. "Where were we coming from right before this?"

"The hotel in Arkansas. We were in some version of reality where everyone was you." He chanced another careful glance her way. "Remember?"

"No. The last thing I remember was when you came back for me."

His brow knitted. "Came back for you?"

"After I escaped the Scarab facility, remember? You got this truck and found me along the highway."

"That was the first time I saw you. Scarab rings a bell, though. This cargo is headed to Scarab."

A chill swept through her. "You're working for Scarab?"

"Not exactly. I accepted an odd job from them before I had any idea of what they got up to. The full extent of their experiments and such. Had I known who captured you, I never would have picked up the job."

Exit signs indicated a large town ahead. "Pull off at the next exit."

"Rachel, I'm telling the truth. I need you to believe me."

"I know. I do. I need to get inside a library. Bigger towns have those. I never looked at the data stick at the hotel, did I?"

"No. I mentioned it this morning, but you said you wanted to leave right away. You seemed a little disoriented. Not quite all there."

"I've felt disoriented for a long time. And my lack of memory this morning means the timelines aren't fully aligned yet. Pull off and map the nearest library. I'm going to put this to bed once and for all and reclaim every single one of my memories."

Timothy listened. Soon, they were driving down a busy street, the GPS on his phone chirping directions in a feminine voice. She tapped her foot when they hit a stoplight, fixing her stare on the red circle and exhaling when it turned green.

The nearest library was a newer building, three stories, heavy on tall windows gleaming in the unclouded sun. He parked in the back of the lot, and they hiked across concrete. She was grateful they'd arrived during hours of operation, as if this precise outcome was meant to be. It wouldn't surprise her anymore if every step along her life path was led by the hand of fate. She crossed her fingers that the guiding force, if there was one, wished her the best.

Twin towers of glass doors greeted them. Inside, the library was cavernous, empty but for a blue-haired front desk clerk in an anime hoodie. Right behind the help desk was a row of desktop computers lined up against a railing overlooking a lower area filled with children's books and colorful furniture.

Rachel was shaky when she sat down. The drive was in her back pocket. She fumbled for it, nearly dropping the tiny device with her sweaty hand. Poising its metal tip against the corresponding USB port, she looked back at Timothy.

He squeezed her shoulder and nodded once. He was here to support her. She could do this. She could handle this.

Rachel plugged in the stick. The hard drive buzzed for a few seconds, and a white box popped up on the screen. Inside it were icons for many files.

TWENTY-FOUR

Not long ago, Rachel had been no one. A blank slate. A tabula rasa. A snowflake melted into nonexistence. Someone whose unique, individual identity survived only as a bygone state, a lost relic, watery remnants floating around in other peoples' memories.

Now, she was overfull. Too much and not enough. A vessel for downloads.

A witch.

An experiment.

The architect of her own destiny.

A mover of many universes.

The lynchpin of a prophecy.

An agent of chaos. Chaos magic incarnate.

Some might say a chosen one, but only a sick joker would choose this trajectory. Perhaps a demented clown was her and her alone, casting the dice of weird, wild magic and letting them fall where they may.

In a slow, deliberate motion, she clicked the red circle to close the window showing the files on the drive. She was numb, yet strangely calm. Her brain buzzed. She steered through the pathway to eject the disk. It may have still been populating. She didn't care. She didn't need to see any more. Before she yanked the drive, she looked up the email addresses for several local reporters. Next, she made herself a fake email and sent the journalists a collection of files exposing Scarab's atrocities. It wasn't much, but perhaps one of the reporters would pick up the case and run with it. This was as much as Rachel could do to keep her promise to the woman at the lab.

Seated beside her on one of the plastic library chairs, Timothy looked on. "What was on there?"

How to even begin to think about how to explain? The story of her, from birth onward. The experiment leaving her with snakes erupting from her scalp. Her chaos magic, dormant in her marrow, activated in the dark lab.

Escaping Scarab. The sister witches. Peru, the first Timothy. Her history with him.

Their reunion on the side of the road. Destiny didn't even begin to describe it.

Her grimoire, the sacred book of magic that'd come to her by mystical birthright.

Found, surrendered, reclaimed, lost, and found again—this time her book of magic appeared as page after page of digital files.

There was no way some random worker in a lab collected all the information and placed those files on the disk.

For a few moments, words escaped her. Finally, she gazed into his brown eyes. How much did he remember of her? Would he ever remember, or was the first version forgotten forever?

It was as if she'd transferred her amnesia to him. As she'd come to remember, guided by the files, his lack of knowing had come to constitute its own kind of forgetting. He'd waited patiently for her to process the raft of context in front of her, even though the more she absorbed, the farther she slipped away from him. "Everything."

Her memories of them returned slowly at first, in gradual trickles. Déjà vu. Wisps of recollection, like the feel of skating rink ice under her blades as they'd whirled around the white oval, their gloved hands joined.

Other worlds. The eyeball under the bunker. She had one idea, and one idea only, for how to route this version of Timothy back onto her timeline. One place to put them back on track. One place to serve as a node, the final meeting point for the six witches and their energetic fields.

"Do you remember?" He held her hand. "A version of us...from before?" His stare looked hopeful, like he wished she did. Like he wished he did.

"I do." She squeezed his fingers. "Let's go to Peru."

Having served its purpose, the library soon ended up in their literal and figurative rear-view mirrors.

Once in the truck again, Rachel's lids sagged, and she slept. On and off at first, groggy and dreamless, then deeper. Dreams rushed at her in waves, magic and memories, reuniting her with herself. When she awoke, she was both parched and calmer than she'd been in ages.

Sunrise spread across the horizon in a bleed of white and pink. They approached a big city where architectural feats scraped the sky with slopes of glass and steel. She drank lukewarm water from a plastic bottle. "How long was I out?"

"The rest of the drive. We're in Austin. One more stop, then we head to Julian's house and we're off."

"How are we getting to Peru from Julian's house?" Shit. In the frenzy, an avalanche of logistics had been left unaccounted for. Rachel hadn't exactly had a moment to slow down and make a checklist. "I don't have a passport."

His smile was cryptic. "Sure you do."

Under normal circumstances, she'd have clocked about a hundred red flags on this guy by now, but she trusted Timothy implicitly. She knew their past. How he'd fought to protect her. "What's the last stop?"

His smile faded into a press of the lips. "There's something I have to tell you. I want you to understand this all happened before I met you and you told me what you've been through."

He exited onto a pothole-littered ramp. They drove past two office buildings, a paper mill, and other staples of an industrial neighborhood before he slowed down at a warehouse loading dock. He pulled into a driveway, rolled down his window, and plugged a number into a code box. With a groan, two panels of a rusted metal fence parted to make way for the truck. The lot was empty, which seemed strange, though she couldn't say why.

The truck hissed as Timothy put the vehicle in reverse and backed it into a port. "I took a job for Scarab when I had no idea who they were or what they were into. I don't ask many questions about these trucking gigs. I think there's something bad back there. Living creatures. I'm so sorry. I didn't want to subject you to this."

"We're not at a Scarab building." She pointed to the windowless slab of sheet metal making up the side of the warehouse. "Look."

The logo was a cartoon beetle with goofy bubble eyes. Curved around the body of the mascot was the brand name in round, childish letters: Polly & Anna's Toys. Rachel giggled. She was starting to get it. This timeline, the one that neutralized Scarab, had a sense of humor.

"What's so funny?" He checked the GPS panel mounted to his dashboard. "This is absolutely the right address. I thought you'd be upset. Or at least have questions."

"Oh, I have questions. Come on. Hurry up and drop this stuff off. I want to see how it plays out."

He lined up the truck and waited until an airy hiss cut through the cab and a jolt let her know the trailer had connected. They got out and walked to a service door where he pushed a red button.

An old man in a yellow construction hat greeted them gruffly and led them into the belly of the warehouse gaping with openness and high ceilings.

Timothy crouched and pulled open the door to the truck's trailer while Rachel watched with interest.

The old man returned riding a forklift. "We'll take it from here." Inside the trailer were stacks of cardboard boxes, stacked high and secured to each other with plastic wrapping. "I have no idea how these ugly things got so popular." He snorted and began to load his forklift. "Must've been social media."

One of the boxes had fallen, the impact having damaged the packing material. A gray hump poked out from a gash in the cardboard. The aged man dismounted his ride and walked to the damaged stock. He squatted, pulled a box cutter from the back pocket of his jeans, and split open the box the rest of the way. "Inventory takes into account a margin for losses of goods damaged in transit. How'd I do with my business-speak?"

The worker pried loose an item about the size of a bowling ball. It took Rachel a few seconds to register what the man held in his wrinkled hands, and, once she did, she had to swallow laughter.

The stuffed animal was hideous. Its head was too big for its body, its centipede legs were too small to support its bulk, and skin the color of rotten hamburger did not suggest "cuddly." Two black plastic beads were all it had for eyes, and white fabric teeth filled the gaping mouth like tiny paper hats.

So much for the Pollyannas. Rachel slapped her hand over her mouth. She wasn't sure whether to laugh or cry.

Timothy met her eyes. "I swear they were moving earlier."

The old man shook the plushie in the air and made a fake, comical spooky noise like he was a restless haunt. "Too freaky for a kid's bedroom if you ask me." He tossed the toy to Timothy, who caught it in a reluctant grab. "But maybe you know someone who's bought into the hype." He chortled again. "Pollyanna. Such a weird name for something like this. Anyway, thanks for delivering the load on time. You kids take care now." He went back to work with his forklift, sliding packs of boxes onto the forks of his industrial vehicle.

Rachel and Timothy looked at each other. A million unspoken thoughts and many lifetimes of emotions stitched a yoke of recognition between them.

Timothy handed her the plushie.

The old man shrugged.

Back on the highway, headed south past sprawling shopping centers and chain restaurants, Rachel rode with the Pollyanna in her lap. Incomprehensible, how she'd witnessed one of these things alive a short while ago, making a snack of a man's face. A short while ago. She thought of time so easily, so neatly, as if its increments were laid out in a straight line made of tidy packets. "Want to hear my theory on chaos magic?"

Timothy appeared unfazed as he drove down a two-lane highway overlooking a mess of trees and underbrush. "Sure."

"It's a deliberate rupture of the space-time continuum disrupting laws of physics and principles of cause and effect. Upending the taken for granted, in every sense of the term."

"Maybe that explains me."

"Huh?"

"I think you put a spell on me." He winked.

"Are you flirting?" If so, he had a strange way of going about it.

"I'll show you once we're back at Julian's place."

"Why are we waiting for Julian's place?"

"It's special."

She was sick of asking questions and posing challenges. There was freedom, and power, in letting things simply be. Especially in the world she was coming to know. Living in harmony with her environment was starting to mean surrendering the urge to fight it. She held up the Pollyanna. "Any memories of these when they were alive?"

"I've dreamt of them."

He hadn't let on a whiff of recognition back at the warehouse. "You sure are a cool customer."

"I've learned to go with the flow."

"Same here. I'm learning, at least."

A couple more turnoffs onto smaller and darker streets, and Timothy approached a wrought-iron gate. He jumped out and opened a latch.

The truck barely fit into what was apparently Julian's long driveway, but it fit enough for Timothy to hop out and close the gate behind them. The gesture had a certain finality to it, making Rachel's chest ache. She sensed they were coming to an end, but an end was okay because endings led to beginnings. Every beginning was born from an end.

The bittersweet essence of the circle would spin eternally.

Suddenly dreamy, spacey, Rachel looked out her window and up to the sky. For a fleeting glimmer, she saw the flaming wheel, a golden hoop whose curls of fire hooked into the firmament to keep it turning in perpetual motion.

The flaming chariot powered them all. Generating, spinning, weaving. She blinked, and the wheel was gone.

"Ready?" Timothy asked.

The unknown beckoned. She had no plan, no outline, no strategy. "As ready as I'll ever be."

He walked around the front of the truck, opened her door, and held her hand while she stepped down. Warmth filled her chest, a soft and expansive feeling. Such a strange moment for chivalry, but strange didn't mean unwanted. In silent acknowledgement of a gentle bond, they walked hand-in-hand as Timothy led Rachel into the backyard.

The lot was decent-sized, an unfenced acre or two flanked by short trees and underbrush. In the middle sat a hut, a domed structure about the size of a garage made of stone or brick.

She ducked to enter through a carved doorway. Glimmers of light drew her attention to the top, where a plate-sized hole had been cut to let in starlight, sunlight, or both.

Timothy joined her on the dirt ground beneath the opening. She felt suddenly vulnerable and clutched the silly, grotesque Pollyanna, which only made her feel ridiculous in addition to vulnerable.

Instead of two beady, black eyes, this doll had one black eye and one eye that was clear and crystalline. Her clear crystal had returned and was safely secured now. "Julian is expecting us?"

Timothy dipped his chin in the affirmative. "Before we do this, I want you to know something. Even though you won't have evidence for what I'm about to say, I want you to trust I'm telling you my truth."

Part of her wanted to ask what it was they were about to do, because the context felt serious and a little scary. But the way Timothy looked at her with those earnest eyes, after all he'd done for her, she'd be remiss to focus on anything but him. She wanted to know whatever it was he wanted to say. His warmth enveloped her. They'd been through so much. That much of their struggle was lost to the primordial soup of their shared unconscious only made their bond more profound.

Chaos bound them, and Rachel was learning to let go and embrace the madness. There was a profound, almost poetic beauty to the crazy. It was theirs and theirs alone. With her silent acknowledgement, she let him know she was listening.

He slipped his hand to her face and cupped her cheek. His touch soothed her into a calm state. She was cared for. She closed her eyes and awaited his words.

"I remember." His deep voice was a lullaby. "Remember is the wrong word because I don't remember our time together in the typical sense. But those memories beat in my heart. My dreams and my blood. I haven't forgotten you, Rachel, and I never will. Even when I'm gone." He sucked in a breath. "I'll love you forever, even after I'm gone."

Her throat went thick. The back of her nose stung. A tear slipped down her cheek in a wet stream.

His lips connected to the corner of her mouth in a dry press as he took away her tear. All her tears. She didn't need them anymore. When he moved his mouth to hers and brought them together in a kiss, she let herself dissolve. Joined with Timothy, her great love, she'd leave the rest behind.

I remember, she heard herself whisper somewhere far away. *I'll remember forever and never forget.*

Her heartbeat accelerated, unless the thrum was his or the combination of their life forces threading together into a series of infinite loops building upon one another and knitting a tapestry of black and purple magic.

He kissed her softly at first, a gentle and closed-mouth exploration, before parting her lips with his tongue to probe her. His tongue was firm, confident, and she nudged her own into his. This kiss wasn't sexual, exactly. It was deliberate, a ritual, a ceremony whose rules were an occulted secret meant solely for the two of them.

She consumed him, and he, her, the comingled flow of their breaths carrying them on a tide of life flowing through the veins of the tapestry to feed the everlasting heart—the new heart.

Rachel was the dark heart now. As she embraced her true love, she dissolved the honeycomb with her chaos magic. The veil to the Other Place firmed up, buttressed by her self-spun network of glowing loops.

As the flaming hoop whirled through the sky, it caught the final scrap of Folly, now no more than a weak slip of energy, and broke her to bits under its spokes of fire.

As the chariot of fire passed over the hut, a blinding light poured in from the roof's opening.

Though her eyes were closed, Rachel had to squint more than she'd ever squinted in her entire life. But she kept kissing Timothy because their union was what crafted this new reality. They were the force filling the dark heart with fresh energy, imbuing her with the lifeblood to halt the prophecy once and for all.

Once the light was too much to bear, Rachel found herself careening through a tunnel of light and color interspersed with pockets of darkness. She flew head over feet, heels over face, all sense of direction lost.

With a collapsed-lung gasp, Rachel rocketed back to consciousness. The air was warm and muggy. Lush forest surrounded her. She was seated, unsteadily. On water. In a rowboat.

Beside her, Timothy pulled a fishing line out of murky water. A large catch flopped on the end of his pole.

Between them sat the stuffed Pollyanna, looking up at Rachel with its comically hideous predator's smile. A universe reflected back to her in one clear crystal.

Her life flashed before her eyes in a breakneck barrage of vignettes. The portal at Julian's. Scarab stuffed animals. A road trip in Timothy's truck. Her run through the woods and prior escape. The defeat of Folly, the lab, the eyeball palace. Ice skating. Helen. Strawberry ice cream not more than a mile from here. The jaguar shifter slowly turning to stone.

"I've been here before." Déjà vu took her for a roller coaster ride. "This exact spot. In a dream, maybe, or the past."

"Another timeline," Timothy said with calm resolve. "We merged them. We did it."

She was almost too stunned to process the weight of his declaration. "What do we do now?"

Timothy put his catch in a bucket, gathered up the fishing supplies, and got out of the boat. He offered her his hand, and she accepted his grip and stepped out onto the riverbank mud.

He brought her hand to his lips and kissed the top, the gesture charming and whimsical enough to make her smile despite the psychic whiplash still making a meal of her.

Timothy said, "We're going to go back to my place and spend approximately the next two days in bed. Then we'll pop a bottle of champagne and listen to Florence and the Machine."

She cast herself into his arms, where they hugged for a long, long time.

Cocooned in the wonderful embrace of chaos magic watching over the witches and shifters forever, they held each other.

A blanket was then woven with the truest love to sustain all their kind with the black and purple lifeblood of the new heart.

***

Thank you for reading! Did you enjoy? Please add your review because nothing helps an author more and encourages readers to take a chance on a book than a review.

And don't miss more in the *Coven Daughters* series coming soon! Until then read EMBERS, the first novella in the *Coven Daughters Origins*, available now. Turn the page for a sneak peek!

Also be sure to sign up for the City Owl Press newsletter to receive notice of all book releases!

SNEAK PEEK OF EMBERS

Thom James couldn't pinpoint, with absolute certainty, when awareness of a void in his heart switched from minor nuisance to undeniable ache. On the latest routine morning in a long string, though, the abyss had stolen more than usual.

He pulled in a drag of cigarette smoke, the woodsy flavor more rote than satisfying as a rush of chemicals cancelled out the minty flavor of toothpaste. An exhale left his lungs in a choppy whoosh, his breath ejecting filmy gray residue. Here he was again, going through the motions.

He touched the cold glass of his hotel suite window and stared down at Nashville. Or Raleigh. Or perhaps his band had played Atlanta last night. Maybe they'd delivered their music to an arena of thirty-thousand cheering faces in Orlando or Dallas.

Didn't matter. This midsize city at morning was the same as any other: paper doll cutouts of buildings, drab redbrick and concrete tones, crumbling infrastructure. The theater of the mundane unfolded twenty stories below while he watched in a fruitless search for affect or even inspiration. A smattering of affordable cars lurched to jobs. A man wearing a backpack scurried down a sidewalk, prompting a cluster of pigeons to lift off in frantic flight.

Nearing the end of his forties and having played cities like this since his teen years, Thom had seen it all.

He'd felt the previous night, yes he had, high on the usual maelstrom of lust and fame.

At night, cities were sexy, glitter-sprinkled light shows teeming with promises, spectacles tailored to cater to the appetites. Come morning, though, they were little more than blight on the landscape. Interchangeable, half-real, used.

He spied a silver arch not far off in the distance, an artistic piece of architecture curving toward the clouds amid downtown buildings that weren't quite skyscrapers. Right, they'd played St. Louis the night before. That's where he was, not that it mattered.

A cynical bark of a laugh jumped out of his lips. Hollow mornings were the price he paid for his indulgent nights. The rock star's debt always came due.

From behind him came a soft, feminine moan. The bed squeaked, and the latest woman occupying whatever he called his bed sighed. The tomb in his chest gaped wider, a mocking reminder that a well-adjusted man would feel tender emotions right about now. His stomach tightened as his head spun. He stubbed out his smoke on the windowsill, snuffing his ennui.

Water rushed from the bathroom sink. Bodily noises of teeth getting scrubbed, gargling, and spitting followed. Thom smiled sadly. If their time together had been intended to be more than one night, the sounds of her freshening up might inspire intimate anticipation.

"Hey." Her voice, thick with sleep, belied a lilt of hope that toppled dominoes of guilt and regret inside him.

He turned to where she stood. A thin, white sheet swaddled her supple form, shielding the soft breasts that he'd enjoyed to the fullest. Her full-chest tattoo peeked out from the top of the material in coy glimpses of flowers crawling through emerald networks of jungle foliage.

His gaze travelled through the artwork on her chest and up to her lips, across freckled cheeks and northward to eyes as green as fresh-cut summertime grass. An inferno of chaotic red waves blazed past her shoulders.

She was quite pretty. Beautiful even, in an unconventional way with her strong features and robust bone structure. Ultimately, though, just another groupie. Another American woman in a city he couldn't place.

He didn't even know her name.

God, she deserved so much better than an empty fuck from the lowlife likes of him.

"Hi." He slid a piece of her hair through his fingers, appreciating the silkiness as he reminded himself not to be a dick. Quality aftercare in these situations kept his reputation sterling. "Sleep well?"

"Yeah. You knocked my ass out. I think it was that second orgasm that did me in. Or maybe the third. I'm pretty sure I'll have sweet dreams of the sexy British rocker for the rest of my life." With a siren's smirk, she snagged his pack of smokes off the nightstand and lit up.

Blowing rails through her nostrils, she jutted her chin in parry. Or defiance, daring him to condescend to her. Bloody hell. This bird was a live wire like none other, crackling with white heat.

Thom tilted his head to one side. Her brazenness, a shameless quality to her, piqued his intrigue. He slipped a finger into the swell of her cleavage and loosened the fabric concealing her breasts. "What's your name?"

She blew smoke in his face, the blast making him cough and blink as his eyes burned, though she didn't resist when her sheet fell to the floor. "You're an absolute pig." A touch of levity to her true statement betrayed affection. "Luckily for you, the accent *almost* makes up for it."

"You're still here. And naked again, I might add." Beneath his unbuttoned jeans, his prick swelled. He plucked the cigarette from her mouth, laid it in the ashtray, and guided her back to bed with two firm hands pushing against the velvety slopes of her shoulders.

"Touché." She walked backward in accordance with his motions, running slender fingers through the mat of hair covering his bare chest. The redhead flopped on the bed and spread her legs, her crooked smile both vulnerable and caustic. "I have a lot of problems."

His hands were busy attacking his zipper when fresh waves of shame and disgust pummeled him. Christ, what was wrong with him, screwing women as if they were mere objects? What a scoundrel he was.

"I'm so sorry." He slashed a hand through his hair, the strands as unkempt as the rest of his life, and pulled his thick mess into a ponytail in some pitifully symbolic effort to order his chaos. "Are you hungry? I can have some room service sent up if you'd prefer discretion, but if you'd like to go out, that's fine too. Or I can call you a car if you're ready to get out of here."

Her smile spread while she appraised him with a knowing, green-eyed gaze. "You don't need to pay me with food. I'm a slut, not a whore.

Nothing against whores, but judge me correctly." Though she spoke in a jesting tone, her words cut like a scalpel.

She hadn't closed her legs—gorgeous pink pussy, trimmed strip of red hair—but now Thom wasn't sure if he felt aroused, embarrassed, ashamed, or some unwholesome mix of all three. He stood there blinking like an idiot, his face hot and a nest of brown pubes sprouting through his open fly while a spotlight shone on his mortified conscience.

"You aren't either one of those." He stammered, his mouth dry. Though he meant what he said—his promiscuous arse had no right to pass judgment—the words came off forced and ridiculous. "You're a beautiful person. I wished I would have gotten to know you a little better before we ended up naked."

He meant that too. Yet some unseen force stopped him, time and again, from seeking out a deeper level of intimacy with women. It was easier to approach them as empty conquests.

Easier to forget them. Easier to keep his emotional wall high and solid.

She smacked her forehead. "A beautiful person? That's the cringiest platitude I've ever heard. Can we please fuck? I don't need to witness you thumping every branch on the way down to rock bottom."

Tension and self-consciousness flew out of him in an inexplicable gust. For all his cavorting and playing the part of boorish lout, Thom never quite felt at ease or at peace. He envied the woman on the bed, how she lay there open and free, unshaken.

"Nice metaphor." He swiped the half-burned cigarette out of the ashtray, drew down a hit, and handed the smoke to his temporary partner. "Were you an English major?" She had to be in her mid-thirties and was articulate enough to be a college grad.

Her ample chest swelled as she partook, falling when she blew out three wobbly smoke rings. He studied the multicolor splash of ink capping her breasts and marveled at the way those inquisitive eyes of hers tracked the vapory hoops as they floated before dissipating. "I'm an English professor."

He sat next to her on the bed, and she scooted over to accommodate. Considering her cue, he trailed three kisses from her shoulder to her collarbone, seeking her scent. Floral and spicy notes mixed with her tang from below. Her exotic scent suited her perfectly, even in the stark light of day. "That's sexy. Will you read to me?"

"Why, can't you read?"

For the first time, he noticed precise details of her voice. Beneath the smokiness and snark lay a melody. She spoke like a song, her rhythm rising and falling. Thom buried his face in her neck, sampling her flesh with teasing flicks of his tongue. She whined a little pleasure noise, and with that he was stiff as a bat again. "Tell me your name. Please."

"No. It's more fun this way. Anonymous."

He urged his cock from his pants and rubbed the swollen head against the soft expanse of her outer thigh, seeking relief from the pressure building in his lower belly.

"Well, you're anonymous to me, sweetheart. I'm a famous bassist, and you know exactly who I am."

The feel of his own hot breath against her skin, the arrogant truth of his cocky words, made boiling cum swirl in his balls. Sure, he got off on his own fame, notoriety, and status. No fool would dare nominate him for sainthood.

"Your ego is out of control." She punched her hips up, and he took the cue and danced teasing fingertips down her smooth stomach. "And I actually don't know you. Right now I have the idea of you, the fantasy. Which is precisely what I want."

"Fair enough." His pulse accelerated. Blood fled his brain and filled his engorged cock. As his eyes feasted upon his partner's inviting form, he took a moment to admire the length and girth of his impressive member, the healthy purple coloring of the swollen tip. He could not wait to feed this luscious, vexing piece of feminine excellence to his hungry beast.

But for now, her pleasure was his priority. Thom might be a cad, but at least he left his bedmates with fond memories of his skills. "What do you want me to do, love? Finger you? Eat you? Rub my dick over your clit?"

"Damn, I'm all about your dirty talk." Her thighs quivered, the musky smell of her arousal intensifying.

He played with the soft curls on her mound, kneeling between her legs to admire her swollen folds and the visible bulge of her sensitive nub. He sunk two fingers inside her, licking his lips at the first touch of pussy, a tease of what his prick wanted so bad. In smooth motions, he moved those two fingers in and out, every ounce of his being committed to holding off on the raging urge to plunge inside of her and take, take, take.

"Yeah," she said, eyes glazed and lips parted.

"You want me to use my fingers?" His rod flexed, a bead of pre-cum leaking out.

Driving women crazy with his talents made him feel like a god. The potent rush of ego beat a quick one-off any day.

"Please." She sat up, her eyelids and pale lashes hooding her eyes when her gaze fell to the piston work of his hand.

"Jesus, I can see your clit. I can see how big and full it is, ripe." He withdrew from her opening and used the two slick fingers to spread her folds, making a V through which the glistening button popped like a red candy apple.

She moaned a reply and began to pinch and rub her own stiff nipples.

"I'm going to stroke your clit now, slowly with my thumb. I don't want you to come too fast, but you're so round and red I don't know if I'll be able to prolong your climax. Forgive me."

Another unintelligible grunt from Ms. Articulate English Professor. Christ, this was fun.

He'd circle back to this very moment every time he felt a flare of remorse about how freely he fucked around.

He brought the pad of his thumb to her target, admiring the smooth, slick feel of the bump as he stroked in a big circle. A few passes around, and her clit went into spasms. She lost control, bucking and moaning as she came apart.

Using his opposite hand, Thom slid a finger back into her, hooking his digit on her equally flush G-spot, and rubbed methodically. Her inner muscles clenched and released all around his plunges, her body's responses proof of orgasm.

With a sharp cry, she froze. Her eyes stretched wide, and her jaw dropped. "Oh fuck, I'm coming."

"You sure are." Once she was done, he grabbed his dick and stroked up and down, slowly, offering a little show. "You ready for more?"

"Hell yes."

"Ah, give me that fiery red pussy, baby." With an unbridled growl, he fell on her and plunged inside her pocket of warm, liquid heaven. She'd sworn last night that she was on the pill, and he trusted that she was telling the truth.

Firm walls molded around his cock, sucking like hungry mouths as he mindlessly thrust in and out. "Goddamn, that's some bloody good snatch." He cupped one of her large breasts, pumping hard and fast in selfish pursuit of release.

"Thanks." She wrapped her legs around his hips and dragged her trimmed nails down his back. "I take good care of it. Only the best."

A laugh, this one earnest and bereft of the poison of cynicism, sprang from his lips. A weird, bubbly sensation cavorted in Thom, unnerving but not unwelcome. He slowed his strokes and gazed deeply into his partner's pretty eyes. "Does this feel good?"

"Yes," she whispered, squeezing his shoulders. His lover smiled at him, and the bubbles in his chest and abdomen swelled larger.

He kissed the tip of her nose before resuming his work, taking care this time to angle his pelvis so the root of his shaft connected with her clit when he withdrew on the down stroke.

When she began to moan again and her walls tightened and released in time, Thom closed his eyes and savored her. Her smell, her sounds, the comforts of her softness and sex. A lump lodged in his throat, and the inside of his nose stung. He'd never made love, but perhaps his current experience of the sex act amounted to a poor man's version.

"Thom, you're so good." She fell limp.

Before he could think too much about those false words she spoke and what it would mean for them to become true, he sped his plunges to the frantic, needy pace required to bring him home.

Her eyes darkened into a dirty, sinful stare. "You're about to come. Your balls are high and tight now, huh? Full of a big load you can't wait to blow."

"You're so fucking hot I can't stand it." He clutched her tit, his skin tingling as he rushed to the end. Base, unspeakable need overcame him, the tension below his waist ratcheting to a fiendish craving.

"Come all over me."

Heat unspooled near the base of his shaft. He gaped at the spot where their bodies joined, marveling at the wonder of his prick slipping in and out, his rigid flesh coated with the glisten of her juices. The second relief tore in, he pulled out and gave three final tugs right below the ridge of the head.

Thom cried out while he splintered into shocks of ecstasy. Blank and blissed with awestruck emptiness, he gawked as thick white ropes splashed her breasts, hair, and cheek.

"Fuck." Aftershocks reverberated through his body. He rubbed his stomach and squeezed his still-stiff member until the final drops of fluid eked out and dripped onto her chest.

"Now lick it off me and feed it back into my mouth."

"Pardon?" He struggled to regulate his breathing, clobbered by the double whammy of a life-erasing orgasm and her request. No woman had ever asked *that* of him.

"You heard me."

Lost in the haze of her thrall, he obeyed, scooping up his own bittersweet semen with eager lips and tongue. When he took her mouth, he forgot all about the nasty, kinky deed and melted into their first kiss.

And what a first kiss it was.

Her effort was predictably assertive, skilled from practice, though more sensual than he would have guessed. But as their tongues stroked, played, gave, and took in a series of caresses and lazy searching, a frighteningly glorious thought sunk hooks into Thom's mind and heart.

I could get used to this.

"Oh, shit." She broke the kiss with a start and lunged for a bedside table, grimacing when she palmed her wristwatch.

"What's wrong? Are you alright?" He reached for her, overcome by an irrational worry that he'd bolloxed something up and caused her to hate him. Absurd that he cared, because if she hated him, she'd leave without a fuss.

She shook her head while bending over, her pale and naked bottom a curvaceous temptation dangling just outside his reach. Last night's clothes flew onto the bed—the red bustier, black leather miniskirt, and matching jacket she'd worn to the Chariotz of Fyre after-party where they'd met. "I missed my flight."

Her body in that outfit had turned his head hard and made his tongue wag with an unspeakable urge to have her. But by now, he ought to have been feeling profound relief when faced with her impending departure.

As his nameless lover shimmied and wiggled into her clothing, the reality of her slipping away lanced him. He glanced at his hands, then the floor. *I do not want to lose her*, Thom thought with an odd and startling clarity.

Normally, he lost interest in a woman after the two of them had had their fill of sex and laughs. Yet here he was moping like a schoolboy in puppy love when he damn well ought to be thanking the good lord above that the groupie of the day was about to bolt without tears, begging, or his insistence. "Can I help?"

"No." She took a cell phone from her purse and rang someone while sliding her pretty feet into danger heels.

"What's up, Megan?" A faint male voice spoke through the line.

Thom clenched his teeth and glowered at a random spot on the wall. Megan. The stupid bloke on the phone got to know her name, but he didn't. What had this wanker done that Thom hadn't to earn the privilege?

"I'm so sorry, Gary, but I'm gonna be late for the setup tonight. I travelled to St. Louis for a work thing, and I missed my flight out. I'm going to rent a car and jet up there right now, so if the drive goes okay, I'll be onsite in time to help with equipment."

What sort of equipment did an English professor need? If he'd conversed with her in more depth than his usual flirtatious small talk allowed for, the context would have meant something. Since he hadn't tried, though, he got to sit on the bed as a clueless outsider, cursing his thoughtlessness and stupidity.

Worse, he was nothing to her. Less than nothing. He was a lie, a "work thing." Served him right, he supposed. She was using him just like he'd assumed that he was using her. Karma was having a right-and-proper point and laugh moment.

Megan popped open a tin of mints and tossed three in her mouth before chucking the box in her bag. "Thanks for everything, stud."

She dropped a chaste kiss to his cheek, a literal kiss-off. He actually felt himself shrink.

He caught her fingers and thought fast. "It's already noon, and the sun goes down so early this month. Please, let me arrange a flight for you." That way he'd learn of her destination, her home state.

"It's only a five-hour drive to Iowa from here. I'll be fine." Glancing at the door, she slung her purse high on her shoulder.

Iowa. Noted. Megan the English professor from Iowa. Might be able to piece a puzzle together from those scraps. College departments had directories with pictures, and with any luck, there was a syllabus floating around out there somewhere with her cell number on it. "Why the rush? Aren't most universities still closed for the holiday?"

Though he'd graduated college over two decades ago, he hadn't forgotten about the existence of a winter break.

"Oh, I'm not going home for my professor job. I have a side gig." She slipped free of his hold and made haste for the exit.

"What's that?" He laid his empty hand to rest on the mattress, clinging to the phantom sensation of her final touch.

"I'm a paranormal investigator. And just so you're aware, when we were at the party I detected a negative entity or presence near your band. I don't say this to scare you, but you may want to think about getting in contact with someone who deals in exorcisms. Thanks again for last night and this morning. Bye."

Before he could ask the first of about a hundred questions invading his confused, vaguely horrified thoughts, Megan dipped out and shut the door behind her.

✳

Don't stop now. Keep reading with your copy of EMBERS available now.

✴

Thom James is tired of his wild but empty rock star life, so when he meets a fan who is as uninhibited and unapologetic as he is, he falls hard. Problem is, she's busy chasing ghosts and has no interest in a serious relationship. Before she says goodbye, the enigmatic groupie leaves Thom with a dire warning about dark forces that are attached to his band.

Freshly fired from her professor job, Megan O'Neil is strictly focused on pouring herself into her side gig: ghost hunting. She can't get her latest hookup out of her mind, though, and her connection to notorious rocker Thom James inconveniently persists when she forgets her demon-trapping watch in his hotel room. When he tracks her down to return the lost object, she confronts her growing feelings for the famous bassist along with a realization that she must tackle a nasty curse that's way above her pay grade. Too bad the curse, which has followed her since childhood, is *not* about to be neutralized without a fight.

Now, Thom and Megan must battle not only a malevolent spirit, but a fierce attraction that feels doomed by the demands of their incompatible lives. When Megan excavates a strange book of witchcraft and taps into a world of magic with ties to a terrifying prophecy, she and Thom face down not only the challenges of making a relationship work, but of somehow halting the machinery of magical fate before everyone pays the price.

✴

special subscriber-only contests and giveaways as well as receiving information on upcoming releases and special excerpts.

All reviews are **welcome** and **appreciated**. Please consider leaving one on your favorite social media and book buying sites.

For books in the world of romance and speculative fiction that embody Innovation, Creativity, and Affordability, check out City Owl Press at www.cityowlpress.com.

ACKNOWLEDGMENTS

Thank you to everyone who has supported the Coven Daughters series from beginning to end!

To my editor, Tee Tate, thank you for your unyielding encouragement and championing of my work.

Shout out to Tina, Yelena, Danielle, and the rest of the City Owl team for their continued support.

To the MiblArt team, you've given each book in this series such a beautiful cover that matches the characters and story vibe perfectly-thank you!

Huge thanks to Jenny, my copy editor for Dark Heart, for her thorough and thoughtful edits.

Thank you to Miranda Owen for providing me with an online space for me to share my latest releases, and to Jesscia Lepe for updating my website to ensure it's always current and looking great.

Thank you to the reviewers at The Paranormal Romance Guild, InDtale, and Reader's Favorite for the review love.

As always, huge thanks to my husband Mark for sharing and promoting my books and otherwise cheering for my author career every step of the way. Love you, babe!

Last but certainly not least, I owe a huge debt of gratitude to my early review team, reviewers, and readers-whether you have read or reviewed one book or stuck by me since the beginning. I couldn't have finished this series without you.

ABOUT THE AUTHOR

KAT TURNER is an award-winning author of paranormal romance and urban fantasy as well as the occasional thriller. Her favorite stories to write are those that combine action and adventure with magic, dry humor, and steamy romance if the situation allows. She lives is Kentucky with her family, where she can mostly be found practicing yoga, taking nature walks, or getting lost in the corridors of her own imagination. Kat loves to connect with readers, so don't be shy about getting in touch!

linktr.ee/katturnerauthor

ABOUT THE PUBLISHER

City Owl Press is a cutting edge indie publishing company, bringing the world of romance and speculative fiction to discerning readers.

Escape Your World. Get Lost in Ours!

www.cityowlpress.com

facebook.com/YourCityOwlPress
x.com/cityowlpress
instagram.com/cityowlbooks
pinterest.com/cityowlpress